W9-CFL-181

# Lost Time

# Lost Time

Catharine Arnold

*VIKING*

VIKING
Viking Penguin Inc.
40 West 23rd Street,
New York, New York 10010, U.S.A.

First American Edition
Published in 1987

LIBRARY OF CONGRESS CATALOGING IN PUBLICATION DATA
Arnold, Catharine.
Lost time.
I. Title.
PR6051.R618L6   1987   823'.914   86-40508
ISBN 0-670-81608-6

Printed in the United States of America by
R. R. Donnelley & Sons Company, Harrisonburg, Virginia
Set in Bembo

For
Robert, Morfa and Graham

# Lost Time

# One

Rain fell with that scrupulous attention unique to Cambridge as Miles Tattershall gazed through his obscure college window. A figure in running kit, skinny and panting, fled through the Quad below, succeeded by the black wheels of two umbrellas.

Bored as usual, Miles turned to Robert Burton, the gloomy seventeenth-century author of the *Anatomy of Melancholy* on whom he had been attempting to finish a characteristically despondent book for the past five years. The text before him concerned the scholar's malady:

> they are most part lean, dry, ill-coloured, spend their fortunes, lose their wits and many times their lives, and all through immoderate and extraordinary studies . . .

This didn't really describe Miles, who suffered chronic tedium, had a modest bank balance and whose idea of danger consisted of a bicycle ride to Fen Ditton in the rain.

In other ways, he fulfilled the physical requirements: Miles might have been considered attractive if anyone bothered to look, which they did not: tall and lean, with hair that flopped over a high forehead, and a bony nose which did nothing to stop his glasses from slipping into the archetypal donnish position, Miles Tattershall at thirty-three had already acquired the characteristics of Cambridge men from previous generations, and concealed himself behind them. The diligent pipe, spectacles, and vagueness bordering on the imbecilic were the legacy of former supervisors.

Or so he believed, though Miles seldom thought about himself, regarding self-examination as somehow distasteful. His lack of interest in himself corresponded with that of other people in him: in fact, apart from a few unobtrusive publications in learned journals Miles often had the sensation that he did not really exist. This was substantiated by the tendency of his colleagues to pass him unacknowledged in the street, only to greet him familiarly at unfamiliar dinner tables.

Miles sighed, trying to light his pipe, and fought the third match as someone knocked at the door. As he muttered through the stem, the knock repeated itself like the opening bars of a symphony, and Miles predicted what would happen even as it did: the warped door flew open and a dishevelled boy fell into the room, landing in an involuntary genuflexion, like a young knight.

"Good afternoon. Do please get up."

The boy did so, apologising to the carpet.

"Do sit down." Miles said this and realised that no chairs were without their weight of papers. Clearing a space, he asked: "What – who – are you? There – sit there – yes –"

"Benjamin Underwood."

"I don't think I know you. Or do I?"

"Dr Ascot – my director of studies – sent you a note to say that I was sending a note to ask if I could come and talk to you – with you – about Burton. Sir."

"Who?"

"Robert Burton."

"Ascot?"

"I'm in the second year English at St Sebastian's. I want to write a dissertation on the *Anatomy of Melancholy*. Sir."

The boy sounded both desperate and laborious.

"Oh. I see. Are you wet?"

"A bit. Just a bit damp." He grinned self-consciously, shy and yet aware of his power to charm.

Miles lay down in front of the gas-fire and finally induced it to light, as the boy dragged his chair forward. Moving away, Miles observed him, the curiously unresolved youthful features at variance with haggard eyesockets and sharp chin. Strong bones were already emerging from a still immature roundness, and his teeth fastened on his lower lip in a way which made him look nervous.

"What did you say your name was?"

8

"Benjy – Benjamin Underwood."

"I'm Miles Tattershall."

"Yes, sir. I know, sir."

"Then call me that. I'm not a schoolmaster." As it sometimes did, shyness made Miles abrupt. Benjy turned full-face to stare at him, wet curls springing onto his forehead above the coldest eyes Miles had ever seen: they suggested the blue vacancy of infinite escape, and created a sensation of unease.

"*Yes*, Miles," Benjy replied, with the faintest suspicion of mockery.

Miles ranged the room as he spoke, an indefinite motion never to be confused with pacing. Movements corresponding to the turns of his mind, he tended to collide with objects: steadying a pile of essays, he looked back at Benjy, who watched as though he had never seen anybody like him before. Disturbed, Miles asked: "Why do you want to write a dissertation on Robert Burton?"

"I'm interested in seventeenth-century prose, especially what they call asymmetrical prose, and I want to do a paper on Burton because he's interesting, and nobody else is doing him. Dr Ascot told me you were the expert."

"An expert on melancholy? It's a dubious distinction."

"I didn't mean –" Benjy sounded anxious, and Miles tried what he hoped was a reassuring smile. Benjy looked more apprehensive than ever.

"Perhaps –" Miles roamed to the window, saw the runner return, flying in the opposite direction, soaked hair clinging to his skull, glasses void. Benjy's presence filled the room like an unspoken question.

"Perhaps –" rounding on Benjy "– you would explain what you mean by asymmetrical prose?"

Benjy tried and Miles recorded the boy's arguments and critical idols with the mechanical part of his brain. Simultaneously, he examined him, intrigued. The boy hunched and stretched, slight in casual, expensive clothes: a button had gone from his silk shirt, one black corduroy trouser was tucked into an Argyll sock in lieu of a bicycle clip; the red Italian loafers were scuffed. Shaggy black hair, growing carelessly out of its fashionable style, revealed pointed ear-tips.

Benjy talked vividly, continuously, and with a faith in his abilities which his arguments did not always justify, but the faults were ones which Miles could remedy. His fascination with Miles' speciality was enough to encourage his warmth: his fascination for Miles was another matter.

"So I thought I'd try and get something written up before Christmas," Benjy concluded, "then you can read it before I do a serious draft."

"What's the first one going to be? Light verse?"

"No, no – I mean I could give you an outline without doing all the joined-up bits."

"Yes, perhaps you should leave the joined-up writing until later. Is there anything you want to leave with me now?"

Benjy produced a sheaf of poor typescript full of emendations. "There's a rough on his use of allusions. I wrote it last vacation."

"I'll look at it for you." Deliberating. "Would you like a cup of tea?"

Benjy looked at his watch, fidgeted, looked again, and insisted on filling the kettle. He went off into Miles' gyp kitchen with heroic purpose, Hobbs gleaming under one arm. Miles found some very old biscuits in a tin and decided against them. Benjy returned as he fed the last Bath Olivers to the birds.

"My God, do you really live here?"

"Why, of course." Miles was puzzled.

"It's a bit – sorry."

"Well, I've always lived here. Ever since I came up."

Benjy looked at him in awe.

"But not always in the same room?"

"I've had a variety of cells."

"Each in his narrow cell forever laid?" Benjy was pleased with himself, so Miles laughed.

"It's just that – you know – the prospect of being here all the time –"

"It never occurred to me to be anywhere else," Miles admitted.

"Don't you feel tied down?"

Benjy asked far too many questions. Miles told him so.

"I'm sorry. It's just that – I'd hate it. I need Freedom Of Action." Speaking in capital letters, so that Miles knew an issue was at stake.

"There's no such thing." Gently, but relieved to be back with the abstract, Miles initiated the argument.

"What do you mean?" He could have been saying: "What do *you* know about it?"

"Freedom of action is impossible. Everyone has responsibilities."

"The only responsibility anybody's got is to himself."

Miles realised from Benjy's vehemence that this was something he'd given a lot of thought to.

"That isn't so. Anyone living by those standards is likely to commit moral or actual manslaughter. On those grounds, you could destroy, or assist in the destruction of, an individual or an institution."

"You some sort of Christian?"

"Not really, no."

"Then I can't see why it matters. You haven't got any responsibilities. You're not married or anything, are you?"

"How can you tell?" A little affronted, but intrigued by this evidence of interest in Miles' personal life, he encouraged the boy.

"Oh, you're not the type." Airily. "So what are you bothered about?"

"I'm still responsible. There's the college, my colleagues, professional ethics, at the very least."

"Do you really believe in all that?" Incredulous, rather than insulting.

The mild, and to Miles inexplicable, euphoria which Benjy's arrival had induced began to dissipate: he felt threatened.

"I suppose it sounds rather pompous," he admitted.

"I suppose it's all you've got."

The accuracy of this shook Miles.

"It's all that matters."

"And does all this –" Benjy waved to the bookshelves "– matter so very much?"

Miles sensed that he was losing him. Well, if he wanted to go, let him.

"Yes. It matters to me."

Feeling that he had said too much, Miles concentrated on filling the teapot. He could not avoid meeting Benjy's eye as he handed the cup.

"I wish I thought it did." Benjy sounded almost wistful. "I wish I had your conviction that things mattered."

Conscious of silence, and of an excitement which he was afraid to betray, without knowing why, Miles stirred his tea a little too loudly.

"I assume that Part One of the English Tripos matters, or you wouldn't be here."

Benjy shrugged.

"Part One, Part Two; like living in a television serial." Miles tried to cheer him up with this familiar Senior Common Room remark. "But surely something is important? What else do you do, apart from reading Robert Burton? I'm not altogether sure he's a good influence on you. Perhaps you should try somebody more positive."

Benjy, as Miles was later to realise, had a provoking habit of waiting for a long time before answering a question, and sometimes never answering it at all. In response to Miles' last remark he got up, carrying his tea in one hand, and walked about the room, looking round. Going over to a framed watercolour above the mantelshelf he commented: "That's rather good. Did you pick it up round here?"

"In a manner of speaking. It's where I was brought up."

"Really? Did you inherit it?"

"I and my sister."

"The Old Vicarage, Bly. And I suppose you had a suitable Brookean childhood to go with it?" Not the egalitarian sneer which his accent would have disallowed, but true bitterness.

"My father was a country parson. I suppose you could say that I had a rather uneventful childhood."

"Rather set the pattern, didn't it?"

Miles did not reply immediately. Undergraduates had said more important things and met with the same refusal to tread on their trailing coats.

12

"There's a great advantage to an uneventful life. It gives you more time to consider other people."

"Er, yes. Sorry about that. I didn't mean . . ."

"It doesn't matter." Vaguely, Miles glanced at his watch. "I'm afraid that I'll have to chuck you out soon. I've someone coming round before Hall."

"Oh – yes, it's getting late. I'm going to the Visconti double feature at the Arts tonight – *Death in Venice* and *The Damned.*"

"That should cheer you up!"

"What do you mean?"

"Nothing. Nothing at all."

"You said something about – considering other people. Lives. What exactly did you mean?"

"Did I?"

"Just a minute ago."

"I've no recollection. Forgive me, I've a hopeless mind. Like a sieve."

"A sponge, more like."

Their eyes met, Benjy glancing quickly away.

"I do think, though," Miles added, "that you should pay a little more attention to the way you phrase things."

Benjy looked down, silenced.

"Now, when are you coming again? I assume you want a couple of supervisions this term, and something next term, after Christmas, when you've done some writing up?"

"Yes. How about in a fortnight's time?"

"That's a little soon – but yes, see what you can do. Try and turn up those articles I recommended. And have a look at Wright's *Passiones of the Minde in Generall*. It's another of these early psychiatric treatises – you should find it diverting."

"Wright. Right. Okay then. Yes."

"Come on the twenty-fifth."

They both wrote cautiously in their diaries. Suddenly Benjy said, with a rush: "Look, I didn't mean – It's just that – I'm a bit offensive. Really."

"I hadn't noticed."

He ushered Benjy out onto the dank staircase. "Come and

13

see me in two weeks. And do, for God's sake, stop chawing your lip."

Benjy clattered away down the wooden steps, and Miles returned to his window in time to watch him cross the Quad. Evening came early to a dark day, pavements gleamed around sodden lawns. Benjy moved swiftly to the archway, a wary progress, collar to his ears, hair given a raven gloss by muted lamplight.

Sunday left Miles, as always, at a loss. He never knew quite what to do with the spare hours between waking and the period when he drove himself to complete minor tasks. Finally, he strolled out of college to buy papers he would never finish, and activity startled him after the silence of his rooms.

Tourists hunted, slung with cameras; choristers flitted in medieval robes; a tiny Chinese boy he always noticed, in a King's Choir School blazer – with a mysteriously part-shaven head and crest of feathers – was vivid in his bright stripes.

Glancing at the headlines, Miles walked through Trinity and paused on the bridge to watch out-of-season punters wrestle with their poles. He glanced up as a familiar figure appeared on Clare Bridge, further down the river. Barbour flapping, head down, the boy did not notice him. He leant on the parapet and gazed into the water until, straightening, he saw Miles.

They stared over water at one another.

Miles waved, slapping his hand down immediately to prevent the *Observer* from flying into the river. Benjy turned his head, walked on, and was gone. Miles shrugged resignedly, turned his attention to the variegated gold of unleaving trees.

"Hello."

Benjy was leaning beside him, voice disturbingly intense.

"Good morning, Benjamin." Too distant. "How are you?" Better.

Benjy shrugged, drooped his shoulders. His pale face and dishevelled curls were almost Italianate, compared with the phlegmatic Anglo-Saxons who passed them incuriously, intent on sightseeing.

14

"All right, I suppose." He produced a packet of Marlboro, pointed it at Miles.

"No thanks. Beautiful day, isn't it?"

"If you can stand the smell of rotting vegetation."

"You sound as though you're suffering from Burton's autumn malady."

"Not limited to autumn." Benjy shelled his hand over a match.

Miles did not pursue the topic, watched instead the mobile gold leaf of the trees along the Backs. "Didn't know whether to come along or not," Benjy continued. "Thought perhaps you'd prefer to be left alone."

Benjy asked increasingly difficult questions: enquiries to which there could be no civil answer.

"Have you ever considered a career in investigative journalism?"

"What?"

"It's only that," Miles continued dryly, "you have an ability – how should I put it – to probe."

"Oh God. Yes. Sorry. It's just that I often find it hard getting an answer out of people."

"It must be."

"I'm *sorry*, Dr Tattershall." He glanced up with a charm which Miles wondered if he were even conscious of.

"Yes, a beautiful day," observed Miles, re-running the conversation like a tape. Benjy muttered something, and Miles walked down the slope of the bridge beside him, Benjy wheezing a little.

"Have you got a cold?"

"Asthma."

"I hadn't realised you smoked. It can't help."

"Shouldn't, should I?"

"Not really."

"I can't be bothered to pack it in." Lighting up again. "I can't get over how it's always the same here. I mean, I'll come back in twenty years, right, and I'll be old, but it won't have changed at all."

"You won't be so very old, Benjy."

"Old*er*. And *different*. But this won't be. It'll be full of

15

people like I am now, and I'll be someone else. A different person."

Miles turned to the young-old face, the hunched figure with knuckles clenched in the pockets of his Barbour, hair straying in the chilly autumn breeze.

"Not entirely."

"I shan't be *me*. You must have noticed it yourself, students changing."

"I've seen a few transformations, certainly. But most people develop, they don't alter overnight."

"You're optimistic. Haven't you known boys who simply get old and reactionary and fat?"

"I haven't been around for *so* very long myself, Benjy."

"Must seem like a long time, though."

"I don't know. What's disconcerting is the way the undergraduates stay the same age, whilst one gets older oneself."

"So you admit it?" As though gaining a point in an argument.

"I admit what?" Miles was slightly irritated, but attempted to conceal it.

"You're getting on a bit, feel life has passed you by, that you haven't really done much with it?"

"Depends whether you'd rather be on a B-road or a motorway," replied Miles, who had only recently, and at the first attempt, passed his driving test.

"*I* prefer life in the fast lane."

They walked through King's, and as Benjy reached into his pockets again, Miles sighed audibly.

"God, can't I even smoke in peace?"

"You understand that I've a vested interest in prolonging the life of my undergraduates."

"You aren't very tolerant, are you? What about your pipe?"

"That's another matter," replied Miles evasively. He thought of offering Benjy coffee, but fearing reaction, murmured about getting back. He consulted his wrist, which was without benefit of a watch.

Benjy's voice had gained its intensity again.

"See you, then."

"Fine. The twenty-fifth, if not before."

16

Both stood, conscious that something else should be said, but uncertain as to what it could be. "Miles –" Benjy began. False start. "Dr Tattershall –" Pause, of inordinate length. "Oh, forget it. See you." Before Miles could pursue the issue he had gone, vanished into the interstices of Green Street.

Miles returned to find the outer door of his rooms standing open, and walked in, puzzled. He noticed a russet leather handbag on his desk at the same time as a woman rose from the sofa.

"Ah, Miles. I wondered when you'd be back."

"Francesca. Yes – I should say that this is an unexpected pleasure –"

"Well, it's unexpected, at least. And inconvenient? Are you anticipating anybody?"

That'll be the day, he thought wearily.

"No – not at all –"

"Oh, Miles –" Their conversation was characterised by the politely vocative. "If I'm disturbing you –"

He kissed her. "I'm always delighted to see you. When did you arrive?"

"About half an hour ago. I didn't know whether you'd be back, but I thought we might have lunch together."

"Yes – yes, of course – let me find my watch – and a tie –"

She held the watch out to him. Francesca, elegant and sleek where he was thin and nervous, scarcely seemed his sister. Glossy dark hair fell in swags about her oval face, and she sat, calm as an Ingres, musician's hands folded patiently, everything that he was not.

"I'm delighted to see you, but why are you here?"

"Short notice. I've been drafted to play the Rachmaninov cello sonata at King's. It was a last-minute booking, and Charlotte's to join me later."

"Charlotte?"

"She's my new pianist. A very talented girl."

"Oh."

He let Francesca square up his tie, bustling round him in an effort to make him presentable, by her standards.

"What have you been up to? I thought you never went out."

"Bumped into a student. An odd boy."

"Aren't they all?" Francesca did not have an idealised view of her brother's occupation.

"He's very intense."

"That's nothing new, either. Shall we have sherry here?"

"I haven't any."

"You're rather distrait, Miles."

"Just preoccupied."

"Are you having teaching problems?"

"Something like that." Miles found his sensations difficult to define.

As Francesca walked beside him through college, Miles felt self-conscious: a colleague collided with them in the Quad, and looked at Miles quizzically before hurrying on. Francesca took his arm, a gesture of protection: the wind which stood his hair on end had little effect on her ordered serenity.

"I'm terribly pleased at the moment. Charlotte and I are very compatible, and she's a splendid accompanist. Do come tonight."

"Well –"

"You of all people can't be doing anything else?"

"There's a Faculty Board Meeting tomorrow –"

"Oh –" Francesca sounded a little disappointed.

"Look – one of your albums. I didn't realise it had come out." He drew her attention to a window display in the classical record shop, anxious to change the subject. Only as he looked did he realise his mistake.

"It's a reissue," Francesca said briefly.

"Yes – of course. You've long hair in that picture." He saw her, airbrushed and polished, poised with her cello on the album cover, her accompanist at a Steinway.

"I've also got Emily in that picture."

Miles looked away, embarrassed. "How's your new contract going with the record company?"

"Oh, marvellous. I've got good terms and I'm going to the States next summer on a promotional tour."

18

"That's excellent. Have you spoken to Hilary Middlemass recently?"

"He's been ill, but sends love. I heard something about a new sonata."

"He's still at Charnwood?"

"Oh yes. Unchanging. You know what he's like."

A legend of their youth, Hilary Middlemass was an ancient though not particularly venerable composer, last of a pre-war set. He lived in seclusion on his East Anglian estate, not far from where Miles and Francesca had grown up, and figured in their childhood demonology.

As they reached the Garden House Hotel, Miles congratulated himself on having let the reference to Emily drop. He concentrated on small talk, which he found taxing at the best of times, until the claret had been ordered, and Francesca asked about his own activities.

"Oh, nothing strenuous. Couple of lectures."

"And the *Anatomy of Melancholy*?"

"Oh, don't."

"I'm sure it would be a wonderful book if only you could get it finished."

"They said the same thing to Robert Burton."

"Ah, Miles." She smiled warmly, and what in Miles' face were gaunt lines turned in Francesca's features to charming modulations. "Look, here's Charlotte. She must have got my message."

Charlotte hesitated, looming in the doorway, before striding forward, firm-jawed and a little military in her belted raincoat. Fresh-faced from the wind, and with the stalwart frame of one who is descended from generations of squire-archal nonentities, she struck fear into Miles. Women disturbed him at the best of times: Charlotte was positively alarming.

"Miles, I've heard *so* much about you," she said as they were introduced, and his heart sank.

"How wonderful to be able to work in Cambridge."

"I seldom do."

"Such an opportunity. The glorious architecture, the heady intellectual atmosphere –"

"Heady's the word."

Francesca caught his eye.

"Well," he added, more circumspect. "And you're here for how long?"

"Just the night. Frankie and I have to get back to London tomorrow."

"Frankie –?" He deplored the name.

"Miles –" Charlotte's tone was challenging, had a constantly argumentative quality – "don't you ever feel cut off?"

"From what?" Several years of teaching had trained Miles to deal with the most irritating of people, but he was calling upon all his resources to cope with Charlotte. He invariably found conversation with strange women difficult, and Charlotte certainly justified the epithet.

"Real life."

Francesca glanced at him across the table, and Miles determined to behave.

"Well, when you've had *our* opportunities to travel, and see the world –"

"From the rather limited vantage point of the hotel room –" interposed Francesca.

"– And see the world," Charlotte persisted, unperturbed as a counsel for the prosecution, "you realise that you're missing so much, and missing the chance of meeting so many people."

Miles suppressed an obvious remark about the advantages of not meeting certain people, and concentrated on his food. "I'd miss a lot if I travelled," he said at last. "Peace and quiet, for instance."

"But –"

He looked up to see her flush, caught off guard, face curiously naked. Miles looked away again quickly.

"Miles doesn't like travelling," said Francesca. "It makes his ears pop. And he doesn't like being away from Cambridge for long. Do you, Miles? Now, Lottie, what will you have?" Her tone was peremptory, and looking at Charlotte suddenly made Miles feel terribly old. Fresh, brash, secure and sincere, she was a completely different proposition from haunted Benjy Underwood.

20

He remembered Benjy, visible on the opposite bridge, then suddenly at his side, eyes blue with the promise of escape.

Charlotte's eyes were hot and brown and didn't know where to look.

Lunch passed unexceptionally after that, Charlotte on best behaviour as if at her first grown-up party, more like fifteen than twenty-five, with her polite enquiries and non-committal answers. Miles was bored, wanted Francesca to himself to not-talk to, resented this bouncing, boring, inadequate girl with her square fingertips and straight eyebrows. He picked through thoughts, unmarked essays, a lecture that awaited revision, Burton, Benjy, until he realised that the latter came too often into his mind.

"Well," said Francesca decisively, folding her napkin. "I have to go and have a word with King's about arrangements for tonight."

"When do they want us to come?" asked Charlotte hastily, moving to her feet.

"Sit down, Lottie. I have to go and see Dr Strachan now, and just discuss one or two things. I thought perhaps you'd like to see something of Cambridge, and join me later."

Charlotte looked from one Tattershall to the other, in a way which made Miles feel self-conscious.

"But —" he began, knowing that Francesca, older and elegant and organised, would already have thought of some answer.

"You can take Lottie round the Botanic Garden," Francesca replied, showing that she had anticipated any protest. "Wouldn't you like that, Lottie?"

Lottie looked depressingly eager about the prospect.

"I'd love to. And it would be wonderful if you could show me Cambridge."

Francesca had always been able to persuade Miles into acting against his better judgement: he knew that it was completely useless to put up any resistance, and with mis-givings said goodbye to his sister and accompanied Charlotte out of the hotel.

"I'd like to go back and get a scarf, if you don't mind," he said, sounding rather elderly. "It's getting quite chilly."

"But autumn in Cambridge is *so* beautiful," Charlotte enunciated, as if in a play. "No wonder you love it so."

Charlotte, whose presence gave the illusion of size although she was of conventional proportions, proved an embarrassment. Undergraduates negotiated her in the entrance of the college like a ship in a harbour mouth. A capacious and unwieldy bag sat under one arm, as though she were running away to seek her fortune.

"Will you leave that in the Lodge?" he enquired.

"Oh – no, I hate to leave anything. It might get stolen."

Unmoved by this touching evidence of her insecurity, Miles suggested they went to his room while he fetched a scarf. Charlotte walked about fingering objects while he found it, and was much taken with the watercolour of Bly. Miles resolved that she would never come to the Old Vicarage if he had anything to do with it.

"I expect you do a lot of work here."

"I suppose I must do."

"It must be so satisfying, having all these young men around."

"I wouldn't have put it quite like that."

"Oh!" All her reactions were infused with this amateur-dramatic forcefulness. "I didn't mean –"

Looking up as he fastened a shoelace, Miles found her staring at him in a way which made him feel vulnerable.

"Shall we go?"

They walked down King's Parade, under bowling autumn skies, avoiding skeins of tourists and ubiquitous bicycles. Miles pointed out places of interest in his donnish way, clumpy Charlotte responding politely but with the continual impression of withholding. At last, in the comparative security of Trumpington Street, she twisted her fingers round the vinyl strap of her handbag and expostulated: "Oh God! I really can't stand it!"

Miles took refuge in his pipe.

"You know what I mean."

"That's debatable." He scraped a match.

"How much do you really know about your sister?"

"Considerably more than yourself."

"Then why can't *you* tell me?"

"I didn't say that I wouldn't."

"Look, Miles – you don't mind if I call you Miles –" He nodded, although she had addressed him as Miles quite confidently an hour earlier. "– I want to help your sister. I seriously believe she needs looking after. But how can I if you don't tell me the real story?"

"What real story?" Miles tried his best to hide his increasing irritation. "Why should I be expected to discuss my sister's personal life with you?"

"Don't say it like that. I just want to know about Emily, so that I can help her."

"Emily is beyond help.'

"I didn't mean that, I meant help Frankie. Why do you have to twist everything I say? You're so clever with words," she added resentfully.

"What do you want to know?"

"Well, Frankie and Emily were very close –"

"They were a professional partnership, as well as being very good friends."

"You know that isn't what I mean."

"You don't seem to know what you mean."

"It's the way you keep changing everything I say."

"What exactly do you want, Miss Perkins?"

Charlotte was almost in tears, but they were not tears that moved Miles. Instead, they inspired disgust. "I want to know about Frankie. And Emily. I want to know what *happened*."

"Emily Deutsch is dead. She was Francesca's accompanist: she had some sort of degenerative illness; and she died. That's all I know."

"Thanks a lot."

They were beside fields which led to the river; horses champed solemnly as Charlotte leant on the railing, and Miles feared that she might actually cry.

"Miss Perkins –" He began to feel a mild, detached pity, but she thrust away, hands deep in her pockets. Miles sighed as damp air seeped into his lungs: despite the shining trees and golden boughs, drops of condensation hung from each grassblade; an infant staggered from its parents' mutual grasp, making for the road. They watched it recaptured, Miles smiling slightly. Charlotte, turning, smiled back.

"Come on," he said. "It's scarcely an hour since we left the hotel, but we might as well have some tea."

Charlotte sat opposite in the teashop, glancing conscientiously at Great St Mary's and King's Parade from time to time, looking more often at him.

"I do wish you'd tell me more about Frankie, Miles."

"There's nothing to tell. You're asking me to divulge things which – which perhaps Francesca wouldn't like you to know. Things which don't concern you."

"I believe that your sister is in serious trouble, Miles. I really am worried about her. Honestly. I just want to get to know her better. I like getting to know people."

Miles suppressed an involuntary shudder.

"Frankie doesn't always know what's good for her."

"Apparently few of us do."

"Why do you have to put everything like that, Miles? You do sound bitter."

"Just realistic."

"You're really blocking me, aren't you?"

"I beg your pardon?" Arms loosely folded, pipe in hand, at his most donnish.

"The whole way you go about things – oh, if only I could get her to talk about it, bring it out in the open. It would be so much healthier."

"Perhaps she doesn't want to talk about it. Had that occurred to you? It could be that after watching Emily die by degrees my sister has exhausted the conversational possibilities of the topic. Now, if you'll excuse me –" Getting up.

"God, you're sour, aren't you?"

Miles looked down at her, exploiting his height, something he rarely did. "Stoical is the word I would have preferred." He walked towards the door.

"No – Miles! Wait!" Rising hastily, displacing a teacup, she followed him. As Charlotte caught his arm with strong pianist's hands, Miles felt hounded. "Don't you understand? I must help Frankie. I *must*."

"Please –" looking round. "Isn't it time you two met up? When is the rehearsal?"

"I'm – meeting Frankie at King's at four."

"Well, it's almost that now. I know it's only across the road, but perhaps you should go now. You don't want to waste any time –"

"Miles – listen –"

Paying the bill, Miles was conscious of being an object of speculation and interest to the other customers. He came out to find Charlotte waiting awkwardly beside the bicycle racks. She had reddened, and an unattractive flush spread from the roots of her curly hair to her thick neck.

"You just don't understand. It's all for her own good. I only want to help, Miles."

"Ever thought much about the road to hell?"

Charlotte looked puzzled, evidently expecting a religious digression.

"It's paved with good intentions." Steering her in the direction of King's Chapel.

As they crossed the Quad, Francesca appeared in the distance, waving graciously in the brilliant autumn twilight, as though acknowledging applause. Miles nodded back, but did not go to her: instead, he turned on his heel and headed back to his own college with profound relief.

Woodville, a tiny college founded in 1480 by the unfortunate Sir Anthony Rivers, basked in obscurity between Caius and Trinity. It rested secure in a reputation for sombre excess and divinity, and had produced a couple of mundane novelists and a defecting intelligence officer.

Walking back to it, reassuring tabby stonework dark against a prismatic sunset, Miles tried to attribute his feelings of depression to beef and cheese, both of which he had eaten at lunch, and both of which, according to Burton, were direct causes of melancholia. But everything caused melancholia, according to Burton, he thought with exasperation.

Wondering what Burton would have had to say about the little episode with Charlotte Perkins, he went up to his rooms and discovered that a record had been placed on the turntable, presumably by Francesca.

Switching on the loudspeakers, he picked up the sleeve and looked into Emily Deutsch's sick-child features on the album cover. He continued to gaze down at it as music and darkness poured into the room.

Miles had been alarmed by Charlotte Perkins, although he found his fears difficult to define. There had been something predatory about the clumsy, tactless meddling in Francesca's past life, the intrusive but no doubt well-intentioned preoccupation with Emily's illness and death.

No doubt it was this very commitment on Charlotte's behalf which Francesca needed and responded to, and which made her a necessary evil. Miles was prepared to tolerate her if she made life more endurable for his sister, but she inspired in him a sensation close to revulsion.

Charlotte was devoted to Francesca, and that Miles could understand. Francesca, with her calm swags of hair, smooth body regulated in silk and cashmere, cool hands remembered from childhood illnesses, older and wiser and more elegant than Miles could ever aspire to being.

Miles longed to be ill again now, racked with asthma or bronchitis, so that she would come as she had done before. On one occasion, when his condition had been grave enough to warrant his being brought home from school in the middle of the Half, Francesca had been summoned from her Conservatoire, his illness deploring her absence. She had come, strange, sixteen, a new shape, and he remembered her, serene, moving above him.

On that occasion, Francesca had presented him with a Chatto translation of Proust, and the blue and white dust-jackets always conveyed an agreeably Marcelian memory of bedridden languor and blue and white packets of Marie biscuits.

The relationship had changed since those days: seldom ill, and knowing it was unlikely that anything short of death would cause Francesca to interrupt a tour, Miles saw little of his sister. He missed her without realising that he did, if only because Francesca was the only woman who did not alarm and frighten him. Miles had little experience of the species.

As a schoolboy, sickly and studious, his disinclination for

any form of affection had gone unremarked. As an equally studious if less sickly undergraduate his innocence had never been appealing enough for anyone to try and corrupt. As he worked for his First, and then for his Doctorate, Miles' studies were an alibi for his failure to introduce a girlfriend among his colleagues. Cambridge is a monument to isolation, and Miles' celibacy was unexceptional.

Sometimes Miles watched families – the orderly, privately educated children of dons, or younger brothers visiting under-graduates – which made him feel wistful. Sometimes he saw quiet, well-bred young women in the college chapel who looked as though they might dust his books and make sand-wiches as he worked late into the night. But feminine reactions disappointed Miles.

Charlotte's burly charmlessness had reminded him of a common phenomenon, for, inexperienced as he was, Miles did possess an attraction for women. The less interest he evinced in a certain type, the more she pursued him. There had been one or two undergraduates of this sort, whom he gently discouraged. One refused to go quietly and another supervisor had to be arranged. There had been a librarian who had wanted to cook for him. Miles left early after a candlelit dinner, seeing her best sheets turned down through the half-open door. Women, for Miles, were like cats: he would greet the ones he knew if met by chance, and ensure they did not follow him home.

Miles had come to the conclusion that his was an asexual existence and likely to remain that way. Occasionally, he wondered about the consequences of celibacy, and sensed a form of loneliness which was more than lack of sexual contact: he found himself envying not only the lovers who walked shamelessly through Trinity Street, wrapped in each other's arms, but the noisy dishevelled groups of half-drunk youths clattering past his door.

Miles would pick up a detective story – he was particularly addicted to the old-fashioned, country house variety – and lose his own worries in anxiety for the characters. For, in general, he found his lack of commitment liberating. Miles' colleagues sometimes expressed irritation at what they took to be deliberate policy, but relented as they realised that his modesty resulted from lack of inclination and opportunity rather than active self-denial.

Most of all, Miles resented the attempts of dons' wives to match him with similarly circumstanced women. He knew that if he ever were to fall in love, it would not be with a bluestocking. Certain incidents in books and films disturbed him, and his dreams shocked him: he was surprised by the nature of the material his imagination produced. But Miles' fantasies remained as such, without any strong impulse to be realised.

Francesca was another matter. She was the only woman with whom Miles felt secure, safe, free from all pressure: she was an extension of himself, and never, as so many women seemed to be, threatening and unpredictable. They had been united in their ambivalent feelings towards their father, and Francesca, two years older, had watched over his development after their mother's defection. Gradually, Miles and Francesca had perfected a near-telepathic means of communication which eliminated distance: he knew it to be illogical when he sensed her to be elated or in pain when she was on the other side of the world; but he knew it to be true.

Even Charlotte Perkins could not do anything about that.

Miles sat up, realising that he had drifted off to sleep while listening to the music. Outside, sky oxidised with night, and his room was cold as a tank. Lighting the gas-fire, he sat in the darkness with a large Scotch, and hoped that Francesca really was going to be all right. He was certain that Charlotte, in her clumsy, well-intentioned way, had over-reacted to the bereavement. Emily had died several months ago, and Francesca was supremely resilient. Anybody, Miles considered, who could sit and play in front of a vast audience – and play superbly – must have nerves of steel. Poor, forthright, abrupt Charlotte. She needed to look after someone, and if Francesca benefited, then he would endure it.

It was just that Miles preferred to have Francesca to himself, to not-talk to.

# Two

Day faded into day, each growing shorter, as Miles beat his habitual track from college to faculty to library and back.

Leaves drifted across the Backs: outside the University Library a group of diseased trees had been felled, and great carcasses lay amid small bonfires, woodsmoke mingling with acrid night air.

On one of these evenings, Miles left the catalogue room and wandered through the revolving door into the cold, the building rising Byzantine behind him. A wind struck up as he unshackled his bicycle and rode along Burrell's Lane. It was the time of evening when Cambridge is deserted, and King's Parade resounded to nothing more than the distant rattle of mudguards over cobblestones as the bells rang out seven.

Miles was about to dismount and lead his bicycle into college when several things happened at once: a fleet of youths sped past from the direction of Trinity Street and a solitary cyclist appeared from the opposite end of King's Parade. None saw the car, which came silently from the recesses of Bene't Street; a youth shouted and the rider, a girl, college scarf flapping in the breeze, turned her head: her bicycle seemed to precipitate itself into the Volvo's path, impact flinging her across the bonnet; a shoe flew through the air and she dropped, to lie still, cheek cushioned by the gutter.

"Christ!" exclaimed the youth, and the group froze by the pavement. The driver emerged from his car as Miles went forward, but a boy was there before him.

"Don't touch her," he warned, and Miles recognised Benjamin.

"You'd better call an ambulance," Miles replied, bending to the twisted figure.

"Is she – dead?" enquired another undergraduate. They stood about, a chorus.

"No," Miles said, taking her pulse, disregarding the driver's repeated protestations that there had been no lights, that she had come the wrong way. Benjy stood a little apart, and Miles realised that he was trembling.

The ambulance came, and the girl was lifted and taken away with professional mercy. Miles, Benjy and the distraught driver found themselves giving statements at the local police station, and the driver was still there when they left, protesting his innocence.

"You're in shock," Miles told Benjy. The boy was white-faced and looked more strained than ever, an oversized overcoat huddled protectively round him.

"I'm all right. Oh God, do you suppose she'll be okay?"

"I've no idea."

"She just seemed to go under the wheels. I've never seen anything like it."

"She skidded, that's all."

"She was so young, Miles. A Fresher. I've seen her in Hall a few times."

"Yes. I realise that she's at your college."

"A thing like that – makes you realise –"

"It's appalling," Miles agreed. He was discovering that his shock had rather more to do with seeing Benjy unforewarned. Miles' elation at seeing the boy again was in direct proportion to his increasing nervousness.

"Are you going back to Woodville, Miles?"

"I was. But look, come and have a drink. You could do with it."

"I was on my way to the Free Press –"

"That's a tiny pub. It'll be packed by now."

"Are you sure – I don't want –"

"I do want. We'll go to somewhere down near the river."

Miles was surprised by his own decisiveness: words came out sounding acceptable, he was able to walk without feeling too self-conscious: it was difficult to understand what was coming over him, and why he was possessed by such febrile intensity.

Dim windows glowed in the dark, and another lone cyclist sped past. They walked down Silver Street, and came to the place where the millrace galloped in its brick confines. A bough had lodged obstinately between the water and walls, and its branches, though lashed with wet, remained unmoved, refusing to be drawn into the maelstrom beneath.

By unspoken assent they stood watching this for some time, only half-conscious of the inky night and strayed revellers wandering beneath the Mill and the Anchor. After a silence, Benjy plunged his hands even deeper into the pockets of his coat and asked:

"Are you used to death? Being older, I mean?" The question had an air of self-conscious naïvety.

"I'm not so very much older, Benjy."

"No, not that old, but –"

"*That* is not an adverb of degree."

"You've had so much more experience of life."

"Far less than you imagine. Probably far less than you, for that matter. But I'm accustomed to death. I've seen it. I don't suppose I shall ever get used to it."

"I've always had this feeling I'll die young."

"It's common to English students. A form of romantic contagion."

"Robert Burton predicted when he was going to die, didn't he? Knew the date exactly?"

"'Rather than there should be a mistake in the calculation, he sent up his soul to Heaven thro' a slip about his Neck'," quoted Miles. "There's a fine example of someone altering events to fit in with his research." He laughed ironically, but did not like the turn the conversation was taking.

"I think about death quite a lot." Benjy said this quite matter-of-factly. "Perhaps it's something to do with studying all these Jacobeans. They are rather a sombre crowd. You're taking it well. But then, it *is* because you're older."

"Benjamin, you are obsessed with my age."

"I know. I'm sorry. It's just that – I'm sick of being the age I am."

"Being?"

"Nineteen."

"I'm thirty-three."

"I'm hoping things will improve with time."

"Why, you haven't got spots or anything." He looked at Benjy again, the haggard eyes, bitten lip, romantic hair springing onto the forehead. "You could probably do with a good night's sleep."

"It's when it happens to someone you know. Something like that. Just seeing her about college – and then under the wheels of that car. I can't get it out of my mind."

Miles realised that the incident was threatening to become an obsession, and that a stop should be put to it. Benjy looked up to see Miles gazing at him, and his stare was disturbingly intense. Miles looked away first.

"Perhaps we'd better go and have that drink."

"I could do with it. I think I need a short after seeing that."

"It'll warm you up," Miles agreed. "Accidents are shocking –" Academically. "– and violent death is perhaps the most –"

"I know." Spoken with such authority that Miles stopped. "I'm not exactly a stranger to this sort of thing."

Of all potential questions, Miles asked: "But you still found this distressing?"

"I've – had problems in the past." Benjy's tone was confessional and Miles did not want to hear any more, anticipating long accounts of therapy sessions and phobias. "I've been ill."

"Do you mean spiritually?" With irony.

"Things happen to you, Miles. Sometimes things happen and you haven't got any control over events. None at all."

"Well, yes." Attempting to sound brisk and failing. "But it's all a question of how you approach life –" Although he received many confidences – perhaps because he had a sympathetic face – Miles felt uneasy with the tone Benjy was adopting.

"You see, things happen," Benjy continued didactically, as if supplying the commentary on some personal vision, and ignoring Miles' reservations. "Things happen, and you're powerless to stop them. You have to stand by and watch while it all goes on, right to the end. You can't do anything, you can't help, and you haven't got any choice." His clichés and flat tone did not diminish the growing, unknown fear Miles began to experience. Miles wondered whether Benjy was suffering from some form of clinical disorder: he had a victim's gaze.

A burst of laughter from a passing group of stragglers brought them to their senses. Benjy was suddenly a pale, strained undergraduate, no visionary but a tired youth who had suffered a shock and needed a drink. He reached out and patted Miles' arm.

"Come on, it'll be warm inside, and we can talk there."

Miles agreed, relieved that Benjy had abandoned his review of some private nightmare. He found it painful seeing the boy in such a state, longed to give reassurance but feared that it might be rejected or misinterpreted. Benjy literally pulled himself together, gathering round him the covert coat which must have belonged to his grandfather, and pushing the straying hair back from his eyes.

The Mill was unusually empty, and Miles settled Benjy in a corner before going to fetch drinks. He was conscious of the boy's stare as he ordered the whisky, and turned suddenly to find that pale blue gaze fixed upon him, enigmatic, challenging, provocative: Miles, whose entire career was based on articulating subtleties and nice distinctions, could not interpret that look.

"I hope she recovers," he said, referring to the cyclist.

"What a way to start life in Cambridge," agreed Benjy.

"I suppose it's better than having no life at all. We must simply hope that she'll survive."

"Not that *you* know much about life, do you?"

Benjy's tone was so unexpectedly belligerent that Miles was startled. Just as he was becoming accustomed to Benjy's mercurial nature, he would act in an even more unpredictable way.

"It's all right for you, nodding away like a mandarin. Why should you care?"

"Benjy, I quite fail to understand —"

"*Exactly.*" And the word came out like a sneer. Miles stared back into Benjy's distant eyes, and without looking away the boy picked up his glass and drank from it. Miles wished that his expression would change, banish the distance between them: the frail, vulnerable Benjy, whom he wanted to save and protect, had fled, and some other being had taken his place. It was enough to make one believe in changelings.

Without breaking the trance, Benjy dug a packet of cigarettes out of his pocket and shook one free. Before he realised it, Miles had reached across, covering Benjy's hand, and the unlit cigarette, with his own. Benjy's lighter clicked involuntarily, and a tongue of flame illuminated both their faces. With a tremor, Benjy put down the cigarette.

"Perhaps you do understand me after all."

"Well, I'm not certain —" began Miles, with his old academic fear of making assertions without qualifying them.

"We must talk some more."

"Well, you're coming for your supervision on the twenty-fifth, aren't you?"

"Oh, next week." Benjy's tone was dismissive.

"You make it sound like a long time."

"It *is* a long time."

That old vulnerable feeling, which he had sensed with Charlotte Perkins and the predatory female librarian, overcame Miles once more. He felt that Benjy was closing in, and that it had become necessary to protect himself from such emotional violation. But at the same time he was fascinated, entranced, by Benjy's fascination with him.

In a thriller, Miles remembered reading about the hard–soft interrogation technique. It consisted of breaking down a witness or suspect by a combination of kindness succeeded by cruelty, and was usually administered by two people. It was such a technique that Benjy seemed to be practising on him now. Stretching out his thin arms, and shuffling off the covert coat, Benjy now lolled relaxed opposite him, black sweatered elbows propped on the back of the bench, red bow tie self-consciously askew.

"You're a hard man to get to know, Miles."

Relieved by this change of tactics, Miles took another sip and replied: "There isn't much to know in the first place."

"I find that difficult to believe."

34

"Do you enjoy being at Cambridge, Benjy?"

"Not much, but it's better than trying to find a job." With fashionable cynicism. "Do *you* enjoy it?"

"I can't imagine being anywhere else."

"I can't imagine you anywhere else, come to that. Still, I'll be out of it after another year. Out in the big wide world."

"Yes – so you will." Miles said this lightly, but Benjy's words reminded him of what he had already refused to acknowledge.

There would be a post-Benjamin age: it had to come. An age where they would not collide on King's Parade, spot one another in the faculty library, when his feet would not be heard on the staircase. An age in which Burton would again be a solitary and perverse study, and he would not prepare new material to be examined and look out articles to be read. An age in which there would be no time spent predicting the boy's mood and wondering how the supervision would go. An age, in fact, where there would be no more anxiety about another person. It was only as Benjy threw these words out casually that Miles realised how much Benjy's existence contributed to his own.

"Are you all right, Miles?"

"Yes – yes, of course."

"I thought you looked a bit unhappy."

"Your concern is most touching, Benjy."

"Oh, I am touching."

This camp indication of flirtatiousness disturbed Miles: again, it implied an intimacy which he found alarming.

"What are you going to do, Benjy?"

"Go back to college, read the *Spectator*, have some scrambled eggs –"

"In future."

"God only knows. Get some sort of job, I suppose."

"As what?"

"You may well ask. Sit behind a desk all day giving people orders. Tear round the country in a company car. Be a brand manager for Unilever or a trainee chartered accountant. You tell me."

35

"I find it hard to see you doing any of those things."

"You and me both." Benjy sometimes resorted to these Americanisms, and they sounded inappropriate as he sat there in his aesthete's bow tie and black V-neck jersey. "There's a bit of money coming, so I can live off that. Perhaps I could stay on here."

"What would you do?"

"Research into Robert Burton?" Drawing Miles into the collusion of a smile.

An influx of hearties, slapping each other's backs in what to Miles was an alarming display of corporate identity, diverted their attention.

"Actually, I must get back."

"I wish we could go on talking, Miles."

You mean you wish you could go on talking, Miles thought. "I'll see you on Wednesday," he pointed out.

"Oh, the supervision –"

"That's the main point of your coming to see me, Benjy."

Miles found it increasingly necessary to impose constraints. Getting up, he led the way out: but he still had the sensation that Benjy was in control.

"It's funny – it's almost as if I expected – to see it." Benjy's comment hung in the air as they walked past the site of the accident, but there was nothing left, apart from arcane chalk marks, symbols of a vanished ritual.

Benjy seemed aloof again now, apart, slender, lonely and unattainable. As though in some science-fiction story, the Benjy he really cared for had been replaced by a creature of unnerving cool self-confidence and awe-inspiring beauty. It was impossible for Miles to attribute his giddiness and thumping heart to whisky alone.

"Will you be all right now?" he asked, as they said good night. "Would you like me to walk back with you?"

"I'm okay. I can manage."

Miles felt that his offer of help had been refused. Benjy started to walk away up the street, and turned to wave once, hair catching a raven gloss from a streetlamp.

Even from this distance, the blue stare seemed to burn him

like a laser, and returning his glance Miles felt galaxies implode in his bloodstream and his mind charged with stars.

Days succeeded one another, each briefer than the last, until there seemed no distinction between morning and night. Miles supervised damp and yawning undergraduates around his gas-fire, drank interminable cups of Nescafé, and was depressed by the mere thought of Robert Burton and all his works. For a brief period, Benjy's interest had revived his own: but that did not matter now.

Occasionally, out of duty, he fetched down the dusty files, considered the notes in his careful, flyblown handwriting, and put them back. He looked at his doctoral thesis, which was to provide so much of the material for the book, and the task of transforming that grim study into a readable text which people would want to buy seemed as impossible as a trial in a fairy tale.

Benjy had not come on Wednesday the twenty-fifth.

After parting at King's Parade Miles had not known what to expect. He walked back to his rooms in curious elation, as though someone had told him an exciting secret. He fell asleep in a state of conspiratorial self-satisfaction, but waking in the night had felt depressed, convinced that Benjy's attentions meant no more than a passing interest, that he would find some other diversion once the novelty had worn off.

Nevertheless, Miles had waited, moved to a sensation which he called curiosity, for Benjy's arrival that Wednesday. And he did not come.

Miles made explanations to himself, and when no message arrived resolved to wait. By Friday he seriously considered ringing Benjy's director of studies. Night brought him strange alarms: dreams of Benjy dead, dying, sent down, lost, three days drunk, indifferent. No undergraduate fatalities were announced in *Stop Press* and Miles survived by reassuring himself that Benjy was not, after all, expressly his student, that he may have been called home, or fallen violently in love. Such things happen.

Tuesday brought a lecture – on Sir Thomas Browne –

37

and Miles glanced up from the lectern at the low tide of undergraduates without seeing Benjy.

It was an erudite lecture, not without wit, but three people left before the end. Miles attributed this to the fact that it was the last hour before lunch, and that he lectured on the top floor of the raised faculty. But he made his way downstairs with the sense that the fates were against him. People eddied about the concourse laden with books and files, and before Miles could concentrate on seeking Benjy out, he appeared.

Or rather he turned round, saw Miles, turned fully, and walked towards him. Relieved, and then angry, Miles wondered what to say.

"Oh – hello, Dr Tattershall."

"Hello, Benjamin."

"Look – I'm really sorry about last week."

"I'm glad to hear it."

"I've been – I've not been well."

"It looks like it," Miles conceded, but he could find no acceptable way of expressing his disappointment and anger, the long and empty afternoon spent listening for footfalls on the staircase.

Benjy looked a little more ravaged than usual, and wore a fuchsia pink cashmere scarf, looped elegantly inside his coat. His hair was crushed and dishevelled.

"I do wish you'd let me know," Miles said finally.

"I couldn't do anything. They stuck me in bed and kept me there." It was a weak excuse, and they both knew it.

The lunchtime crowd disappeared, and within a few minutes Sidgewick Avenue was deserted, as if by magic. Miles walked towards the cycle racks and Benjy followed, anxious. "Look, I can explain. Where are you going now?"

"Back to Woodville."

"Come to the Granta. We could have lunch."

Miles was already half-tempted, but he unshackled the ancient bicycle without catching Benjy's eye.

"I'm lunching with a colleague, actually." He could not bring himself to speak Benjy's name, and started walking away.

38

Benjy followed, half-running to keep up with Miles' stride. Despite the anger, which he could feel beating in his face, Miles realised that Benjy's presence transmitted an indefinable hilarity, a sensation that they shared a secret. If he had really wanted to get away, he knew, he would have ridden off by now.

"You didn't come to my lecture."

"'Fraid not."

"Have you given up lectures? Is it no longer fashionable to attend them?"

"I went to one on *Cymbeline*."

Miles glanced at him.

"I read it in bed. In fact, I've done quite a lot of reading, and some work on my dissertation. I meant to get it round to you, but on Tuesday night my asthma started getting really bad."

"How much have you done?"

"Two thousand words."

This was such an improvement on Benjy's initial essay that Miles stopped.

"Two thousand words on what?"

"Macaronic equivocation."

"No wonder you were ill."

"Well, it's all starting to mean something to me. I'm really getting interested. Before, it was simply a question of passing the exams but now – I begin to see what you mean."

"Well – that's splendid. Obviously, you've risen transformed from your sickbed."

"I was only there a few days. But –" catching Miles' eye, and looking charming and anxious "– I think it must be working with you. At my college, nobody is really interested. But you bring it all to life."

Miles thought of himself, drearily thumbing through old research notes.

"I suppose we'd better arrange another supervision, hadn't we?"

"Can I – have one now?"

"What, today?"

"After lunch?"

39

"An emergency appointment?"

"Well, sort of."

"In the face of such boundless enthusiasm, how can I refuse? But I've got a class."

"When?"

"Three thirty."

"Two, then?"

"Benjy, is this strictly necessary?"

"Yes, look, I'm all excited. I want to get on and finish this thing, and we've only had one supervision so far. I've got all sorts of new ideas I want to talk to you about."

Flattered, self-conscious, Miles was in no position to refuse. He thought of the faded, blank-faced students in his lectures: he looked at Benjy, intense and crackling with psychic electricity, and had to smile.

"Two thirty," he conceded. They stood looking at one another for a moment, hesitant. "By the way, have you had any news about that poor girl? The one who was knocked off her bicycle?"

"Yes. I heard a couple of days ago that she'll be all right, but she's got a broken collar bone."

"At least she's alive."

Benjy nodded, smiled. There was another pause, then Miles got on his own bicycle and rode away.

While they were apart, Benjy had become, if not an ideal student, then the nearest Miles would ever get to one.

During the afternoon Miles' old ideas and dusty theories stirred, his flagging interest revived, their discussion revolved around concepts which before he had only vaguely considered, and the new research that he had worked on, in order to amuse Benjy, was taken up and examined.

Comparing approaches, they often made the same observations identically, speech rushing on to a simultaneous conclusion. The Benjy who had fallen through his door six weeks ago stretched, talked, relaxed before him, lips unchawed. Both jumped when the three-thirty class knocked on Miles' door.

"Time's flown. Right, Benjy, I'll look at what you've

written and perhaps next week we might discuss presentation."

"Yes. I've got to do my bibliography. Could I borrow the original of your paper, *Physician Heal Thyself?*"

"How did you know about that?"

"I looked it up in *Review of English Studies*, but I'd like to see the original. I got the impression perhaps you'd cut it because of the length requirement."

"That was perceptive of you, Benjy." Naturally flattered, Miles promised to find the manuscript. His practical criticism group infiltrated the room, looking about with their customary whey-faced incuriosity. Benjy left, and Miles stood at the window to watch him go.

Brilliant December light struck across the Quad in Blakean rays, and the runner panted by, glasses steamed and blind. Benjy paused to wave from the archway, the fuchsia tips of his scarf dancing like pennants on the wind.

Miles waved back.

Practical Criticism (Part II), Unwin, Berman and Physshe, looked at their director of studies with sheer incredulity.

# Three

In the last week of Full Term, Miles woke to a changed world. Whiteness blotted Trinity Street, detailed each beam and turret of the opposite shopfronts, damped all sound but the clatter of skidding bicycles. The runner, in crimson tracksuit, skirted the white napkin of lawn in the Quad; Miles' windows were engraved with frost.

Miles shivered into clothes and went out, scarved, to the baker's. King's Parade, with its small dark figures and grey sky, reminded him of the Brueghelian Christmas card Benjy had sent, with its imperative signature: *Love Benjy.*

Tourists, undeterred by the cold, fluffed out with jumpers like the birds with ruffled feathers, clustered resolutely outside the Senate House. Miles stepped into the road to avoid them, and almost collided with a bicycle. The rider was shawled in a fall of snow.

"Why the hell don't you look where you're – oh, hello, Miles." Benjy stopped, the bicycle slipping beneath him, one foot on the ground.

"What's happened to you?" Miles enquired. Benjy made an attempt to brush off the snow.

"Oh well, I was coming over the bridge and it sort of – dropped on me. I'm seeing you today for the second supervision, aren't I?"

"Yes." He watched Benjy remove the hood of his Barbour. Pink-cheeked, elf-locks flying, he seemed designed to counterbalance the whiteness of the street. "I've finished the last draft."

"Where are you off to now?"

Benjy was evasive, avoiding Miles' eye. "What about you?" he enquired.

"Just going to get something for breakfast."

"Let's have something together. I haven't eaten yet and I'm starving. I had to come up to drop an essay in."

"Well – I'm not certain –"

"Come on, you aren't doing anything, are you?"

Miles wasn't, and they went off to the Blue Boar, a hotel unpatronised by undergraduates. Miles had an obscure anxiety about being seen in public with Benjy. Once there, he ordered liberally and fed Benjy with pedagogic indulgence, as though to compensate for this fear.

"I often think you don't get enough to eat," he explained. Benjy shook his head.

"Hall food's lousy, but I don't do too badly. Do you want that slice of toast?"

"I expect you make up for it when you go home."

Benjy spread marmalade studiously. "Home?" he said at last. "I have no home."

"I see. My apologies."

"Why be sorry? Nothing to do with you." Concentrating on his toast. "I've been uprooted quite a while now."

"And your parents – are they dead?"

"My mother died when my sister was born. My father was killed in Cairo eight years ago."

"Cairo?"

"He was in the Diplomatic Corps."

"I see. Of course, out there I suppose it's pretty dangerous –"

"Oh, it wasn't anything like that. Nothing political, terrorists or anything. He fell off a roof. It was an accident."

Benjy announced this with disconcerting flatness. Miles stirred his coffee and remembered Benjy's clichéd attempts to describe his fears after the bicycle accident. His face showed no fear now: it was impassive.

"And so you came back to England?"

"I was sent back here, with the furniture, and sent to school. In the holidays, they farmed me out to relations. Luckily for them, there are quite a few. None of them had to put up with me for more than once a year."

Moved by his bitterness, Miles asked: "And your sister?"

He wondered what insouciant disclosure Benjy would make as soon as he enquired.

"My sister? Oh, they keep us apart."

A group of residents, breakfasting late, arrived and these distracted his attention. Miles was glad of the relief, though he felt driven to question Benjy further, to discover the cause of his cryptic nightmares.

"What's your sister's name?"

"Olivia. She – she might be coming up here next year. If she passes all the exams."

"That's splendid. You'll be together, and Olivia will have someone to look after her in Cambridge."

The effect of this conventional remark, intended to be conciliatory, was astonishing. Benjy put down his cup.

"What do you mean?"

"Exactly what I said. You'll be able to guide her through the first term. I expect she'll be rather lonely at first."

"You don't know Olivia," he replied darkly.

Miles demurred.

"*Your* sister didn't come up, did she?"

"Do you mean Francesca? I didn't realise that you –"

"I went to one of her concerts once, in London. She doesn't look much like you, does she?"

"Benjy –"

"I know, I'm not much like my father, come to that. I'm not very diplomatic."

"Perhaps I should be getting back. I've got some essays to mark –"

"Oh Miles, don't be offended, please." Benjy gave a pleading smile, brushing a stray croissant crumb from his cheek. Miles wondered, not for the first time, how conscious Benjy was of his charm. Depending on Miles' mood, Benjy was a fascinating Jacobean princeling, or a self-conscious Italian waiter; but whichever he resembled, he always won Miles over.

"What will you be doing this Vac, Benjy?"

"I'll be in London. There are some relations up in High-gate."

"Do you get on well with them?"

"They're all right. Not there, most of the time. They let me have the run of the house and I can get on with some revision, go to the cinema, you know the sort of thing." His face was set, with the underlip drawn in. If he had not seemed so distant, literally and figuratively, Miles would have reached out to him.

"And in the summer?"

"I'm not going to worry about that yet."

Miles was already making his plans.

"Well –" He got up, paying despite Benjy's protests. "I'll see you this afternoon."

He walked out of the hotel without looking back.

Miles knew it to be the last time he had a legitimate excuse to see Benjy. The course of supervisions was over. The essay itself, splendidly entitled 'Macaronic Equivocation in *The Anatomy of Melancholy*', needed only retyping and one or two alterations. It would be completed long before the Lent Term deadline and leave Benjy plenty of time for revision. Miles' task was finished.

Benjy now sat in his chair, fiddling with a lock of hair and Miles stood at the window.

"I wonder if that chap ever does anything else?"

"Who?"

"The one who runs around the Quad."

"Where? Let me see." Benjy was across the room and at his side in an instant. Briefly, his arm brushed Miles, before he took up a position some distance away, arms folded, closed in on himself. Miles felt the panic of desire, surprised by the physical response triggered off by Benjy's touch, and bewildered by the fact that Benjy, so distinct and self-possessed, seemed unaware of it.

"Does he always do that?"

"Every single day." Managing to keep the quake out of his voice. Miles, unaccustomed to such demonstrations by his body, was convinced that his affliction must be evident.

"Miles – is anything wrong?" Benjy enquired in the tones of the polite undergraduate he so evidently was not.

"Nothing at all. It's just rather hot in here." Miles, appalled at himself, sat down firmly and crossed his legs.

"I hope we'll meet next term," Benjy said, refilling the teapot. He moved around Miles' room with heartbreaking familiarity, taking down books, offering him the plate of biscuits.

"I expect we'll run into each other." Gradually Miles was bringing himself under control. "We always seem to."

"I'll miss our talks."

"There's no reason why there shouldn't be more."

"I'm sorry if I was rude this morning – about Olivia."

"That's perfectly all right."

"I – I sometimes find it difficult to get on with her. Sibling rivalry, I suppose."

"What does she plan to read?"

"Modern Languages, I suppose. Or at least, that's what she's taken the entrance exams in. She's been educated in France – at a convent."

"Cambridge will be a bit different after that."

"Maybe you'll meet her."

The conversation turned to other things, films Benjy had seen, a novel both had read, intellectual gossip.

"By the way, I've been meaning to ask you," Benjy enquired, "who *is* Sir Hilary Middlemass?"

"How did you know about him?"

"I noticed your sister plays a lot of his stuff."

"He's a composer. You know the sort of thing – English mysticism, backed up by a spell in the Party in the thirties. Lots of folk tunes, and an obsession with William Blake. He lives near us in Norfolk, but he's a bit of a recluse."

"I saw a programme about him recently. He wasn't actually on it – refused to be interviewed."

"That's fairly typical. He's on the arrogant side, I'm afraid, but he's been very good to Francesca."

"So he lives near you at – where is it?"

"Bly."

"Bly." Benjy smiled and stretched luxuriously, so that Miles wondered if he were aware of the effect he had, and said that he must go. Miles accompanied him to the top of the staircase, prepared to say goodbye there.

"No, come and look at the snow," Benjy insisted. There

had been a fresh fall since lunchtime, covering all footprints, and the Quad was a half-completed canvas under the wash of dark sky. Miles found an old envelope in his pocket, scribbled hastily on the back of it, and offered it to Benjy.

"Francesca has a house in Campden Hill Square. I usually stay there for Christmas. You're welcome to drop in when you're up in London –"

Benjy smiled, grinned. He looked about twelve years old. "That's marvellous. I'd love to –"

"Then give me a ring." Miles drew back automatically from Benjy's enthusiasm. "Have a good vacation. And don't work too hard."

"Miles –" shaking hands, mock-stalwart – "thanks for everything."

Benjy turned and walked away, leaving a neat trail of footprints, turned at the arch to wave, and disappeared.

Benjy had gone. Miles stood looking out into the Quad, where his footprints were still visible in the early starlight. Turning back to the room, he saw, as in a trailer, Benjy falling through the open door, Benjy pacing the room, Benjy self-contained and aloof beside the gas-fire, profile sharp and definite. He saw himself meeting, losing, Benjy among the narrow streets and bridges, *like some East Anglian Aschenbach*, he thought severely, and resolved to ring Francesca.

Miles was caught in the cross-current of elation at Benjy's recent presence and depression at his absence: he could not concentrate, could neither go out nor stay in, was scarcely able to decide whether to go into Hall for distraction or work himself into oblivion with a pile of supervision reports.

The telephone rang at that moment.

"Francesca! I was just about to –"

"I know." Matter-of-factly, as though telepathy were a normal method of communication. "How are you?"

"A bit dazed, really."

"That's what I thought. You sound rather confused."

"I am rather confused."

"I simply wanted to know whether you're coming up to London."

"I expect I shall be –"

"You can't spend Christmas alone."

Miles had often thought that spending Christmas alone was probably the best way to endure the festive season, but said nothing. He could sense Francesca's silent impatience.

"I don't know if I could spend it happily with Charlotte," he said.

"Oh, Lottie's gone."

"Gone? Gone where?"

"I'll explain when we meet. It was a personality clash. I'll be on my own at Campden Hill. You will come?"

"Of course I'll come." And Francesca's voice continued, beautiful and calm, detailing her programme of concert bookings, evenings when she would be at home, dinner engagements; Miles scarcely listened to what she had to say, only hearing the voice, melodious as her cello, and longing to be with her.

"I'll come as soon as you like," he said, when she had finished her disquisition on the acoustics of the Queen Elizabeth Hall. "It all sounds wonderful."

"Miles, have you been listening to a word I've said?"

"Every word."

"I said, I need a new accompanist."

"I'm sure you'll find someone. You always do. I'll see you at the weekend."

Now he knew that she would be alone, Francesca's professional problems were of no interest to him. Miles would have his sister all to himself – that was really what mattered.

It was true that Miles had never liked any of Francesca's companions: her accompanists, invariably female; the conductor, whom Miles had regarded as a sinister, Svengalian influence; Clarice, the Canadian feminist writer who could roll cigarettes with one hand and had propositioned Miles in the kitchen; and Emily Deutsch.

Emily Deutsch had been different: Miles had arrived in London one afternoon three years previously to find her installed, Francesca absent, and Emily's possessions disposed about the house.

Emily Deutsch had been cooking, and the entire house smelt of fresh bread. Geraniums glowed in the area, and, searching for the cause of all these changes, Miles had clattered downstairs to find what on first sight appeared to be a child of twelve standing at the kitchen table, a girl with a china doll face and black velvet dress.

"Who are you?" she had asked directly, just like a child.

"I'm Miles. I live here – occasionally."

"So do I. My name's Emily. I live here all the time."

She shook hands like a stiff little infanta, leaving a dust of flour, so that Miles was reminded more than ever of a Victorian doll brought down from an attic.

"Where's Francesca?"

"Out."

"Yes, but where?"

"Rehearsing."

"Shouldn't you be with her?"

"She is rehearsing a concerto, so that would not be necessary."

Miles fetched out the pure malt, and Emily gave him a glance which suggested that he was in the advanced stages of alcoholism.

"How long have you known my sister?"

"For a time."

"Where did you meet?"

"We were introduced by a mutual acquaintance." She rolled pastry, deftly, precisely. Miles felt uncomfortable, knowing that he had a certain degree of charm, even knowing that he attracted women, although he often regretted the consequences. But he could never have charmed Emily.

Francesca had arrived soon after this episode, but Miles had made his excuses and left. For the next eighteen months, every time he met his sister, Emily Deutsch seemed to be with her, regarding him with the same quiet contempt, replying to his social inconsequentialities with the calculated insolence of a Henry James creation.

"She's dreadful. How can you put up with her?" he had asked, on one of the few occasions when he and Francesca were alone.

"But she's brilliant. You've heard her play."

Miles thought that she played exactly as she spoke: cool, precise, dispassionate, giving away no more than was necessary. She seemed incapable of passion.

Miles was never certain if Emily and Francesca were lovers. He tried not to think about his sister's personal life too much: once or twice, imagining the two women together, he had experienced a powerful and debilitating frisson, almost as strong as that occasionally sparked off by Benjy.

When he had learnt that Emily was dying, by degrees, of some unspecified tumour, Miles' lack of compassion had made him feel guilty. Perhaps it was how doctors felt, he had thought, simply watching another specimen go through the progress from clinic to clinic, the curtailment of personal liberty, the eventual confinement to bed. She was merely another statistic, her case gaining additional pathos by virtue of her talents.

Articles appeared in one or two papers, delineating her gifts: a solo album was re-released. Miles could not avoid seeing her from time to time, noting that she had become thinner, now seemed a nightmare doll, that her silky hair had started to fall out as if uprooted by a spoilt child.

And still she recognised him, knew who he was, stared with resentment when he last saw her, speechless with painkillers, the dummy keyboard on which she had been practising abandoned. Emily had seen Miles and Francesca standing by her bed, seen Miles put his arm around his sister's shoulders, clenched herself, and died.

The very fact that he had felt no pity for Emily made Miles guilty for her death: that, and the resentment which had been Francesca's response. She had treated the world as though it were to blame, and instead of bringing them even closer, as Miles had hoped, Emily's death drove them apart. She retreated to France for six months, leaving no address, no telephone number. It was the longest interval for which they had ever been separated.

And then, in the middle of June, she had reappeared in

Cambridge, brilliant, plumper, and as though Emily Deutsch had never existed.

Now, Miles looked forward to the comforts of London: warm rooms, sybaritic armchairs, gold and plush theatres, familiar dinner parties at which he would be known for his reticence and left in peace, to watch and listen. He would have Francesca to himself, to walk with across Hyde Park on grey, blustering afternoons after lunch. And, perhaps, Benjy.

Miles sat in the Cambridge station buffet, stirring his tea and waiting for the train to Liverpool Street. He was lost in the *Times* crossword when a quiet voice named him, and he looked up to see Benjy.

"I thought you'd have gone down, ages ago," said Miles. Benjy was swathed in his covert coat, and stood protectively beside a tall girl with burnished hair. She was dressed in the usual amalgamation of styles he recognised from other students, but her boyish jacket, baggy trousers and soft felt hat were worn with considerably more élan. Miles found her striking and slightly ambiguous.

"This is Mel. I've been showing her round Cambridge. Melissa, this is Dr Tattershall, one of my supervisors."

"Hi. Benjy's told me a lot about you. I recognised you right away." She smiled benevolently, as though bestowing warmth on a mortal.

"Miles has done a lot for me. Miles, Mel is my cousin. I'm going to stay with her family for Christmas."

"That sounds nice. How were your supervision reports, by the way?" He took refuge in academe, conscious of Melissa's benignant scrutiny.

"They weren't that bad. Much better than I expected. Thanks for putting in a good word, Miles. Cheered my tutor up no end."

All discourse was interrupted by the baleful tones of the public address system, and with a conditioned reflex everyone reached for their luggage.

It was rush hour, and in the resurgence to the train, Miles, Melissa and Benjy were separated. He recovered a dropped case to see the tips of Melissa's scarf disappearing from view, climbed into the nearest carriage, and settled down with a sigh. It would be best not to pursue them: after all, they would want to be alone. How long, he wondered, had Benjy known her?

The door of the compartment slid open: Benjy and Melissa sat opposite, taking over the seat with their belongings and the characteristic Underwood manner of sprawling across the largest available space. Melissa's trousers and cowboy boots had the paradoxical effect of making her seem more feminine; she also wore a thin leather tie, and had the appearance of an active heroine in a Western. Melissa and Benjy made a strange couple, young, slightly disturbing, and not quite like anything Miles had come across before.

"So you're at Woodville? Sometimes I wish I'd gone to Cambridge," said Melissa happily, obviously not regretting the lost opportunity. "It must be great to be clever."

"But you are!" protested Benjy. "Mel is a designer, Miles. She works for this advertising agency in London. You should see some of the things she comes up with."

"What do you design?" Miles asked cautiously. He had only the vaguest idea of what Melissa's occupation involved.

"I'm what's known as a finished artist," Melissa laughed. "Yes, I've heard all the jokes. Still, it pays. I'd love to live in a place like Cambridge, though. Seems to be so quiet and peaceful."

"Far from that, isn't it, Miles?" Benjy enquired. He seemed relaxed, happy, a little intoxicated, and while Miles liked and responded to Melissa, he envied her for the effect she had on the boy.

Melissa appeared confident, unselfconscious, and outgoing, as if there were no reason why she should not approach life with complete optimism. Cambridge would soon have robbed her of such convictions, Miles realised.

The journey passed quickly, although Miles felt a little as though he were being exhibited to Melissa as a freak. Benjy and his cousin chattered to each other, cheerfully planning what to do in London, and Miles realised that if anyone were going to spend a lonely Christmas, it would be himself. As they drew into Liverpool Street, and Melissa turned to fetch her leather satchel down from the luggage rack with strong amazonian arms, Benjy touched Miles lightly on the shoulder.

"Don't worry," he said hoarsely, dramatising the scene ridiculously. "*Don't worry*. I'll see you before long."

Francesca lived in a Georgian house with a blue plaque by the door which had once sheltered a minor Victorian poet. Miles paid off his taxi in a state of mild euphoria, supplemented by the promise of dinner, wine, and the low, soft sofa. He experienced an unusual sense of well-being.

The hall was in darkness as Miles made his way inside, and he wondered if Francesca had gone out. Then, a stroke of light thickened and Francesca stood in the drawing-room doorway.

"Miles?" She sounded apprehensive.

"Who else?"

"You sound very pleased with yourself."

This was not the reception he had been expecting. But perhaps she was tired. Francesca switched on the overhead light and Miles saw that she was pale and drawn. This was not unusual, and the house gave no signs of disorder: the armchair received him, the decanter was put into his hands in the familiar ritual, Francesca was as beautifully dressed as ever in bottle-green silk and a Victorian paisley shawl. Yet somehow these indications of normality served only to emphasise her air of disturbance. Miles took her hand and found it clammy.

"Whatever is it?"

"Nothing. Oh, it's silly really – I –" She shivered suddenly, and in lieu of anything else, Miles got up and wrapped his overcoat around her shoulders, coaxing her to sit down and drink some whisky herself. "There's been a disturbance," she said at last.

"A disturbance? What, some sort of riot, you mean?"

"That's what they call it. A disturbance."

"Who? What are you talking about, Francesca?"

"I came downstairs the other morning – about nine. Miles, something had got into the kitchen and smashed half the china."

53

"Something?"

"It couldn't have been a person. I've had the police round – that was the first thing I did. There were no signs of a break-in."

"Could it have been cats – something like that?"

"I didn't leave any windows open. You know how careful I am – especially after I bought that Guarneri last year."

"And you don't know anyone – I mean you haven't –"

"I don't go round giving people keys to the house, if that's what you mean. Oh, don't worry, they asked me all that."

"Then I simply don't understand."

"I think I do. That's why I used the word 'disturbance'."

"Well, I'm perplexed. I don't see how on earth –"

"I'm not talking about on earth."

"Then what are you talking about?"

"Psychic activity, Miles. Ghosts, kinetic energy."

"Really, Francesca –"

And then he remembered.

Something like this had happened to Francesca before. Miles had been away at school, but there had been reports of inexplicable incidents, curious lights and noises in the middle of the night, breakages. Francesca had been found wandering, oblivious and half-dressed, in an orchard on more than one occasion. It was six miles from the vicarage and no-one, including Francesca, ever discovered how she got there. At first, Miles had learnt much of this indirectly, from a school-friend; but later witnessed the occurrence for himself. His father refused to discuss the subject, but the word 'disturbance' had been employed.

In his later reading, Miles realised that occasionally adolescent girls attracted this form of unaccountable manifestation, and when he considered their childhood at the Old Vicarage, such events were quite explicable. Nevertheless, he always made a conscious effort to avoid thinking about them.

"Why?" he asked at last.

"I don't know. Things started to happen a few months ago – a window got broken, a looking-glass cracked –"

"You haven't been having any runs of bad luck, have you? But tell me, is this why Charlotte left?"

"She couldn't stand any more of it, she said. Or perhaps she just couldn't stand any more of me. I don't know. But she got on my nerves, Miles, she was so worried about me and I couldn't stand it. So we agreed that she should go."

"When did she leave?" Miles had not expected to spend the evening discussing such a bizarre dilemma, and slightly resented it. Francesca had no right to have problems, when he needed her there to be calm, and soothing, and ready to listen. Resigning himself to the situation, he took up the position of a good listener and poured another glass of the excellent pure malt Francesca always got in for him.

"A month ago. She – she told me some ridiculous story about a recurring nightmare. Something was trying to strangle her. Anyway, we agreed to part, because it was ruining her concentration. She simply couldn't play properly with this going on."

So Francesca shared his own basic selfishness: Miles was reassured by this. The fact that his sister had turned Charlotte out because of her failure to fulfil her professional commitment convinced him that she must still be well-adjusted, despite these events. Francesca sat opposite him now, a little colour tinging her face as the whisky began to take effect. Presently she suggested that they have dinner.

"There's veal, and a raspberry meringue," she said, the calm, detached Francesca of the concert platform returning visibly. And the meal *was* as he had expected, the kitchen, just like the rest of the house, undisturbed and tranquil.

Francesca's house had none of the attributes of a haunted one: well lit, with its white woodwork and biscuit-coloured carpets, it defied any horrors in the cellarage, or presences above the highly polished banisters which curved into a stairwell. The minor Victorian poet had lived an apparently prosperous and uneventful life there, dying peacefully. Which was probably, Miles had once remarked, why he had been a minor poet.

"How did you manage to explain all that broken china to your insurance man?" he asked.

"Well, it certainly wasn't an Act of God, whatever it was. We finally put it down to the Underground. They've been doing things to the Central Line and we decided it must be earth tremors. It looks satisfactory on paper. I only wish I could believe it myself."

"That still doesn't explain Charlotte's nightmares."

"Oh God, Charlotte. Don't. I liked her, Miles, but she was a tiresome woman."

"I think she's very fond of you, Francesca. She spent a lot of time talking about you."

"Yes, I'm sorry about wishing her on you like that. But you know what it's like. However fond you are of someone, you just want to get away from them once in a while. Oh. Perhaps you don't," she added, catching Miles' eye.

"I can understand your feelings." But Miles was lying to spare Francesca's. He could never imagine wanting to get away from Benjy. Every moment spent away from him was spent wondering how long it would be before he saw him again.

"By the way, why are you so cheerful tonight? You're positively incandescent."

"I met some people on the way down."

"Is that all?"

"A student of mine, Benjy – you've heard me mention him before – and a girl."

"What was she like?"

"Very nice." It was rather a tame way of describing Melissa. "A designer of some sort. Terribly trendy, with boots and a jacket three sizes too big for her. Quite endearing, that."

"Not your type at all," replied Francesca firmly. Miles looked at her in surprise.

"I don't have a type – do I? Anyway, don't suppose I shall see her again. Benjy might pop round – he's staying in London."

"I'll look forward to meeting him. Perhaps I can get you some tickets, and you can come to one of the concerts." Francesca was smiling again. Perhaps Miles had imagined it, but it had seemed to him that she had tensed at the mention of Melissa. Surely she could not be jealous?

56

"Isn't Benjy the boy who was working on Burton?"

"That's right. Rather a sad case, in fact – his parents are dead, and he spends all his holidays staying with relations."

"You must ask him here," said Francesca. "He could have the spare room. As long as he doesn't disturb the vibrations."

"The what?"

"The psychic meteorology."

"Let's hope he won't."

Miles had never been afraid of ghosts: there were far too many material threats without coping with an unknown fear, and besides which he felt an instinctive affinity with those members of a twilight world which he would have found difficult to explain, but which perhaps was the consequence of his own, shadowy personality.

Flitting about his own imaginative half-world, absorbed with figures from the past and forgotten authors, he had nothing to fear from other spirits only slightly more ethereal than he. At present, his major preoccupation was that Francesca must be on the edge of some form of nervous breakdown: it would fit in with Charlotte's concerned if intrusive warnings. Conceivably, she had broken the china herself; and perhaps been the cause of all the other mysterious disturbances. Miles was quite prepared to find a clinical explanation for her behaviour, and wondered if it could have been triggered off by Emily's death and some long-suppressed grief.

But there had been the stories at Bly. Francesca found wandering in an orchard at dawn, moving lights in the darkness, furniture displaced. There was even a rumour that she had got into the church and been found in the organ loft.

But rumours spread in villages and schools, so that Miles could never be certain that any of them was true: he wouldn't have been surprised if another Norfolk boy in the Classics VIth had come up to him and said that his sister had been discovered giving demonic performances on the organ, clad in a black silk cloak.

However, Miles worried. There was the fact that none of her companions remained with her for long; there were the sudden, unexplained rifts between herself and her friends, the acquaintance who turned into a bosom-friend overnight, the old friend suddenly declared an enemy. For all her outward appearance of serenity, Francesca was a difficult person. The poise was a form to which she attained, rather than the unreflective good nature which characterised Melissa.

Melissa belonged to a distant, prosaic world. It was far removed from his own way of life, and slightly intimidating. Putting out the light, he prepared to sleep.

Miles was not afraid of ghosts.

The few days leading up to Christmas were enjoyable, despite shopping crowds on the tube and the press of bodies in Charing Cross Road as he combed the few remaining anti-quarian bookshops with professional vigilance. As he had hoped, Miles and Francesca attended undemanding dinner parties (where he was not expected to make conversation with a single female of his own age cunningly invited to put him at ease), walked in Kensington Gardens and on Hampstead Heath together, went round galleries. They would sit in front of some arbitrarily selected painting and gossip, just as they had done in the school holidays when Francesca's already demanding professional commitments had allowed her only a weekend in London instead of a month at Bly.

In public, Francesca seemed serene as ever; very occasion-ally, she would be recognised and unlike Miles, who would have felt cornered and shy, would extricate herself so adeptly that her admirers assumed she could scarcely tear herself away. "I'd loathe it," Miles said, after just such an incident, when they had escaped to the Friends' coffee room at the Royal Academy.

"I know you would. I know you hate strangers."

"I don't mind strangers. It's when they try and get to know me that I'm afraid."

Francesca smiled to herself, smooth and unruffled as a glossy cat. It was then that Miles realised how much happier his sister was when out of the house. He had resolved not to sense any atmosphere, any suspicion that he was in the company of supernatural beings when alone in the house; he had turned over another page, watched the play of sunlight across the floor, or rapped away at the piano.

However, sometimes he realised that his sister did not possess the same ability to switch herself off and ignore any sensations of unease. Miles would look up from his book and see her staring into air, the way cats do, as though seeing something which he could not, or gazing at a corner of the room with an expression of modified hopelessness. When she caught him watching her, she would smile, distractedly, and look away.

"Have you ever thought of moving?"

Francesca turned to him. Miles realised that the words were peremptory in this rarefied atmosphere, and felt that the coffee room rebuked him.

"Moving where?"

"Getting another house. Or a flat. Somewhere without any memories."

"What for? I'm perfectly happy where I am."

"I simply thought –"

"I don't know what you thought."

Francesca turned away, hugging her collar, although the room was far from cold. Miles wished he had not mentioned it: it took tea at Brown's to bring her round.

Christmas passed off much as Miles had expected: he and Francesca attended sedate parties, and Francesca gave her services in a series of charity concerts as she always did during that season.

One evening, soon after Boxing Day, Miles sat alone with an espionage novel set, with questionable veracity, in Cambridge. He was waiting for Francesca to return from St John's, Smith Square, and looked forward to the domestic commonplaces: the brandy nightcap and scornful viewing of some film on television before bed. In fact, he anticipated this all pleasantly when the doorbell rang, and rang again with prolonged violence.

Miles jolted up, ran down from the first-floor sitting room: the hall was a lake of darkness into which beams from the streetlamp spilled through the fanlight. The ring came again, and with similar intensity, as, puzzling at the locks, Miles finally got the door open.

"Who's there?"

A bedraggled figure, thin despite its swathes of winter clothes, stood silhouetted in the porch: beyond and above, a winter moon fled through the sky.

"Who's there?" he repeated, questioning the air, and, for all his ease with the half-world of shadows, wondered if he were about to see an apparition. The answer, when it came, was almost what he expected. A figure named him, hesitantly.

"Benjamin?" Miles found the light, and at the sudden illumination Benjy threw his arm across his face in a melo-dramatic gesture, darted inside, slammed the door behind him and fell against it wheezing.

"Have you run all the way?"

"Something like that." Patting his chest histrionically, Benjy added: "All the way from High Street Ken tube."

The boy looked awful: his pale face was pointed and strained, the skin beneath the eyes puffy and blue. His clothes appeared to have soaked and dried on his back.

"Whatever's happened?"

"Don't ask." He looked round. "Is your sister here?"

"She's out. Playing."

Benjamin shivered.

"Look, you'd better come and get warm. Come and have a drink."

Benjy followed him upstairs, a dark and spectral figure against the expansive carpeting and glossed woodwork. He watched like a stray cat as Miles built up the fire and poured out whisky, apprehensive and grateful. Benjy sat nervously on the edge of his chair at first, but when Miles returned from the kitchen with mineral water, it was to find him crouching close to the fender, almost on top of the flames.

Demolishing his pure malt, he held out the glass for another, with a desperation that deprived the gesture of rudeness. Shrugging, Miles poured it, diluting his own. When Benjy was on his third, he turned from the fire and looked up at Miles.

"Nice to see you again, Miles."

"Don't tell me you came here in this condition on a social call."

"You don't mind me coming?"

"Of course not. But you seem to be incubating a dose of flu."

"Yes – yes, I know. Hang on a minute." Benjy produced a small inhaler from his voluminous pockets, and held it between his lips. After three or four puffs, he breathed deeply and put it away.

"Aren't those things dangerous?"

"Yes. I think I probably overdo it. But there we are." He sighed, suddenly languid and relaxed. "I didn't come – straight here. I've been sort of – wandering about. I don't know for how long, but I found your address and suddenly realised I could come here. I got a bit lost on the Circle Line."

"Have you been drinking, Benjamin?" Miles wished that he did not sound so sententious.

"No. Something happened." He gulped, shook, but whether this was on account of the whisky or past events, Miles could not tell.

By an association of ideas which he was unable to follow, Miles found himself asking: "Is Melissa all right?"

"Melissa?" Benjy seemed surprised. "Mel? Yes, of course. Didn't really affect her that much."

"What didn't?"

Miles visualised a series of appalling events, road accidents, house fires, Benjy and Mel arrested by the Drugs Squad. "If you give me some indication of what's been happening, perhaps I can help."

"My sister's back."

"Is that all?"

"We don't always get on. We're too alike."

"So have you had a disagreement?"

"Yeah, there's been a row. There was a lot of hassle about me staying with Mel, for one thing."

"I *see*."

"No, you don't. Melissa and I – well, Mel's nearly four

years older than me, and she's into all these macho types –
guys in leather jackets – freelance copywriters working in
Covent Garden, you know the sort."

"I can't say I've ever met anybody like that, Benjy."

"No, but you can imagine. I mean, she's not interested in
me. But we do get on really well, and she's great, very
sympathetic and *normal*. I like being with Mel. She makes me
feel good."

"I can understand that. But why would your sister resent
it?"

"She's just difficult, Miles. It's hard to explain. She has this
mercurial temperament, and it's hard to live with."

Miles did not comment that they both shared this characteristic.

"Where is Olivia, now?"

"She's gone off somewhere, with a friend."

"Your family life seems arbitrary, to say the least."

"I'll phone Mel's mum later. She can tell me whether it's
safe to come back. Mel's gone to earth in Putney."

"Are your family reunions always like this?"

"Almost always. When we have them, which is seldom,
because that's how they end up. Mel's family are very under-
standing, though. Not like us at all."

"Look, I think I'd better be off. Thanks for the drink –"
Staggering to his feet.

"You can't go back in that state."

"I'll be okay," Benjy replied, collapsing. He slumped quite
slowly to the floor and lay there, almost at Miles' feet, hair
over his eyes and mouth slightly open, a modern shabby
Chatterton.

Wondering whether to make him comfortable there, or try
and drag him onto the sofa, Miles bent down and attempted
to lift Benjy. He was surprisingly light, seemed bonier than
previously. As he disposed him over the sofa, Miles considered what to say to Francesca. And almost on cue, Francesca
arrived, vivid and laughing, music case under one arm, scarf
bright against her dark hair.

"Miles! What *are* you doing?"

"Come and see."

62

She looked with concern over the sofa-back, where Benjy slept like a haggard child.

"But who is he?"

"Benjamin Underwood."

Francesca put her hand to his pale cheek: the touch must have wakened Benjy, for he opened his eyes and looked from one to the other of them, then he took Francesca's hand and kissed it.

Benjy had been given the spare bedroom, where Charlotte used to sleep, and had retreated politely if shakily to it, as Miles and Francesca sat opposite each other that night.

"He said there'd been a misunderstanding."

"A row."

"He did call it that," Miles agreed.

"But he seemed shocked. Terrified. Surely one's own sister can't have that effect on one –"

"You never know."

"No, it must be something else. Unless he's given to imagining things."

"He was acting as though something were after him." Miles glanced down at the spy story which he had thrown down beside his chair. "Perhaps he's been reading too many of these," he suggested, picking it up.

"Do you think he's unstable?"

"He's very sensitive. But then, with his background –"

"Didn't you say his father was killed – in some odd sort of way?"

"That's right. The circumstances were – rather unusual."

"How peculiar."

"Yes. So peculiar that it must be true."

Morning hung bright and frosted beyond the black trees. Miles dressed and went down to the kitchen, surprised to find Benjy there, half-sprawled over the table as he read the more recondite reviews in *The Times*. Looking up briefly, he smiled.

"Have you had breakfast?"

It seemed extraordinary that Benjy was there at all, elbows

among the coffee cups, shining morning face lowered over the newsprint.

"Yes, but I can always eat more."

Benjy's mercurial changes of mood continued to surprise Miles: he still looked crumpled, but his flushed face and air of well-being made it seem like wilful eccentricity of dress.

"Sleep well?"

"Eh? Oh. Except for one of you moving around, yes."

"Moving around?"

"Somebody was. Just outside my room – in fact I got up and had a look, but I couldn't see anybody."

"What time was this?"

"Don't know – my watch stopped."

"Have you seen Francesca?"

"She came down for a cup of coffee. I think she's practising."

Francesca appeared at that moment, as if summoned; she tapped Miles on the shoulder as she passed.

"Aren't you going to make some more coffee?"

"Oh – I'm sorry – I –" He had been standing there in a daze, bewildered and delighted by Benjy's miraculous ordinariness, the gesture with which he slicked butter over toast, or stopped with his cup halfway to his mouth, arrested by some sentence.

"Miles is always standing about like that," Francesca told Benjy. They seemed to be on excellent terms.

"Miles – Francesca – look, I think I'll have to be going soon –"

"How do you feel?"

"Oh, I'm fine. Fine."

"Did you telephone –"

"Yes. And I spoke to Melissa. We're meeting for a drink at lunchtime."

"And Olivia?"

"Olivia is on her way back to France."

"You all seem to lead what Stella Gibbons called rich emotional lives," commented Miles.

Benjy agreed equably, and added: "Do you want to come to the pub? Mel would be pleased to see you again."

"Where are you meeting?" Cautious, as he did not like the sound of Covent Garden.

"We'll take you somewhere that isn't *too* alarming, Miles. Not too trendy. Don't worry. Somewhere in the piazza, where there are lots of copywriters and journalists."

"That sounds even worse."

With misgivings, Miles accompanied Benjy to the windswept expanses of WC2. His anxiety was mitigated by his pleasure in the boy's company: even waiting at High Street Kensington tube, usually a dreary experience, was a memorable event because they were together.

Miles actually found Covent Garden reassuring: the milling tourists, marketplace, and oddly dressed pedestrians reminded him of Cambridge. Benjy and Melissa had made a wise choice.

They found Melissa sitting at an outdoor table in the Rock Garden, hands in the pockets of her battered leather jacket, hair stirring like a scarf in the wind. She smiled at Miles, as though eager to see him; but she probably greeted everyone like that, he thought.

"There you are! We were wondering where you'd got to. Miles, this is Tony. We work together."

Tony, Benjy later commented, looked like the hero of a nineteen-sixties bike movie. His glowering features, lean jaw, and thirty-six-hour growth of beard all added to the impression: but the whole image was shattered the moment he opened his mouth and uttered the strangulated, slightly diffident syllables of a public schoolboy attempting to live down his education and become a black sheep in black leather.

Melissa, after some protest by Miles, bought the first round of drinks, and Tony concentrated on a sandwich. Miles, out of place, self-conscious, but intrigued by his surroundings, watched her. The ambiguous clothes, slightly provocative air, reminded him of Benjy; he could see now that they were related. But Melissa had warmth, an openness, which Benjy lacked.

Benjy's ambivalence perplexed and confused: but the same trend in Melissa had made her an honest tomboy.

"How are things at home now?" she asked, working

through a bottle of chianti with a dispatch which shocked Miles.

"I haven't been back. Miles and I just came straight here. Miles and Francesca have been really kind – looked after me."

"Are you from a large family yourself, Miles?" Melissa saw him shake his head, continued: "Then you don't know what these family reunions are like. Christ. We have this every time. I've come to regard it as normal. Anyway, Olivia's out of the way for a bit, so we can *all* get some peace and quiet."

"What time did she go?"

"Late last night. We all crashed out after that. God, I was glad to see the back of that girl. She really gets up my nose."

Miles was interested. Melissa didn't strike him as the type to be annoyed by others; and he hoped that he would never need to meet Olivia.

Melissa, as egotistic in her own way as Benjy, turned the conversation to her interests, and talked mostly about the agency. Apart from the fact that he could not take seriously a profession where the sales of toothpaste or pet food were a topic for profound concern, Miles found many similarities between Melissa's world and his own.

The political intrigues, animosities, personality cults: all these reminded him of the English Faculty, the only difference being that in the agency they were overt, not covert, and that most of the people concerned seemed well paid.

Finally Melissa prodded Tony, who, perhaps afraid of revealing his non-proletarian origins further, had remained silent during the meal. Melissa stood up, tall and jangling with cheap jewellery, swinging the satchel onto her broad shoulder.

"Have to get back. We're doing a pitch next week, and there's a lot on. They've buggered up the separations again."

Miles nodded: Melissa's world possessed jargon as obscure to the uninitiated as structuralism. Benjy, who had also been unusually silent, started to fidget.

"I'd better get back, too. I want to do some reading this afternoon." It sounded like a poor excuse, and Miles wondered whether he wanted to get away, or was simply afraid of imposing on his hospitality. "Thanks for putting up with me."

Trying to think of something to say, Miles ended up as usual saying nothing.

"Give my love to Francesca. Tell her how grateful I am, Miles."

"Yes – yes, of course." He shook Benjy's hand formally, slightly at a loss, and watched him walk away with Melissa and Tony, Melissa tall and brazen, Tony cultivating an appropriate slouch.

And Benjy, slim and huddled, striding beside them with his pink scarf glowing, talking but managing to look singular and alone.

The unaccustomed wine at lunchtime had slackened and re-laxed him: he wandered about the piazza for a time, wondering how to spend the afternoon, unwilling for some reason to return to Campden Hill Square and spend it with Francesca.

Miles tried not to drink during the day: his nerves, when they were not tensed, generally led him to discontent and daydreaming, longing for the impossible. At night-time this did not matter, and he could allow sleep to take over, but this afternoon as he roamed the streets he found himself wanting things he could never have, feeling that he had missed vast chunks of life which were commonplace for other people; and feeling that he would never be like them, happy and ordinary and doing as they liked.

He tried not to feel like this, dissuaded by his father from introspection at an early age: the practice had been condemned as 'unwholesome', the mental equivalent of masturbation.

But after only a moderate intake of alcohol, he found it difficult to suppress his instincts: perhaps it was a form of self-abuse, but as the body longs for sexual satisfaction, Miles longed for spiritual warmth, an intimacy with some other person who would accept and comfort him. And if anyone offered this, whoever it was, Miles would have been patheti-cally grateful.

He stood on Victoria Embankment, looking out across the bitter river, wind tugging at his collar, and realised what he

67

had hesitated to admit for years: Miles wanted desperately to be loved.

Miles arrived back later that afternoon to find Francesca asleep on the sofa, covered by her paisley shawl, hair released and spread across the cushions. Benjy had looked younger in sleep, a haggard child, whereas Francesca was marmoreal, hands folded like a figure on a tomb. She looked like her fifteenth-century ancestress, Inez, Lady Tattershyl, whose image, cobwebbed now and mazed with cracks, lay in a recess in the church at Bly.

Miles sat down beside her, covering the folded hands with his own, which were so different. Francesca's fingers were beautifully manicured, but short-nailed, powerful and un-equivocally purposeful, whereas Miles bit his nails and would absentmindedly crack his prominent knuckles. He covered her hands, just as he had covered Benjy's on a previous occasion.

Francesca, eyes still closed, gave a little sigh where she lay stretched beneath him. He wondered what she was dreaming about; her hair fell across her face and he lifted it gently away, remembering that dawn, years ago, when she had been found wandering in the orchard. She clutched his arm, muttering to herself, eyes still firmly closed, and her grip tightened until she woke, an instant later, blinked to see him sitting above her, murmured his name in recognition.

"Miles – where have you been?"

"Hatchards. You've been asleep."

She yawned, languid, stretching out again. "Asleep? Yes – I thought I was back in Norfolk. I dreamt about that orchard – do you remember?"

Francesca had never mentioned the incident directly before. "Do you remember?" she continued. "I couldn't think how I'd got there. I simply woke up and saw you. There you were."

Miles disengaged himself. Hands in the pockets of his jacket, he walked over to the window.

"Good sunset out there," he commented.

"Miles?"

He turned to her in the unlit room, saw her swathed in her shawl, propped by cushions, like an invalid: it was as though roles had been reversed. He remembered her coming to see him, as he lay ill, returning from her Conservatoire, distant and remote. Now she was calling him, almost pleading.

"Miles? Don't you remember what happened? *Miles?*"

In the twilight, diminished by shadows, she did not look so very different from her fifteen-year-old self. But she chose that moment to disperse the effect by sitting up and tossing back her hair. And the girl who had been his sister, bony and angular as himself, vanished into Francesca's elegant body.

Miles knew now that there could only be danger for his own peace of mind – and their fragile relationship – in his admitting memory, a total recall of events. Neither had referred to the incident before, and he was determined that they never should. Francesca's vulnerability, her soft, freshly woken eyes, induced cruelty in him.

"I don't know what you're talking about. You must have been dreaming."

Downcast, she looked aside and wrapped her shawl round her shoulders. Miles began to feel guilty, and went to sit beside her. But she turned away, settling the shawl more firmly about her shoulders like a protective cloak in a fairy tale, and walked out of the room.

Exhausted, and tired by the after-effects of wine, Miles lay down on the sofa himself. He did not dream, or even fall asleep, the nagging ache for Benjy keeping him awake. Sometimes it seemed as if Benjy cared: he had already made such a difference. And sometimes it seemed as if Benjy did not give a damn.

Trying to think for a change about someone else, Miles reflected on the fact that he and Francesca seemed to get on so much better for short periods. The extended interval of his stay had caused them to see too much of each other: he thought of their mutual trespass as she lay sleeping beneath him, and he touched her hair: and he remembered Benjy's gesture of kissing her hand. So many tentative movements, so little warmth: but he feared that if anyone were to treat him with tenderness, he would become totally addicted, totally dependent, and totally at the mercy of whoever chose to manipulate that tenderness and control him.

Francesca returned, calm, anger professionally mastered, and Miles announced that he would return to Cambridge that night. This news improved Francesca's temper so much that they shared an enjoyable dinner, and Miles described the lunch in Covent Garden.

"I wonder if Benjy's jealous of this Tony," Francesca commented. "Melissa sounds very attractive."

"She is. But not in a way you'd expect. She doesn't dress in a feminine way, or anything like that."

"Being feminine, as you call it, has nothing to do with appearances." He had the sensation that Francesca was laughing at him, but her face remained serious, and he wondered again what her predilections were. He knew better than to think further about it.

"Will you see Benjy next term?" she was asking.

"He seems pretty determined that I will."

"He's rather sweet, Miles."

"That's not the word I would have used."

"I shall have to start looking for a new accompanist, you know."

"Well, just make sure she isn't psychic. Or perhaps it would be better if she was. Benjy heard noises last night, you know."

"What sort of noises?"

"Someone moving about. He had Charlotte's old room, after all."

"Yes. Yes, you're right." Francesca put down the cream jug, and sat for an instant, one finger lying along her cheek.

Miles caught the last train from Liverpool Street and arrived at Cambridge in the early hours of the morning. The porter was still about, and his room was clammy as a tank.

As he lay down to sleep, too tired now to be kept awake by anxieties, Melissa, Francesca, Tony, receded as though on a railway platform. But Benjy's face was still with him, the image in the pane.

# Four

The following months passed paradoxically in an intense ordinariness, a brilliant, prosaic sequence during which Miles taught, lectured and read with an enthusiasm which amounted almost to inspiration; he actually began writing the first draft of his book and generated an excitement which affected even the apathetic third years, Unwin, Berman and Physshe.

Miles' colleagues noticed the change, but were unable to ascertain its cause: the heavy rains of February, beating down on his shoulders as he cycled to the Faculty, failed to depress him; he rode about Cambridge whistling, so that acquaintances who as a rule scarcely noticed him turned to look in amazement; he made inroads into his Heffer's account, stimulated to buy books which he would formerly never have read; and most of all, he dusted off the little manual portable and tackled Robert Burton.

Benjy would never change the world: he was not outstanding, no embryo genius, but he had changed Miles. His flawed arguments, over-insistent remarks, even his wilful misreadings, inspired Miles as a more proficient student would not have done. He felt intensely responsible for the boy, determined that he should succeed at something, even if it was simply obtaining a good degree; Benjy had some indefinable quality which eluded Miles, but he was adamant that whatever this quality was, it should be moulded to fit the demands of Tripos: he wanted to harness Benjy's brooding energy, his dark grief, gain him attention, applause even, in the narrow world of Cambridge.

Benjy for his part seemed to enjoy Miles' company, which was flattering; and Miles could never resist the offer of his companionship. Benjy would appear, sometimes during a supervision, sometimes just as Miles was on his way out, and demand conversation. At first, soon after January, Miles supposed that he wanted to discuss Francesca, convinced that Benjy had transferred his affections to her. But after polite enquiries, Francesca's name dropped from the interchanges.

Often they would sit in Miles' rooms, and though both were wary about supplying personal details, they seemed to discuss everything: school; Paris (as far as Miles had travelled, since a chance to lecture on Burton at Yale had to be cancelled at the last moment); spiders; poetry; the romance of railway stations; loyalty (a topic suggested by the recent defection of a don); cricket; Nostradamus; dreams; nuclear power; the sea; Proust. Benjy would alternatively sprawl and curl up as he talked, often fiddling with an unlit cigarette, whilst Miles tended to wander interminably up and down the room.

Sometimes they walked. Benjy had an appetite for metaphysical speculation over beer, and for reciting poetry under the starlight, running together bizarre and inapposite lines:

> With heigh! the doxy, over the dale
> Underneath the greenwood tree
> Like a rat without a tail
> Who is Sylvia, what is she?

Their conversation developed in width and range as they met and talked. Miles remembered one fragment of dialogue as particularly illuminating: it had been a late spring evening, with the sun vanishing in the ellipse of silver, as they crossed Midsummer Common.

"Why do those horses stay there?" Benjy asked, looking at the phlegmatic cobs which cropped the grass.

"Because there's nowhere else to go," Miles replied, indicating the heavy traffic on two sides, the Cam on the other, and the surrounding houses. "It's like that bit where Philoctetes asks Neoptolemus to let him go and Neoptolemus says: 'Where?'"

"'There is a world elsewhere'."

"Where?" Miles repeated.

"I suppose that's how you feel about Cambridge."

"I suppose it is."

"I thought I'd like to be an academic, when I was younger. Or a writer."

"Like to be? What's stopping you?"

"Talent, or rather lack of it. I used to create long rambling plots, and titles, but I never got round to writing the novels."

"What sort of titles did they have?"

"*Garlic and Sapphires* was one. Probably just as well it never got written. What are your ambitions, Miles? What do you really want out of life?"

Miles had never thought of life as something that one could get things out of, rather as something to be endured and got through with as little disruption as possible. He said so.

"But that's an awful attitude."

Miles shrugged, and gave no excuses. "It's how it strikes me. Oddly enough, I used to want to be invisible."

"Like a voyeur, you mean? So that you could watch people?"

"No, like the Invisible Man. It seemed to offer such freedom. Then I realised that I could be invisible after all: I could be inconspicuous, and that isn't far off."

"Why would you want to be?"

"Saves an awful lot of trouble. Shall we try the Fort St George?"

Benjy did not pursue it, and Miles was grateful but at the same time disappointed. He wondered why something in him cried and begged for an attention no-one could give, and a reassurance no-one could provide, and why at the same time he resisted, indeed resented, all attempts at intimacy. He built barriers, challenges for someone to break down and reach him: but these barriers were so firmly and solidly constructed that it never occurred to anyone to try.

There were many occasions like this: if Miles' first recollections of Benjy, at the end of Michaelmas, had been like a trailer, his memories came to resemble footage from the main feature when he thought back to these months. On a similar evening, soon after the beginning of Easter Term, they had been leaning on Trinity Bridge, watching the punters disturb green water, the play of light across the Backs. They had not seen each other for weeks, Benjy having spent his vacation with unspecified relatives, while Miles went on with his book, and Miles had missed him.

In fact, Miles had been desolate, had found himself inadvertently looking for Benjy amongst shoals of tourists, seeing his face on the opposite pavement only to discover that he had been deceived by a trick of the light or a fall of shadow. Spring matured, warmth returned, leaving Miles isolated: he had thrown his energies into Burton and completed half the first draft by the time Benjy reappeared, and reappeared subtly changed, although Miles could not tell why.

"Big term, this," Benjy commented.

"Do exams worry you very much?"

"Not a lot. I wasn't thinking of that." He leant on the parapet, turning to face Miles: his dark hair snaked over his forehead giving him, with his white, open shirt, the look of a Jacobean miniature. Despite the strong sunlight, his skin remained pale as marble. "I saw Olivia last week."

"How is she?"

"Very well. She's left her convent, and she's definitely coming up this autumn."

"Which college?"

"King's."

"And what will she read?"

"Modern Languages. We got on all right, this time. I didn't see her for long, but she's coming up for the day soon. I thought we might all get together, see a bit of Cambridge. She's only been here once before, for interviews."

"I'm not exactly an authority on the local hotspots, Benjy."

"It would be nice to do something, though. Oh, and another thing. I got a letter from Melissa this morning – we didn't have a chance to meet while I was in London. She's moved in with that Tony guy."

"Well, he struck me as very nice. Rather taciturn, but I'm sure he's eminently suitable."

"I'm not so sure. In fact, I'm really pissed off about it, because if I went round to see her now we wouldn't be able to – talk, you know. Before I met you, she was the only person who understood me, and there aren't many girls around I *can* talk to."

"I wouldn't have thought you'd have any trouble finding women, Benjamin."

Benjy gave him a look as if to say that Miles didn't know what he was talking about, which was probably true.

"It's just that we can have a discussion, and she knows how my mind works. It's special, I can't explain it. There aren't any – complications."

"I don't suppose you can talk to Olivia –"

"She's the last person."

Benjy patted Miles' arm, where Miles sat on the parapet, long legs crossed, and unusually conscious that he looked attractive, hair bleached by the sudden sun, the first freckles of summer breaking through. He always attempted to discourage any physical demonstrations of affection, as their effect on him was catastrophic, and this incident followed a familiar pattern. He had almost convinced himself that Benjy did not realise the consequence of his actions, the pang of desire. Except that Benjy would catch his eye in the progress of arousal, so that some conventional movement, a shaking of hands or a pat on the shoulder, was charged with sexual electricity. He would hold Miles' gaze, as Miles struggled to master himself: emotional responses could be concealed, but physical ones were harder to hide.

As always on these occasions, Miles isolated himself quickly. He made an abrupt goodbye to Benjy, half-convinced that the boy was conscious of and gratified by the effect he had. Once alone he resorted to self-abuse, still with a schoolboy guilt, but shocked and exhilarated by the excitement the encounter had produced.

Benjy disappeared soon after the interchange on Trinity Bridge. At first his absence did not strike Miles as such: after all, it was exam season, Benjy had Part I of the English Tripos within a few weeks, and most undergraduates either went to ground at this time or compensated for anticipated disaster in wild bacchanals that echoed through the streets of Cambridge.

Physshe developed a mysterious rash the night before his

Tragedy paper and insisted on sitting up with Miles until two in the morning for an in-depth discussion about Euripides. A Woodville scholar was intercepted in an attempt to barricade himself into the cellarage, with the announcement that he had been offered a job in the Inland Revenue. Miles had to invigilate, looking down from his dais upon the sea of bored and distracted faces, and then to mark scripts; so that at first Benjy's absence consisted of no more than a desire for his presence: Miles was at once relieved that Benjy was not there to disturb him, but at the same time wished that he was. He could scarcely tolerate the emotional demands which Benjy's tapering, shabby elegance and deep eyes made upon him, the unanswered question of his presence: but Benjy in abeyance produced phantoms, shadows like to him of strangers in the street, imagined footsteps on the stairs.

Benjy's disappearance came to be regarded as such after exams finished. Miles had checked his attendance, and knew that he had sat the papers; and had planned a mild celebration, although they had not decided what form it should take. He expected Benjy to come and discuss the matter, and wanted to know how he had coped, whether he felt elated – like Berman and Unwin, who whooped and stamped in the Quad, annoying the runner – or exhausted and melancholy, like poor Physshe, who was confined to his room with shingles.

As Tripos finished Miles waited, keeping watch in the street, expecting a knock on the door. He almost went to St Sebastian's. And, one evening, when he had almost given up expecting it, the knock came.

Miles opened the door himself, aware of the curious con-striction in his chest which characterised recent encounters with Benjy. A stranger stood on the threshold.

"Dr Tattershall?"

"Yes?"

The messenger was short and thickset, with a conventional, dependable face: he already looked like a well-intentioned GP, or a chartered accountant. "Sorry to bother you, sir, it's about Benjamin Underwood."

"What about him?"

"He sent me to fetch you. We've just found him."

"We? Who? Why? I mean, where?"

"Down near the railway station."

"I don't understand."

"Can you come with me? Now?"

In reply Miles picked up his jacket and keys.

"We only found him an hour ago," the boy continued, as they approached Miles' car. This was a recent acquisition, a battered Morris with a folding roof inherited from a clerical cousin, and he had been amazed to discover that the vehicles were now collectors' items. Erratic and rather quaint, and very unlike modern cars – he felt it suited him.

The boy climbed into the passenger seat with a muscular asperity far removed from Benjy's lethargic gestures. "He's been trying to contact you for ages, and in the end he rang me at college."

"How long has he been missing for? You make it sound like a considerable period of time."

Even in the panic which the prospect of Benjy injured, intoxicated or insane inspired in him, Miles spoke accurately, selecting words with care.

"He turned up for his exams –"

"I realise." Miles was impatient.

"Afterwards – well – we thought he'd gone to London for a few days."

"You're a close friend of Benjy's?" Something about the boy was familiar. "What's your name?"

"Robert. Robert Dee."

Miles remembered the previous autumn: the wheels spinning through the air, the girl's head pillowed on the kerb.

"I remember you from the accident. Benjy's always talking about you, you know."

"But where exactly is he? And what has he done?"

"Someone came and told me he was on the phone – we've got a telephone at the bottom of our staircase. I'm the one who answers it, usually," he added, accepting without rancour his role as one of nature's doers. It would never have occurred to Benjy to answer a public telephone, Miles reflected. "Anyway, I rushed down and couldn't make out half he said –

sounded terrible. Not himself at all – he's in some hotel, but I know where it is."

As he occasionally did, Miles picked the inference out of the air.

"You mean he tried to kill himself?"

"We think he might have OD'd. Overdosed, that is." The boy sounded suddenly desperate, less assured. "I'm a medic, but I don't know anything about this side of things. We haven't covered anything psychiatric yet."

Rain spattered the windscreen and tattooed on the skin of the roof. Miles swept along Mill Road, over the humped railway bridge, down among the streets of narrow blackened cottages which tourists never see.

The 'hotel' was no more than a boarding house, the 'Floribunda', with withered eponymous blooms around the door. Miles had a brief impression of a group of people standing in a close hall, of a steep staircase and a reproachful noise as he tripped over some article of furniture. Robert bounded up after him.

"I think he's in there."

The effect would have been less disturbing had the room not been so determinedly cheerful: white paintwork shone against psychedelic wallpaper; carpet muffled his footfalls. Benjy seemed to demand a seedier deathbed, cobwebbed lampshade and sagging curtains rather than home decorating and the cosy candlewick bedspread.

He lay as though he had been thrown down, one arm spread out as if reaching towards infinity: his head had flung back, and the brilliant light accentuated hollow cheeks. Fortuitously or by design he was dressed entirely in black, a Jacobean spectre in the homely room.

Robert hesitated by the door and Miles was reminded of his presence. "I'll wait downstairs," he murmured, disappearing with an impressive tact. Both had seen the open bottle of Paracetamol, the white dots strewn across the purple cover which gave the impression of a bier. Both had seen the whisky bottle, nearly empty.

Miles sat down, the bed giving a little beneath him so that Benjy was thrown imperceptibly nearer. He looked down, at the individual black hairs of the eyebrows on their white ground, the shading of beard beneath the bones over which skin stretched tightly, the damp lashes. He took Benjy's wrist, pallid and thin beneath the shabby cuff: and he felt Benjy's pulse beat, just, like a soft drum.

Miles slipped his arm beneath the narrow shoulders. He remembered lifting Benjy before, when he had seemed weightless. Now his very heaviness gave a material actuality: it was not a phantom whom Miles raised gently towards him, head lolling, a wetness spilling onto the cheeks; it was not a ghost who touched him, as though reaching towards infinity, and wept on his shoulder.

"But what prevented you from taking the pills?"

They sat in Benjy's room, which Miles had never visited before, Benjy, much against his will, in bed, and Miles in a creaking wicker chair by the gas-fire. The cold summer dawn quickened beyond an arched window.

"I didn't have that in mind. Really I didn't."

"Everyone else appears to think so."

"I don't know what I was doing there. Honestly. I woke up and saw you and wondered where the hell we were."

"Selective amnesia? But Benjy, you haven't been seen for days."

"I went off somewhere, forget where. I do, you know."

"So I've heard. And think of all the trouble you've caused. Poor old Robert had to send away the ambulance and I had to settle the bill. The landlady was most upset."

"I didn't *do* anything, did I? It isn't as if I did away with myself in her sodding hotel."

"I always seem to meet Robert in violent circumstances."

"He's good like that. I'm sure he'll make a very good doctor. I mean, he always knows what to do. He – kept an eye on me for a while. We've known each other from school."

"But what was this escapade in aid of?"

"I just wanted to be alone."

"With a bottle of Paracetamol and a bottle of Scotch?"

"I didn't take the pills."

79

"You still made heavy inroads on that whisky bottle, though."

"You know what it's like after exams."

"I would have understood your need for isolation, except that you appeared to require a companion in your solitude."

"What do you mean?" Suddenly alert.

"What about the girl who came to see you?"

"What girl?"

"The girl the landlady mentioned."

"No-one came to see me. She must have got it wrong."

"She saw the girl arrive and told her where your room was, but she didn't see her leave."

"That's because she didn't exist in the first place."

Miles sighed, wishing that Benjy would trust him enough to admit what had happened. He wondered who it could have been, whether he would ever know. Benjy sat opposite now, throned in pillows like a sickly prince, eyes glazed slightly with the after-effects of alcohol. Examined by the college doctor, he had been found to be suffering from summer flu and a massive hangover. Miles, accompanied by Benjy's tutor, had overseen his return to college and installation in bed.

"I must go," said Miles, watching a dim sun emerge over King's. "There's an examiners' meeting this morning." He moved up and down the room, looking at the Japanese prints, Samuel Palmer's Chestnut Tree, the photograph of Nastassja Kinski; the books: *Doctor Favstvs*; *Pale Fire*; *Seven Types of Ambiguity*; *Four Quartets*; the stack of tapes, including Jean-Michel Jarre, Monteverdi, and something called *Tainted Love*; and the battered panama hat. He turned back to the window and saw the impulse of light striking along the dorsal spines of King's Chapel.

"Benjy," he said at last, "would you like to come down to Bly for a while?"

Benjy's voice came back, soft and mocking, so that Miles could imagine him smiling and narrowing his eyes.

"I thought you'd never ask."

# Five

Miles drove into the haze of evening, a clatter of leaves disturbing the frequency of light across the windscreen, the road curving and gesturing before him, lanes filled with brilliant chlorophyll green.

He drove with as much abandon as the little Morris would allow, plunging through pools of shadow flung into his path by trees, meeting no other vehicles, exhilarated with freedom. The car, its canvas hood rammed back, had been filled with books, holdalls, and delicacies unobtainable in East Anglia; Benjy had occasionally to prevent the contents from falling into the road, turning in his seat to rescue a stray tin of pâté or packet of Bath Olivers.

Despite the wind, Benjy wore his battered panama, attaining raffish elegance in his frayed striped shirt and faded linen jacket. Miles could scarcely believe that he sat here, beside him, commenting on the landscape, pointing at roadsigns: he was here, in Miles' country, with its cloud-filled fields and ranks of distant poplars.

They had been late setting out. The initial plan had been to start straight after lunch, but they had been sidetracked by a final tidying of Miles' rooms, which took longer than either anticipated. Miles kept finding things which he'd mislaid, stopping to read old newspapers discovered at the bottom of the wardrobe, being interrupted by colleagues who had been perfectly content to ignore him all year and now arrived in deputations demanding his views on the redecoration of the College Chapel or why someone had raided the contraceptive machine.

Benjy was not much help: he sat on the windowsill in a

flood of sunlight, watching the dust motes dance, offering useful observations from the English poets.

Miles looked up from his packing late in the afternoon, to see Benjy silhouetted in gold; he glanced round the room, which seemed dingy and confined, with its old files and sagging armchairs; a spider which had tenure in one corner of the ceiling emerged in alarm. Miles identified with it: there he was, among his piles of dust and accretions of paper, whilst Benjy sat on the sill, a bee charged with golden light.

And now here he was again, beside Miles, laughing into the breeze, which did not sweep off his hat as it should have done, half-muttering something under his breath.

"What did you say?" Miles enquired.

If one speaks in dreams, one wakes. He wondered whether he would receive an answer.

"'Boundless and bare the lone and level lands stretch far away'."

"Sands," corrected Miles automatically.

"Lands. I haven't seen the shore yet."

"You will. Bly's about half a mile from the staithe."

"The *what*?"

"The shore. Where the weekenders go down to the sea in yachts."

Benjy stretched languorously, then exclaimed: "Look! A windmill!"

Miles, to whom the sight was familiar, did not register surprise, but he enjoyed Benjy's enjoyment, his comments on the little villages which approached and receded, the self-conscious antique shops and rural squalor, the timbered excesses of Lavenham, where Benjy insisted on stopping for a drink.

It was only as they walked into the pub that Miles suddenly wondered how their relationship would seem to an onlooker. In Cambridge, the association was explicable: tutor and student. But how would it appear to the outside world? They were obviously not related in any way, and Benjy didn't bear the mark of a younger partner in professional or business terms. In another age teacher and pupil, master and apprentice, would have been acceptable; now, the companionship seemed a little sinister.

Or so Miles thought, although to outside eyes he looked innocuous: shy, bemused, elegant in his grasshopper way. The patrons of the pub, in carefully laundered fisherman's smocks and Guernseys, took little notice of them, and soon Miles was back on the road, under a vast sky.

"So this is Bly?"

A village street, a row of cottages strung out along the road, an accumulation of Georgian houses, and then the Old Vicarage itself, set slightly apart from church and people, superseded by the New Vicarage, an Edwardian innovation.

"Why are there two? It doesn't make sense."

"People didn't want to live in the old place. Claimed it was too big and draughty. My father was the last incumbent to live here, and when he died, Francesca bought the house off the Church Commissioners. I think they were only too glad to be rid of it."

Benjy looked at the vicarage in awe.

"Not haunted, is it?"

"Not for me."

The gravel path had been inundated with weeds, and a heavy creeper, already tinged with russet, stretched across the Queen Anne brickwork; the Old Vicarage was an assemblage of architectural styles, each generation having improved upon the Elizabethan original. The Queen Anne frontage merged into bleached timbers; the Regency had supplied a summer-house in the Chinese taste, and thrown out a bow window; Victorians had left a minor influence, but at the beginning of the century, the Tudor barn, which stood close to the main building, had been incorporated into the structure as a studio.

The Old Vicarage, Bly, looked as if it had been designed by a committee, or for use as a film set in an historical drama.

Strange now, Miles thought, to come back: the countryside lay silent, as though in wait. Light drained beyond the steep incline where the land dropped to the village street and the darkling chestnut tree. Windows, some leaded and lozenge-shaped, others sashed and austere, regarded him blankly. A

83

yellowed series of paperbacks was visible above a sill; a terracotta flowerpot lay in fragments on the mossed terrace.

"Are you *sure* it isn't haunted?"

He had forgotten Benjy. Miles turned round, swung a bag out of the car.

"Let's go and see if any spirits have moved in while I've been away."

The house stirred to life as he heard Benjy rattle along the gallery which joined the upper rooms; the distillation of silence dissipated with vibrant footsteps, the clatter of drawers along their runners, the banging of a window in the breeze. As he rearranged his books in the study, putting out the typewriter, Miles heard Benjy exclaim, his tread on the stairs. Any ghosts present must have been puzzled, he thought, though the interior of the vicarage did not suggest the super-natural. Any more than Francesca's house in Campden Hill Square.

The rooms had been swept and dusted that morning by a woman who came up from the village whenever Miles or Francesca was at Bly. Apples sat in a silver bowl on the oak chest; a sprig of rowan had been placed on the mantelshelf, whether from superstition – the mountain ash is reputed to ward off evil – or decorative ingenuity, Miles could not tell.

Miles could never get used to the idea that the study was now his, to work in as he wanted, that he knew the contents of the applewood desk and that the books ranked in dark shelves were his own. The room retained an essentially Anglican smell, compounded of beeswax and damp bibles; he expected to see the strained faces of first communicants, awestruck boys sitting upright on the horsehair sofa. Miles knew that he could banish the ambience for good with a few coats of paint and some furniture shifting, but he could never get round to it. Instead, he wandered into the drawing room.

This room, too, had scarcely changed since his childhood. The copper-fronted fireplace, the rugs from India, the chintz sofa with its sagging back and tendency to groan when sat on; the french windows which had struck him as stagey even as a boy, through which he half-expected a marcel-waved heroine to appear, waving a tennis racket.

Then Miles noticed a further difference: Mrs Sedge had placed another bough of rowan in the Chinese vase on the piano; red berries danced faintly in the draught. Miles shrugged and went upstairs. His room, at the end of a panelled passageway, had a doorway surrounded by Gothic carvings which had been the source of nightmares in his childhood. Despite the apple tree which grew beyond the dormer windows, the bedroom was surprisingly light.

Miles' room reflected every stage of his development. He had never sorted the books on the shelf above the chest: *A Greek Accidence*; *Prince Caspian*; *The Observer's Book of Larger Moths*; *Urn Burial*; *Lucky Jim*; *The Turn of the Screw*; *The White Divel*; *The Golden Bough*. The same patchwork quilt covered the brass bed, bought long before such items became fashionable, to accommodate the six-foot-two he attained at fourteen. A Hornby train, like a forlorn idol, stood between the china candlesticks on his chest of drawers. A pair of elderly watercolours, an eighteenth-century print of a hare and an old map of Norfolk, hung on the white walls. Miles sighed, feeling as though he had never been away.

Lying on the bed, to which he'd always been so glad to return after every Half, Miles remembered the irresponsibility of childhood. Though when he considered it, life was scarcely full of commitments at present.

A breeze sent shadows of leaves hurrying across the ceiling.

"So there you are."

Benjy stood in the doorway, leaning on the lintel, hands hooked into his pockets. "Thought you'd disappeared and left me here with the *dobrymov*."

"The what?"

"*Dobrymov*. House spirit. You know."

"Where on earth did you acquire a knowledge of Russian folklore?"

"From a relation. There's a whole bunch of us who got chucked out in the nineteenth century."

"Jewish?"

"Yes, suppose so. Though I'm not, strictly speaking. It's

just another family connection." He walked about the room, so various, so beautiful, so new, and Miles could scarcely believe that he was here. Slightly frightening in his composure, Benjy paused by the window. "This place is like something out of James."

"Henry, M. R. or P. D.?"

"All three. What was your father like, Miles?"

Getting up, he polished his glasses on the curtain.

"What was he like? Rather like me, I suppose."

"Couldn't have been."

"Essentially, my father was a scholar." Miles led the way downstairs. "And being a country parson didn't suit him a bit, at first. He felt as though he'd been exiled among the Scythians. He tried to get a fellowship at Woodville, and he wasn't, perhaps, quite good enough. So he came down here."

"Disappointed?"

"Yes, I think he was. Though I had no standards to judge him by until I went to school and heard about other people's fathers. And by that time I realised that he was – rather odd."

"What did he do, drown choirboys in the font or something? He's beginning to sound like an intellectual Peter Grimes."

"You have a Gothic imagination, Benjamin, and you let it run away with you."

They were in the stone-flagged kitchen, clammy as a crypt even at the height of summer. Mrs Sedge had left loaves, a cold chicken, fruit pies, and a triangle of cheddar on the scrubbed table.

"No, he simply became more and more of a recluse." Miles fetched willow-pattern plates and a pack of lager cans. "I didn't notice at first. But then, one summer, when I was about fifteen, it became obvious. I heard rumours that the Church intended to replace him with a younger man."

"But what did he do?"

"He performed his offices, but seemed less and less concerned with his people. There's one story about him preaching in Greek. New Testament Greek, of course," Miles added absently. "I don't think I gave as much attention to matters as I should have done. I know I didn't."

86

"Well, it wasn't your fault. You were away at school. You couldn't be expected to know what was going on."

Miles smiled, mildly. "Yes, I realise that now. Anyway, soon afterwards, during the Autumn Half, his letters stopped. My father had never been a particularly good correspondent. The odd postal order, perhaps, or a Loeb edition – I was in the Classics VIth. Anyway, towards Christmas there came the summons to the Housemaster's study. I think that I guessed what it would be. I had a fairly uneventful career at school and couldn't think of any misdemeanours. Apparently, someone went to the vicarage after my father hadn't shown up for a fortnight – a long interval of seclusion even for him – and found him at the foot of the stairs. He had fallen, and broken his neck."

"But how horrible!" Benjy spoke with feeling.

"I suppose so." Miles shrugged. "And yet – he seemed so distant that death scarcely seemed to alter my feelings towards him. Perhaps it's because he never exactly seemed vital in the first place."

"But how did all this affect Francesca? You've scarcely mentioned her."

"Francesca is a few years older than I am, as you know. And she was very sensible, even then. When she came over from France, where she'd been studying, she insisted on buying the house. The Church was happy enough to be rid of it – the bad associations didn't make it very popular with new incumbents."

"I thought priests weren't supposed to be superstitious."

"Well, it was a difficult house to bring up a family in, and the new chap was very philoprogenitive. Francesca had already accumulated money from various professional engagements, and said that it was very important that we both had somewhere to come to. She pointed out that if everyone abandoned a place simply because someone had died in it, there wouldn't be a historic house left in England."

"She's right, of course. But what about your mother? Where does she come into it?"

"My mother –"

"Did she die when you were younger, like mine?"

"She left my father when I was about two years old. She just – disappeared. Nobody knows what happened – she might have drowned and been washed out to sea, or simply run away with somebody else. Nobody knows for certain."

"Which is why you distrust women."

"That's rather glib, Benjamin."

"Yes, but I bet it's true." Benjy looked down at his feet, elegant in Italian white moccasins, scuffed at the toes. "Perhaps I have overstepped the mark. I've asked too many questions again, Miles. I'm sorry."

"Oh, that's all right. It's ancient history."

"To you."

Miles smiled, gesturing to a chair. "To me. Isn't it about time we had something to eat?" He wondered how these disclosures would prompt Benjy to talk about his own background, which had been the object of this exercise in autobiography.

"We're similar, in a way. Both our parents are dead, and they keep us apart."

"You mentioned this before. But who are they, Benjy? Why do they keep you separate?"

"They just do. Our relations. They keep us apart."

They finished the washing up, and, since it was past midnight, went to their rooms. Miles heard Benjy moving about for some time, waking the house. He lay in bed and watched the pool of moonlight on the floor; the new moon herself sailed past, reflected in the glass-faced map.

It had been a long time since he had discussed the family with anyone; Francesca refused to talk about their father except in the terms of heredity, as in "Your Father's books" or "You sound just like Your Father"; never his mother, whom he could scarcely remember. Occasionally, he tried to imagine what she must have been like, wondered if she had been the source of Francesca's musical gifts. There had been exotic blood there, he always assumed, something Celtic, Italianate, a dark romanticism which had come out in Francesca but left him untouched. Even her name, Francesca, instead of the plain serviceable Frances, had a dramatic flourish to

88

it, resonant of opera and papism and curiously at odds with her surname. Francesca Tattershall: it sounded like the title of a swashbuckling historical novel. Dr Miles Tattershall conjured up exactly what he was: academic, lengthy, and slightly shabby. They had called him Eggshell at school, and Miles had not minded, because he thought the nickname accurate.

Their mother had escaped: whether into death by drowning, or another, more mundane, more bearable life, they never knew; but she had left the solemn Edwardian constraints of life at the Old Vicarage and their embittered father. When he came to read *Middlemarch*, Miles recognised Reverend Tattershall, he had been another Casaubon. And, fond as he was of casting everyone around him in literary roles, speculated on his mother as a latterday Dorothea Brooke, finding eventual happiness and fulfilment with some virile, younger man. Francesca and his mother had escaped, as he never would; Miles felt as if his father's influence would remain with him for life.

Desertion was another term for his mother's act, but he could not bring himself to blame her for leaving. Why should he feel any loyalty to a father who sent him away to school, despite the fact that he could not afford it, and who treated him with greater reserve than he did the curate? School had been isolation among crowds of contemporaries, but Bly had been good training for that. Miles had learnt early to tolerate his own company.

Which was why it was strange to have Benjy in the house: he almost believed that he could hear him breathing. He felt his presence, lying sentient in the moonlight. The house, and perhaps its *dobrymov*, settled round him.

Miles woke early, sunlight streaming across his bed. He realised that it would be a hot day, and dressed in clothes too old and worn even for Cambridge: the cord trousers he was fond of, the comfortable frayed shirt, sleeves rolled above his elbows. He looked better, according to the shaving-mirror, than he had for some time: the sun had worked its old alchemy, lightening his hair, strengthening inchoate freckles, giving him a weathered, quintessentially English look, like a certain type of explorer, or a minor Bloomsbury in an old photograph.

Wondering whether to call Benjy, he went downstairs. Miles realised that it would take time to adapt to the demands of another person at Bly: he was not accustomed to entertaining. Francesca, determined and independent, never needed cups of tea in the morning or polite enquiries about her night's sleep. If something did not suit her, she could be relied upon to say so. But Benjy might require such attentions, and he might also become bored, tiresome, disaffected. Perhaps it had been unwise to invite him; living with other people was not Miles' strength at the best of times.

But Benjy was already up. The kitchen door stood open, and Benjy walked among the apple trees of the orchard, passing through tall wet grasses which clung to his calves; a vast pigeon settled in the branches above him; Miles stepped into an illuminated manuscript, and any doubts about Benjy's presence disappeared.

They cooked breakfast, sat drinking coffee for hours, and, just as in Cambridge, fell into one of those long discussions which encompassed everything. Mrs Sedge came, was introduced to Benjy, whom she treated with respectful distrust, and went. After lunch, Mrs Sedge's handsome young nephew came to mow the grass in the orchard, and in the stretch of green behind the french windows, and look at Benjy. When Miles and Benjy walked down to the post office, Miles realised that he had become a cynosure and had to make introductions all round. He stuck to his story of tutor and student, which the residents seemed happy to accept, though he wondered whether Benjy was not being assessed for any faint physical resemblance to Miles.

"Is it always like this?" Benjy asked, as they sat on the terrace. The term was an idealisation of the slabbed shelf which projected over the one hill in the area, but there was a balustrade and a mottled urn.

"Like what?"

"Nosey. I feel rather exotic, the way they were watching me."

"It's because you're a stranger. And they haven't seen

anyone quite like you before. They don't have so many weekenders in the village. The holiday cottages are a few miles away."

"But I'm a friend of yours!"

"Even then. They probably think we're going to conjure up shades, or perform experiments in alchemy."

Benjy shrugged, sipping his wine and soda-water. He had caused consternation in the village shop by asking for Perrier, and had to make do with carbonated drinks instead. The experience was repeated when they went down to the Chestnut Tree.

"I feel like a freak," insisted Benjy, as they sat outside in the twilight. "You should have seen the way those darts players looked at me."

"It wasn't at all uncomplimentary, Benjy."

"I'm sure I heard one of them mutter 'queen'. Christ, I haven't heard the word for years."

"Of course they don't think you're – effeminate." Miles tried to sound soothing, but he was sure that the darts players had meant exactly what Benjy thought. Benjy, dressed entirely in white and with a blood-red sweater knotted idly around his open-necked shirt, looked exotic, dark and glamorous compared with the local men. Tonight he was friendly, approachable, but still retained a little of the air of a graceful alien, perplexed by the rituals of life on earth. Miles, flattered by his company, by his being here at all, was a little self-conscious of all the attention Benjamin attracted.

"Those *looks* they were giving me, Miles." Benjy seemed disproportionately irate.

"It almost made me jealous," Miles replied.

The remark surprised Miles more than it did Benjy. He had never made a comment like this before in his life, and later attributed it, and much else, to the strong local bitter.

In acknowledgement Benjy raised his glass.

"I don't know that I like being treated as a student. They don't seem to be popular round here."

"The novelty will wear off," Miles assured him. "I'll introduce you to Hilary Middlemass soon. That'll be rather different."

"Yes, you keep telling me about him."

After their drink, they wandered the half-mile to the staithe. The winding road, surrounded by desolate fields, gave way to sand and marsh. The bulk of dike rose among rushes which moved ceaselessly in the sharp breeze. Miles snuffed the brackish air, stepped onto the sand where dinghies and small yachts had been drawn up, halyards zinging in the breeze. The marshland curved round like an arm, encompassing the little shore; beyond, the sea stretched into grey infinity. A distant bird described an arc against the metallic and swiftly moving sky.

"Isn't it rather desolate?"

"Yes," replied Miles, with an unusual degree of passion. "That's why." Further explanation seemed unnecessary. He was completely content, aloof on the pathed banks, pools and reeds beneath him on one side, the sea beckoning on the other; he merged into the landscape, thin and blanched as a reed, silent as a shadow.

"I can imagine you," said Benjy, "in a place like this, centuries ago. Slipping away secretly in your boat among the reeds, lying in wait."

"For what?" Miles admired his perception.

Benjy shrugged. "*Fuge, Late, Tace.*"

Then Miles saw that he was shivering, and they turned back.

"This countryside's addictive," he explained as they arrived back at the vicarage. "Especially when one's brought up in it. It's the scale, and something to do with the isolation. I don't feel anomalous here."

"You aren't," Benjy agreed, as they cooked the meal which Mrs Sedge had prepared. The table had been laid in the dining room, which featured more of the elderly watercolours that hung everywhere, and Benjy insisted on lighting candles.

There was an excellent beef stew, quantities of vegetables and a blue Italian bowl overflowing with ripe strawberries. Miles discovered a forgotten bottle of Rousillon in the larder. The walk had given them terrific appetites, and while they prepared the food, Benjy chattered on about Crabbe, whom he had read the night before. "He's rather unpopular, so I think I'll do a dissertation on him for Part II."

Benjy had done quite well in the English Tripos, and Miles took some of the credit. His dissertation on Burton had been awarded an A, enough to lift him securely into the 2:1 bracket, and Benjy had been surprised and delighted by the result. It had given a lease of academic energy, and he planned to spend some of the time with Miles getting through the daunting reading list for the final year.

Miles watched him, in the candlelight, black hair falling into his eyes, the strawberry glistening between his fingers, as he rolled it in castor sugar; the white, open-necked shirt flattered his dark skin, and the red sweater blazed like a flag. Propping his chin on his hand, Miles thought that he could never look for long enough, though Benjy's appearance turned him to stone, paralysed his will. A harpsichord recording plucked away in the background, appropriate to these sonneteer's sentiments.

Benjy seemed to read his mind. Producing a cigarette – one of the Sobranie Black Russians he had lately affected – Benjy pronounced: "'All who love not tobacco and boys are fools'."

Miles felt obliged to protest, make a token attempt to prevent Benjy from realising how accurate his statement was.

"Why not tobacco and girls?"

Benjy shook his head, curls dancing.

"I don't think we've either of us got much time for girls, have we, Miles?"

They had never discussed the subject: by consent, sex had been ignored as a topic of conversation, and Miles would not in any case have wanted to know of Benjy's activities, if he indulged in any. Benjy had never mentioned a girlfriend, not that that meant anything; he gave the impression of having very different tastes, but that again might only have been undergraduate bravado. Perhaps, and in this instinct Miles was closer to the truth than he realised, Benjy loved to arouse and excite; perhaps he enjoyed enslaving, regardless of sex or age; perhaps he enjoyed the power that inciting strong physical attraction brings.

93

Miles did not admit to himself that he knew all this: could not. Benjy's influence over him at the moment was too potent, too irresistible.

"Shall we have some coffee?" Miles felt banal, elated, and frustrated all at the same time. The knowledge that Benjy would leave him in this condition and retreat to his own room for the night depressed him deeply. This must be what it was like, he thought, to be teased by a girl. Benjy was a male flirt.

When he returned from the kitchen, Benjy had installed himself on the drawing-room sofa; he lay abandoned, carefully distributed over the broken springs, one arm behind his head, the other hand holding a second cigarette. Miles remembered seeing him lie unconscious in Francesca's house, remembered raising his body gently in the Cambridge hotel. The scarcely acknowledged desire which had touched him then was now impossible to ignore, but he felt guilty and humiliated at the prospect of himself alone again, stretched out on the patchwork quilt upstairs and struggling for relief. Miles also had the sensation that Benjy knew exactly what he was thinking.

The harpsichord clattered some haunting tune he half-remembered, enhancing the speechless silence between them. Miles was frightened – quite literally so – that at any moment Benjy would ask a question, and one which he would have no choice but to answer.

Miles set down the tray and walked to the french windows, open onto the terrace. The moon shone down across flat countryside, and the distant glimmer of the sea; a faint susurration of grasses rose, accompanied by the creaking apple boughs. And still Benjy said nothing, although Miles heard him rise and move towards him. Miles could not have said anything; his mouth was dry and his body pulsated with sexual excitement. And then, silently, dextrously, Benjy was at his side, self-assured and masterful, taking charge of him.

Miles could never afterwards recall events precisely; the sequence had been like many dreams, and Miles was not certain if this was another of them. Benjy's skilful fingers had tantalised Miles, before he moved forward and led Miles along the dark passages, along the panelled gallery, until they reached his bedroom. Benjy had cast his clothes off like someone about to jump in and save a drowning man, and emerged lean-bodied and erect.

By enlightened standards, the night's events were puerile in the extreme, but Benjy's lips and fingers brought Miles greater release than he had ever experienced before. Miles also achieved the even greater satisfaction of pleasing somebody else, of seeing Benjy stretched and ecstatic, or threshing like a fish, as he squeezed the boy's penis. And when they eventually fell asleep, Miles drifted off in a state of relaxation and tranquillity which was enhanced by this warm and breathing body lying beside him, one slender arm thrown across Miles' shoulders.

Miles woke to the fractured light which spilt through branches. He felt curiously hot, and bits of him hurt, as though he had been engaging in strenuous exercise. He tried to imagine why, and turning his head saw that someone lay sleeping beside him, turned slightly aside, black hair visible above the cuff of sheet. Miles tensed, and realised that the fragments of dreams caught at the back of his mind were recollection, not imagination.

He looked at the sleeping back humped under the patchwork landscape, the tumulus which rose and fell almost imperceptibly as it breathed, listened to the faintly asthmatic respiration. Miles was confused with tenderness, felt his face stream with shame. Absurdly, Francesca's voice came to him: *"What would Your Father think?"*

As Miles tried to imagine, Benjy woke up. It was too late for Miles to feign sleep, and now that they were both here, he could scarcely pretend that none of it had happened. The novelty of the situation led Miles to further disclosures. He already felt like somebody else.

"Do you know, this is the first time I've slept with anybody?"

"I gathered that."

Benjy looked soft and tumbled, strange yet familiar, the

same, but different. Miles could scarcely believe that their skin touched, that their limbs lay tangled. He felt flattered and deeply embarrassed. "Never in my wildest dreams –"

"I don't suppose your dreams are all that wild, Miles."

"But –"

"You've never had it with anybody? Anyone at all?"

"No."

"Not even at school?"

"Certainly not. I was too frightened, if you must know. Look, I don't think you should do that. Not here, not now."

"Where would you suggest?" Benjy's voice sounded muffled.

"I don't think –"

"Why not?"

"Because –" Because this had gone quite far enough; because Mrs Sedge might come in at any minute; because they might find out in Cambridge; because his father would not like it; because Benjy's lips sucked forth his soul "– because your teeth are rather sharp."

Benjy apologised.

Breakfast, when they finally reached the kitchen, was exuberant. They shared a very private joke which Mrs Sedge could not possibly appreciate, although she smiled politely as Miles and Benjy were simultaneously shaken with fits of laughter, and when she had gone they amused themselves further by contemplating her ignorance.

"She probably thinks we conjure up the dead," said Benjy.

"Engage in nameless acts."

"Well, we're going to, aren't we?"

"Perhaps she thinks we raise up incubuses."

"Shouldn't that be incubi?"

Sunlight fell like a benison; Benjy sat, framed in the doorway with the orchard a backdrop, a boy-Cleopatra tempting his appetite with honey on his lips. Miles bit sensuously into a shower of toastcrumbs, hunger provoked and satisfied. But he still could not resist the demand for explanation.

"Why?" asked Benjy. "Why? Because I wanted to. Because you wanted to."

"But why did you want to? What provoked you?"

"God, what is this, a seminar on Cartesian theories of desire? All right, if you really want to know, I fancied you. Will that do?"

"But – you couldn't. Nobody ever does."

"Have you ever asked them?"

"Well, no," Miles admitted.

"There you are, then. How can you tell?"

"I'm sorry, I just can't accept that. It's not enough."

"I like you, Miles. I admire and respect you. I owe you a lot. I'm attracted to older men. What more can I say?"

Miles looked down, self-conscious and unaccustomed to such declarations. "And why shouldn't I?" Benjy was almost hostile. "Why shouldn't I like you? Don't you like me, or something? Do you think I'm some sort of freak? Don't you care for me? Don't you?"

Irritation with Benjy's habit of reiterating questions mingled with more tender feelings. "Benjy, I don't think you're a freak. What a thing to say. That upsets me more than anything – it's simply that I find it difficult to imagine any-one – caring much about me." Benjy was downcast now, sulkily fiddling with the rush-binding on the arm of his chair.

"You're impossible!" he said finally.

"Please define your terms."

"You're enjoying this, aren't you! Come on now, admit it. You are, aren't you?"

"I don't think we should talk about this any longer, Benjy. I think it's a waste of time."

"Up to you," Benjy shrugged.

"And this has got to stop."

"I never thought I'd hear you use a cliché."

"That isn't a cliché, it's a pronouncement."

"Give me one good reason."

Miles could not think of one single reason why it should stop, and his senses were already giving him numerous reasons for it to continue. He felt relaxed, happy, fit, and pleasantly excited; he was already looking forward to taking Benjy again, seeing the cool sullen face flushed with exhilaration and desire. It should stop if Miles were not to get involved: but he did not intend it to stop. Not for the moment.

"I suppose you do this sort of thing all the time," he said.

"What, seduce my supervisors? More than my life's worth. Anyway, have you *seen* some of them?"

"I meant – sleep around."

"I'm very fastidious. You should be flattered."

"I'm very flattered, but really –"

"Think of it as something inevitable, Miles. It would have been me, or someone else. I don't even know if you're basically straight, or gay. I don't really care. What difference does it make? You've got to get round to it sooner or later, and you've left it later than most, so the sooner the better. Everybody's got to learn some time."

"You make sex sound like swimming."

"That's *exactly* what it's like," said Benjy, with evangelistic fervour. "It's the reverse of Stevie Smith's line. I'm not drowning, but waving."

Miles spent the subsequent days adjusting to the demands of another body: he had never before woken beside someone else and sensed him lying silent; he had never had to consult anyone else about his plans, outline his intentions to boil a kettle or go for a walk, because they might affect anyone but himself. Even at school, he had maintained his isolation; an invisible barrier had surrounded his corner of the dormitory, his study had been a preparation for the retreat of Cambridge rooms, his behaviour challenged any attempt at friendship, a challenge which was never taken up.

Now Benjy, whilst retaining his mystery, systematically broke down Miles' defences. He asked intimate questions which demanded answers, coaxed and cozened his physical resistance so that Miles lay shaken and drained, washed up among the sheets like the survivor of a shipwreck. Lithe and tanned, Benjy instructed with his slender thighs and firm buttocks; his surprisingly strong fingers had virtuoso talent; he introduced Miles to desire, the delight of possession, provoking and tantalising him into acts he had never imagined in those rather tame dreams. Benjy made him sentient, raised every hair of his body with perception, increased the frequency until his existence was concentrated within a few inches of flesh.

Of course, there were shifts in tempo. Mrs Sedge's visits usually coincided with their mutual exhaustion. She would arrive to find them yawning blamelessly over coffee cups, or lying among orchard grass with open books. Once she had arrived unexpectedly to do the ironing, and Miles had lain silent on the bed upstairs, hand across Benjy's mouth, the prospect of discovery intensifying his excitement.

Benjy had exhibitionist tendencies as well as an appetite for danger. Some evenings after Mrs Sedge's unscheduled visit, after dinner, they had walked down to the staithe and along the dike. Samphire swayed under the viscous pools, reeds bent against a metallic sky. Miles led Benjy along the high path over the dunes, among clumps of sharp grasses, to the white sand. A few yards further, and the deceptively calm North Sea sucked at the shore.

Benjy stepped forward, letting the tide pull at his bare ankles; he stumbled back in mock-alarm, as Miles called out.

"My God, that current's strong."

"I tried to warn you –"

"Nearly swept me off my feet," he gasped, clutching Miles, soaked with spray. Sand clung to his damp legs, and suddenly his grasp shifted, became more pronounced. Before Miles could stop him, his hands had slipped down to find the erection which waited for them: the alacrity of his body in responding to Benjy's demands never failed to amaze Miles.

"No – not here – don't –"

But Benjy did, dropping before him on the sand, fingers caressing as he applied his lips in a parody of resuscitation, tongue rasping a little. Miles buckled, with no choice but to throw Benjy down beside him, there among the dunes, appalled by himself, but unable to resist.

During that period, Miles and Benjy lived quite literally in a world of their own, a metaphysical earthly paradise, in which they turned the leaves of books beneath waving branches, in which they read, talked, knew each other; in which they lay as open volumes, face to face.

It was Miles' domain, territory shared now with Benjy, that extended to the staithe and along the shoreline, down the swift dip of hill and to the Chestnut Tree. When they stepped beyond the boundaries, to the pub or village shop, it was in disguise, those concealments which nevertheless indicated their relationship: tutor and scholar; master and pupil; for, after all, their exchanges still consisted of learning and teaching. And Miles was learning all the time.

Their world encompassed Bly, the tunnels of leaves above dry paths and blanched reeds, the canopy of oak giving way to marsh, the harvested fields which made Benjy sneeze; the cool echoing vicarage with bedroom curtains drawn against hot noon sun as they lay in dark, beamed rooms listening to the clatter of harpsichord music. Miles looked back on those days and realised that he and Benjy had created their own, revolutionary calendar; familiar dates in an old Cambridge University diary reminded him of the pre- and post-Benjamin age. Although he never made entries more revealing than 'visit library' or 'get aspirin', each day, with its nugget of information – Moon's First Quarter or Scarlet Day – became suffused with recollection. 'To Bly. Underwood. 2 p.m.' His own personal Bastille Day.

Their retreat remained undisturbed: Miles had been accustomed to solitary summers, occasionally relieved by Francesca's visits between tours; the villagers and local families had never enticed him from the vicarage for long, and in outward appearance Benjy had merely joined him in this studious and ascetic life.

Both were content with each other's company, though it struck Miles as strange that they never encountered another person in their long fenland walks, not even a lone birdwatcher or a self-conscious weekender in a brand new Husky. It occurred to him later that perhaps this solitude had been policy, that rumours of his activities circulated. He knew that in the village the Tattershalls were considered a little odd: his father preaching in Greek, Francesca's alleged ghosts and poltergeists; yet there was almost a tact in the way that Mrs Sedge loudly announced her presence every morning, as though she were giving them the opportunity to return to their separate beds. Perhaps Mrs Sedge and her family – who constituted two-thirds of the village – knew of their union and blessed it with rowan berries. Miles could never really tell.

Their retreat remained undisturbed, for a fortnight. After this their little world was disrupted. Miles and Benjy returned from one of their long walks, yawning under the blue glass of night, while Benjy recited extracts from *High Tide on the Coast of Lincolnshire*.

"God, that's a miserable thing," Miles commented. "Can't you think of anything more cheerful?"

"'But two are walking apart for ever'," returned Benjy, heartlessly, "'And wave their hands for a mute farewell.' No, I don't think she wrote anything exactly sanguine. You said Ingelow was your father's favourite reading."

"That doesn't mean I have to like her."

"What's this?"

They stood by the front door as Miles detached the sheet of manuscript which, in a cavalier gesture, had been fixed to the wood with a penknife.

"Who's it from?"

"Wait until we're inside."

Miles held the paper under the standard lamp. It was a sheet of music manuscript, obviously torn from a notebook. Across it, with complete disregard for the stave, had been scrawled:

Although you appear to be INCOMMUNICADO come to dinner FRIDAY – and bring your protégé.

Middlemass.

"But what does it mean?"

"It means we've been invited to dinner by Hilary Middlemass."

"Is this how he always delivers his invites?"

"I expect he rode over." Absently Miles folded the pearl-handled penknife.

"With a mask, you mean, and flintlock pistols?"

"He has a very – idiosyncratic way of doing things."

"Where's he live?"

"About five miles from here. I imagine you'll get on very well."

"*He* won't think I'm peculiar?"

"He won't even notice."

They drove to Middlemass's house through a swift, chilled evening. Light filtered from the banks of cloud, making the landscape grey as a steel engraving. Silhouetted stems of cow parsley choked the lanes.

Benjy sat beside Miles, as he had done those weeks ago, looking raffish and tatty. He had produced a dinner jacket, bought in Cambridge Market for five pounds, a wing collar, a greenish bow tie and a white silk evening scarf. These clothes, with his tumbled hair and the garden rose in his lapel, gave a curiously pre-war air.

"You look like a dissolute junior diplomat," commented Miles, and then remembered.

"Probably the image of my father," Benjy replied. "It's all right. I do talk about him sometimes, you know."

"Not very often. And what about your mother?"

"I told you. She died of Olivia."

The statement had a Jacobean ring.

"How is – Olivia?"

"I wanted – I want to talk to you about that."

The Morris ran along beside a lichened park wall for another half-mile, and then Miles swung into the gateway of Charnwood. The wrought-iron gates stood forever open, anchored by weeds and ivy; rose bay willowherb encroached across the lawns. Distantly, a goat cropped by an alley of yews which had grown grotesquely out of shape and now resembled huge, abandoned hats. A cedar tree, massive on crutches, shaded the turn of the drive. When Benjy saw the house, he gasped.

★　　★　　★

"Christ, Miles, what will you produce next? You're like a conjuror."

"I'm not the conjuror, Benjy. He is."

Both Sir Hilary Middlemass and his house were impressively ruined. Both were well proportioned, with decent groundwork and a distinct impression that they had once been beautiful. Both combined a certain derelict charm with a slight suggestion of the sinister; each complemented the other, Hilary in his balding black velvet jacket standing before the peeling stucco of the Georgian façade, propping one of the cracked pillars of the portico. The pose struck Miles as familiar; then he remembered it from one of Hilary's rare photographs. It had been as impressive in the restrained monochrome of *The Times* as now in the evening light.

"Miles, I'm delighted to see you. You've got your own transport now, instead of having to get around on that bicycle? Very good." He inspected the car with interest. Miles knew that in one of the disused stables a black Porsche waited. Hilary liked to pose as a highwayman, but one who favoured modern methods of travel. Then he turned to Benjy, who in his own efforts at elegance was outclassed. There were some stilted introductions.

Middlemass ushered them in, and they followed him through a darkened hall, across tessellated black and white floors, into a long drawing room with windows open to the overgrown park. White-painted, bare-boarded, the room contained the minimum of furniture. A dusty chandelier tinkled in the breeze. Benjy made towards the uncurtained windows, awestruck.

Hilary Middlemass poured gin and vermouth and stood beside them at the open windows. His shadow loomed across the far wall in the last light, and Miles turned to look at him. Tall as Miles, but far broader, Middlemass was physically imposing. As one music critic had written, he 'bulked large' in every sense. Cropped grey hair suggested asceticism, heavy eyelids sensuality; solemn black, and his cadaverous cast of face, reminded Miles of some worldly divine; this impression being heightened by bright green eyes and the velvet jacket.

Miles had never known what to expect from Hilary Middlemass. As a boy, he had been terrified by Middlemass's presence, the remarkable impact of his personality even when he remained silent. But Middlemass had also instructed him, had been more of a father than his own, and curiously less distant, although he never concealed his contempt for Miles' ignorance of abstruse quotations or recondite librettists; and he had encouraged Francesca, inciting her to fight for a musical career despite the Reverend Doctor Tattershall's protests.

"How long have you been down here?" he asked. Miles could never overcome a childhood conviction that Middlemass knew everything that he was thinking.

"A fortnight or so – I – I've lost count."

"No doubt you've been preoccupied."

"Well, I'm trying to get on with that book –"

"Academic life no doubt offers other distractions."

As usual, Miles was silenced by Middlemass.

"I'm sorry I can't tell you more about Francesca," he said at last, anxious to change the subject. Changing the subject was one of Miles' talents. "She's in the States – I haven't heard much myself –"

"She sent a postcard from Manhattan. I believe that she's still trying to find another accompanist."

"Yes. It was bad luck about Emily Deutsch."

"Conceivably." Middlemass seemed to suggest the reverse, but, having gained a little ground, Miles was unwilling to take him up on the implication. "I'm glad to see that you've brought your protégé along. He can meet mine."

"Your –"

"A member of the family. We haven't seen one another for some time but we have – interests in common."

Right on cue, a rap of heels echoed from the staircase which swept, dim and cobwebbed, beyond the open door. Miles had no idea who, or what, would appear. Middlemass's brief entry in *Who's Who* concentrated only on his career, carried few personal details. Francesca, out of loyalty, had always refused to speculate about his tastes.

They all turned to the doorway at the same moment. Miles had been prepared for anything – a busty singer, a slender clarinettist, a countrywoman in cashmere and pearls, a devoted amanuensis. What he did not expect was the creature who appeared.

Small and thin, wearing what looked suspiciously like an old school dress, the girl tapped towards them in ankle-socks and sandals. Two plaits, brown and glossy, hung below her shoulders, and gold-rimmed spectacles, poised circles, gleamed above her well-scrubbed face.

"This is Louise," said Middlemass briefly. "She writes string quartets."

Dinner took place in a dining room as sparsely furnished as the rest of the house; white paintwork, and the bristol-glass blue of the night offset the Sheraton table and the unexpectedly superb food and wine. They were waited on by an ancient *ayah*, an Indian woman in a resplendent sari who had had some connection with the family years ago. The dishes were a blend of occidental and oriental, and Miles remembered that Middlemass's relations had had many connections with the subcontinent; a fortune had been made there generations ago, and Hilary had spent many years in India long before it became fashionable. This accounted for his ability to step aside from English life, to see it at a remove: he had an outsider's insights.

Miles looked again at Louise and wondered where she fitted into the curious pattern of Middlemass's household. She presided at the other end of the table, dignified but buoyant, like a young princess in an old regime, giggling at Benjy's remarks. By the light of Hilary's tarnished candlesticks, she looked younger than ever, a child at her first dinner party. Although she did not sound like one, he admitted, overhearing the comment "Fuck early Schönberg" in her precise Edinburgh accent.

Hilary Middlemass was eager to discuss Cambridge, although he seemed to dislike everyone Miles mentioned. They ran through university gossip together, Middlemass asking with concern after individuals whom he proceeded to damn with faint praise.

After coffee in another dim, white room, they walked out into the grounds. Overgrown trees, branches distorted, were silhouetted against the night sky. A few ghostly clouds sailed past a flood of stars, and as the party crossed the park, it separated into pairs. Miles and Middlemass were left near the yew alley, as Louise and Benjy faded into darkness. Middlemass watched the two young people indulgently, and Miles laughed to himself.

"You know, I expected a number of things of you, Miles, but sodomy wasn't among them."

"That's rather a biblical way of expressing it."

"I suppose that's what it is? Nothing more juvenile?"

"Well – I – well, that is to say – yes."

"I might have known. When are you going to grow up, Miles?"

"Look –" He had never contradicted Middlemass before, and it took some courage to start. "Why don't you –"

"Mind my own business? It's in order to escape that that I mind other people's. It's curious –" he added objectively, sounding like a criminologist in the dramatic reconstruction of some old tragedy "– I would never have thought that you would turn out this way. I wouldn't have said that you were constitutionally perverted, either."

Miles muttered at the epithet.

"It's a term which you'll get used to, Miles, if you pursue this form of gratification. Of course, you've never belonged to a minority group before, have you? You aren't a Jew, or a Catholic, or a member of the Communist Party of Great Britain." For a moment, despite his detached tone, Middlemass sounded as though he had been all three at some stage of his life. "You're letting yourself in for centuries of opprobrium and some rather unpleasant words. Queer; pervert; faggot; gay –"

"For as long as I can remember," Miles replied, "I have belonged to a minority group of one."

"My dear Miles! At least you're going to benefit in one respect. I can see that you're about to develop the notoriously sharp tongue of the persecuted."

"Now wait a minute –"

"You're going to ask me why I should set myself up as your moral tutor?"

"Why do you always know what I'm going to say before I've said it?"

"I'm familiar with your thought processes. As the great detective said: you know my methods. Apply them. As for your question – who else would bother? Who else would care?"

Miles sighed. "I never did like confession sessions. Straight talks."

"Straight is not the word."

From the distance a laugh rose, precise, feminine, and with a faintly Scots intonation.

"Where else," asked Miles, "would you find an elderly nympholept giving advice to a retarded adolescent?"

Possibly the most revealing speech about himself that Miles had ever made, it left him feeling shy and self-conscious.

"I think you're being rather unjust, Miles. Both to me, and to yourself. Louise is eighteen, and admittedly, I like the company of – young people. But that's common enough. It is also a great deal more innocent than you imagine."

"It won't last." Miles resorted to cliché, already losing interest in Hilary Middlemass's private life and concerned only with his own potential suffering. "It won't last."

Miles was off in his own world, walking past the fantastic sets he had constructed for their future together, some shared house in Cambridge and a life of books: he knew that these drop-scenes and flats would be towed away, leaving a dark stage, Miles alone, night and silence, blackout. Benjy would be gone, and although he wanted to believe otherwise, he was too sternly trained in intellectual rigorousness to entertain the possibility. "It can't. Nothing like this has ever happened to me before. This love – this warmth, this comfort and joy."

He sat down beside Middlemass on the stone bench. Above them, birds transmitted their last coded messages of the evening. "I can't explain how much this means to me," he added, wondering if people spoke in clichés so often because they were so true. That was another cliché, he thought, absently.

"I think I can," said Hilary Middlemass, distant and compassionate. "It's simple. You're making up for lost time."

"Did you like him?" Miles asked, as they drove through the darkness. Branches swung forward into the headlights: small creatures scampered into the car's path and had to be avoided. Benjy, a black silhouette against blacker night, seemed distant. He had a way of switching off, refusing to accept emotional transmissions, ignoring Miles, which left the latter devastated. In these gestures, Miles foresaw the end: a state of incommunicado, when it would all be finished, and Benjy would turn to him with bland incuriosity, like a stranger watching someone making a scene in a restaurant. The vision tormented him.

"Very much," Benjy replied, finally. "I was impressed."

"I've always been impressed." Relieved to have found some reception, Miles continued. "How about Louise? I noticed that you spent quite a lot of time together."

Benjy turned to him sharply.

"Oh – I – not that I – got the wrong impression. Nothing like that. I just wondered if you – took to her, that's all."

Benjy replied, in the slightly constrained tones of one who wanted to say "What *is* the matter with you?": "Louise is very nice. She's at the Royal Academy. She knows someone I was at school with."

"I hadn't expected her to be there."

"Yes, it's an odd set-up. How old is he, Miles?"

"Sixty something." It was another of the obvious omissions in the *Who's Who* entry. "Let me see – about sixty-five, I should think."

"It's not as if she was very good-looking," Benjy persisted. "But on the other hand, one has to admit, she's got sex appeal. Oh yes."

Miles was on the point of asking Benjy what he knew about it, but realised that he really did not want an answer. Instead he commented: "You have the oddest notions of sexual attractiveness, Benjy."

"Don't I just." Benjy reached out in the darkness. "Will we see them again?"

"Probably. Although I don't know how and when. Hilary Middlemass likes to be elusive."

"He likes Francesca, doesn't he?"

"They've always been very close. Hilary was instrumental, if you'll forgive the word, in Francesca's going to music school. If it hadn't been for him, I don't think that she could ever have outfaced my father."

"Didn't he approve of Francesca becoming a musician?"

"He disapproved very strongly, Benjy. But Francesca has a strong character too, and in the end she won. She went off to Paris, against considerable opposition."

"When's Francesca coming to Bly?"

"I don't know. To tell you the truth, I'm rather worried. She usually keeps in touch with Hilary. But only a postcard. I hope she's all right."

"Don't you always come away from Middlemass feeling rather – ignorant?"

"Very ignorant," Miles replied, dissuading Benjy's hands.

"I think he's *wonderful*. So mysterious and – fascinating."

For some reason, Miles remembered Benjy's comment about older men, and was rewarded with a flare of jealousy. The sensation blazed, fast as petrol on a bonfire, wreaking havoc as it always did on Miles' untrained emotions. One moment Benjy talked about Louise, the next it was Middlemass. Why did he always turn to somebody else? Why was there always somebody there, ready for attention, ready to be looked at, ready to be admired? This had been the side he had not mentioned to Hilary Middlemass; this had been the side he chose to ignore, the consuming envy and anger, the fear that Benjy would go from him.

Miles tried to concentrate on his driving, which was erratic at the best of times. He slowed down as they approached the village, passing the New Vicarage, the darkened shops and cottages, the exemplary council houses, the square-towered church.

"You've never shown me round the church," said Benjy.

"We'll go round tomorrow, if you like."

"Why wait until then?"

"Benjy, it's after two –"

"We haven't got to get up in the morning. Come on, I'm sure it'll be open."

Miles stopped the car reluctantly, and Benjy sprang out into the long grass by the lychgate.

"Perfect churchyard atmosphere," he observed, as an owl called to the full moon. He darted ahead through the tombstones, a slender ghost, silk evening scarf fluid over one shoulder. The parish church of St Peter at Bly was a stocky, fenland church set with pebbles; it had been designed as a fort as well as a sanctuary, and sat thickset among the graves.

"There's a torch on the ledge," said Miles automatically, as Benjy fumbled for lights. Shapes sprang and quivered on the whitewashed walls; from the simple altar the crucifix cast a lateral shadow high as the vaults. Figured monuments shot forward and receded again into the gloom.

"What are those?" Benjy asked, moving towards the figures in the transept.

"My forebears," said Miles.

"My God, so they are. *Hic jacet Milef Tatterfhalluff anno domini MDCCLXII* – Miles Tattyphallus, that's quite good. And this one's even older. She looks just like Francesca." Benjy hung over the effigy in surprise, playing his torch along the mazed stone. "You must have been big people round here."

Miles shrugged.

"I suppose so. We've always lived in this area. That's one of the reasons why my father took this living. Of course, there wasn't much money left by then, so he didn't have much choice."

"But weren't you powerful once?"

"I believe so. But we just sort of – died out."

"Wasn't there a house?"

"Yes – the Government bought it about thirty years ago. I believe they train Intelligence personnel there now."

"It's rather sad. I hate to think of these families all dying out."

"Ah well, I suppose we just ran out of steam. And I'm the end result. There won't be any more, after me."

"No more Tattershalls?"

"Not from this line."

"You'd better get married quickly, and start producing a few." Benjy knew that he hated jokes like this, but he still made them. "Don't worry. I can see you alternate weekends."

Miles yawned, as much to indicate to Benjy that he was being tedious as to demonstrate tiredness.

"Yes, I'll come in a second." Benjy was still looking round. "I haven't been in a place like this since school chapel." He walked up the aisle, paused before the altar, then turned. The torch illuminated his dead white features, pale in spite of the tan, the winged collar and wilting rose: Miles caught only a glitter from his eyes as he switched off the beam. Immediately, the sky beyond the thick-leaded glass became nacreous and Benjy came forward in the dank darkness like a spectre, the fringes of his white scarf trailing in the draught.

Distinct yet shadowy, distant yet accessible, he had never seemed more desirable. He came closer, and Miles noticed that the second-hand evening trousers had button-flies. On another occasion, this would have been intriguing: but here? No.

"What's wrong?"

"I'm tired, Benjy. I need my bed."

And Miles was lying: how could he tell Benjy that here, of all places, he sensed his father's reproachful presence, and that Benjy's approach seemed like blasphemy?

# Six

Next day the rain came, and stayed. Miles woke to hear it trickle down the open window, blowing in to soak the row of paperbacks along the sill. He rescued members of the local moth population who staggered inside with waterlogged wings, and, though it was early, dressed and went downstairs. Miles realised that it had been some time since he'd begun a morning alone, enjoyed again the solitude of placing his cup on the table, and of opening the back door to see if the milk had arrived.

The orchard shone beyond, drenched in moisture, each blade of grass feathered by water, the globes of apples bright as an illustration. Miles sniffed the air like a cat, loving the smell of rain.

The postman, who came seldom, had been early that morning; a postcard and an air-mail letter lay bright on the mat. The postcard, of the Pan-Am building by night, was from Francesca.

> Dearest Miles, Everyone here marvellous despite. Wish you were here with me. F.

Despite what? The message seemed more exaggerated than usual; the intensifier was uncharacteristic: he had never met a professional musician who described his or her associates as marvellous. The postcard had every appearance of representing Francesca's bright, brilliant self, and yet, like her manner at Christmas, in supposedly haunted Campden Hill Square, its very normality disconcerted. The letter, in staggering spiky handwriting, was for Benjy.

Miles sat with his tea and studied the postcard. It had an

East Side postmark; he seemed to remember that she was staying in a friend's apartment, but no address had been left. The F was unusual, too. Francesca had always delighted in her name, its baroque grandeur, signing with an italic upstroke of delight, a mounting flourish which tilted, running up the scale.

He put the card in front of the milk jug, sighing with the faint melancholy which always follows dinner parties. It had nothing to do with Hilary Middlemass's Montrachet or his cognac, and everything to do with that brief exchange in the dark park.

"Hangover, Miles?"

The dishevelled aesthete had disappeared; Benjy was once more in faded jeans and checked shirt, hair standing on end; even with sleep in his eyes he possessed a matutinal beauty. Fly-button Levi's, too, Miles noticed; apparently this style was favoured among the cognoscenti; anybody who was anybody, or wanted anybody, wore fly buttons, according to Benjy. Miles had expressed an ignorance of the trend, and been reprimanded. "But you *must* know about these things, Miles. You're one of us now."

Miles had consented to learn, but in this respect was a bad scholar. He could not remember all the complexities of buttons left undone, handkerchiefs, the rules every self-respecting man must know. And, to be honest, could not be bothered to learn them: it would mean admitting membership of the club to which he did not wish to belong.

"Hangover?" Benjy enquired again, sitting down and gulping tea with appetite. There were only thirteen years between them, but in his exuberance Benjy could have been from another, younger, planet.

"You could call it that."

"I was flat out. That stuff of Middlemass's certainly packs a wallop. He's got a good cellar."

This remark reminded Miles of Benjy's previous comment about Louise's sexual attractiveness: he wanted to know what sort of a judge Benjy thought he was. But again, resisted the temptation to ask: let the boy have his affectations.

"There's a letter for you."

"Really? You sound pretty pissed off, Miles. Suppose it's the rain."

"No, I like rain."

"Who's the postcard from?"

"Francesca."

"Nice."

"No it isn't."

"Oh all right, it isn't. You're spoiling for a fight."

"I'm worried."

Benjy opened his letter with a knife; he smiled, laughed, sighed, then: "Miles – c'n I ask you something?"

"You can try. But don't expect a civil answer."

"Olivia."

"I thought it might be."

"Miles – is it all right if she comes to stay?"

He had half-anticipated the question. Perhaps that was why he felt such relief.

"It would mean so much to her. We haven't seen each other for ages, and perhaps we can get everything sorted out now. We're older and I'm sure we can adjust –" Benjy stopped, realising that his persuasions were unnecessary.

"I'd be delighted to meet your sister." Miles was belting up his old Burberry.

"I know it's asking a lot – a bit much, really."

"I've already told you. I'd be delighted."

"You mean you will? She can come?"

"Of course." Knotting the belt, Miles prepared to stride off into the rain. Benjy was conscious of the theatrical nature of the gesture.

"Miles – wait a minute – hang on –"

"I could do with some fresh air."

He had always enjoyed walking in the rain. Now moisture clung to him, flattening his hair and misting his glasses; wet weeds brushed his legs in passing. He strode off in the direction of the staithe.

"Miles – wait – come back!"

He felt disinclined to turn, enjoying the drama. Water ran down his neck, and spattered his old brogues; he observed the infinite variations of cloudscape above soaked marsh, bowed his body against the wind. In the distance, he heard Benjy's unsure feet stumble and falter.

"Miles! Wait for me!"

He didn't wait; instead, he walked along the edge of the dike, looking out to grey sea. Along the staithe, rain beat on tarpaulined dinghies and rang the halyards: waves responded to the blow of drops. On the other side, samphire swayed in its beaten pools.

"Miles, what's the matter?"

He turned, to see Benjy soaked to the skin, hair sleeked on his forehead; he looked reassuringly unattractive.

"Miles, what's the matter? What is it? What?" Again, those reiterated questions which so infuriated him.

Miles shrugged.

"For God's sake! Miles! Say something!"

"You're very wet, Benjy. I think you'd better go back."

"Well, do you want her to come or not?"

"Of course I do."

And he did: which was what confused him. The prospect of having a woman in the place, let alone a prim convent girl, should have thrown him into consternation; and a third party placed inevitable restrictions on his association with Benjy. Yet he welcomed the presence. Perhaps, he tried to tell himself, he was tired, satiated with Benjy's charms; after all, he was physically unaccustomed to any sort of active sex life; perhaps he needed a rest.

But as they walked back to the vicarage, Miles admitted that the reaction had set in; he flung his arm round Benjy's shoulders, but without desire. Was it possible that one could be argued out of the irrationalities of passion?

Hilary Middlemass had disturbed him and Miles understood, turning from the boy as he went upstairs to change, that nothing at Bly would ever be the same again.

"I don't know what to expect," said Miles.

"You might get on, you never know."

Benjy did not sound convinced. It was a week after their visit to Charnwood, and Miles was driving down to the station to meet Olivia Underwood's train. The rains were over and gone, and Benjy had become a little restless, as Miles had predicted and feared.

"I'm sorry, I'm rather busy at present," Miles had told him a few days earlier, "I really must get back to those notes"; and, "I'm sorry, but I've really got to get up early in the morning and work." Benjy had received these rebuffs with irritation; he had demanded explanations and been offered none; he had accused Miles of coldness, and regarded the Burton manuscript almost as a rival. Miles' elusiveness, his obvious relief at evading Benjy, distressed the boy.

"Anyway, you can show her round," continued Miles. "It'll give you something to do while I'm working. You could go over to Norwich. Or take out those bicycles from the shed."

"I expect she'll want to talk to you. She'll want to know about Cambridge."

"I doubt it. In a few months Olivia will be able to find out for herself, and I'm relying on you to keep her –"

"Under control?"

"I was going to say occupied."

"When you meet her, you'll know how impossible that would be. She needs a lot of attention." Miles looked apprehensive. "I think she's going to find you irresistible."

"Oh, shut up, Benjy."

They reached the station as the barriers were coming down over the level crossing. A bell sounded across the deserted platform, and a train rumbled in the distance.

"That's her!"

Benjy leapt out of the car and ran into the station. Miles followed more slowly, through the blaze of willowherb which sprouted beyond the white clapboard. The little halt had the gentle melancholy of empty waiting rooms and buffets quiet in the afternoon sun. He remembered meeting Francesca here, as he returned from school, Francesca changed and strange from her time in Paris, waiting in front of the tea-urn and the faded advertisement for Apollo Table Waters.

The train pounded quickly into his thoughts: it stopped for an instant to allow a figure onto the platform, and was gone.

116

Miles had not known what to expect. As with Louise he was prepared for almost anything, although he had in mind some feminine Benjy, a Shakespearian twin, distinguishable only by costume and with the same black and white beauty. Or otherwise a dowdy convent girl, all plaits and sandals.

Olivia Underwood had plaits and sandals: she also had khaki shorts and long, brown, bare legs; from a distance her features were of the same cast as Benjy's, but more strongly tanned, a bronze counterfeit. She stood completely still as Benjy hurled himself at her like a dog, and detached herself to shake hands with Miles, looking up at him with sly, appraising eyes, head slightly to one side. Her light brown hair had a curiously green sheen.

"Dr Tattershall, how nice. I've been so looking forward to this." Her accent was entirely English, and as her long fingers curled into his palm, he dismissed any comparison with Louise.

"I'm delighted – to – Benjy's – well, yes, won't you come to the car?"

She confused him: they both did, standing side by side like two halves of an apple, or coins, one bronze, one silver. "Do you have very much luggage?"

She shook her head, so that the plaits danced, and led a minor procession to the car. Insisting on the passenger seat, she made herself comfortable beside Miles and made remarks about the countryside, noting windmills and flatlands just as her brother had done.

"I hope that it isn't going to be too boring for you here," Miles said. In reply, Olivia smiled, making it difficult for him to keep his eyes on the road. "I'm never bored," she replied. "I make my own entertainment."

"I'm sure you do. Did you have a good journey?"

"It took hours from Dieppe. Then there was a *manifestation socialiste* so that we were delayed at the docks. I was in a trainload of Northerners, all thrutching away –"

"Doing what?"

"Thrutching. It means fussing and threshing –"

"But you weren't?"

117

Olivia laughed, stretching her arms across the seat. Miles jerked forward instinctively, but leant back again.

"Don't you believe her," said Benjy. "She's got the worst temper I've ever seen."

"You keep out of it." Without malice.

"When did you leave your – convent school?"

"Oh, back in June. I've been staying with a friend in Paris. He lets me use his apartment."

"Very nice," commented Miles.

"Well, he *is* away a great deal, and likes someone to be there. Just to keep an eye on things. It is useful," she admitted. "Having a base of operations, so to speak." The formal language sounded odd in her casual, lean-lipped mouth, and Miles realised that she had her brother's ability to disconcert. He wondered who the lucky apartment-owner had been, and what he was doing now.

"Actually, it was rather sad." Olivia was off on another tack now.

"What's that?"

"At Sacré Coeur – the convent up in Normandy – one of the novitiates committed suicide."

"That's dreadful."

"Mm. Of course. A mortal sin, and all that. I'd rather not talk about it, actually. She was one of my friends."

"Of course." She turned to look at the landscape, and in the driving mirror Miles saw Benjy open his mouth to speak, think better of it, and glance down.

"What a steep hill," Olivia commented, as they drove up to the Old Vicarage. "Rather unusual round here."

"That's why the church is up here. They always selected the highest spot to build on."

"It dates back to prehistoric practices," said Benjy. "They used to sacrifice –" He was suddenly quiet. Olivia sat staring into the distance, chin on hand, the plaits stirring on her shoulders like green corn.

Far from being a distraction, Miles soon came to find Olivia's presence a relief. The enforced isolation of his weeks with Benjy had produced a tension which he only now appreciated:

sexual frustration, once dissipated, had been replaced by a more profound mental suffering; fears of Benjy's leaving him had developed into a longing that he would actually go, and leave Miles to feel sorry for himself in comfortable, familiar solitude. There were so many threats, actual and half-imagined, of desertion, that every day brought the prospect of new pain. On a recent occasion, before the advent of Olivia, they had been lying at noon on Miles' bed, sated and languid in the manner of many lovers, and vaguely wondering who would be the one to get up and fetch a drink. Miles could not remember how the topic of conversation had arisen, but suddenly they were discussing women.

"One or two, perhaps. But they would have to be special. Very special," Benjy was saying, stretching like a young cat.

"I suppose – I don't know, I suppose most women alarm me," Miles admitted. "The whole business – the prospect of failure – and all that flesh –" He spoke academically, unwilling to admit further personal reservations and anxious to change the subject. But Benjy wished to pursue it.

"I like a lean girl," he was saying. "The thin ones, all leg and hip – the kind you see trotting down to the boathouses on misty mornings in tight little shorts. And I love to see them in stockings – I could quite go for that. Have you ever been into the lingerie department at Joshua Taylor's? Christ, I wouldn't mind that myself. All those suspender belts –"

Benjy had been mocking, another elaborate joke; but his body had obviously responded to the fantasies, and Miles watched him, humiliated and rejected, as Benjy touched himself.

Miles turned aside, unwanted, unable to compete with such illusions; and knowing that he would be unable to compete with the real thing, too, if she came along.

He was glad of Olivia's presence now: the insistent demands of another personality were alleviated by a third party. Miles retreated into his work, content to hear conversation from the next room or laughter drifting up from the garden. And, despite Benjy's warnings, he found no evidence of a temper in Olivia: she generated a sly amusement, which tended towards the anecdotal, and Miles was grateful for her presence at mealtimes, when she recounted various episodes from her life in France. As she said, Olivia made her own entertainment, and absolved Miles from the strain of conversation. He found her physically pleasing, too; not beautiful so much as graceful, a bronze complement to Benjy.

Olivia's presence made one essential difference, however; Benjy no longer came to Miles' bed. On the first evening, after a meal which seemed to last for hours, and a discussion of the French cinema which consisted mainly of Olivia's reported sightings of screen actors on the beach at Cannes last summer, they had gone to their respective rooms.

Benjy had been unusually quiet throughout the meal, and Miles had glanced across once or twice to see him scowling. When he did speak, it was to add some rider or a wry commentary to one of Olivia's anecdotes, a tendency which Miles came to resent. At bed-time Benjy had clumped upstairs last, *Barchester Towers* ostentatiously under one arm. And Miles lay in wait, beneath the patchwork quilt, arms behind his head, watching the pattern of leaves across the ceiling and comfortably expecting footfalls on the landing.

Perhaps, he thought, he had overestimated Hilary Middle-mass's remarks; after all, if he were so constituted, it would be ridiculous to suppress his instincts. The fact that these instincts had been quite content to remain in abeyance for the previous thirty-three years did occur to him: but presumably they had lain dormant, waiting for the appropriate person to awaken them.

Miles smiled at the prospect of himself as a sleeping prince – last year the thought would never have occurred to him. But last year, he would never have foreseen the events of this summer. Being able to think about himself, even to consider that as worthwhile subject matter, was a recent innovation. He remembered his father's injunctions: "*I will not have you absorbed in your own processes, Miles. You must think less of yourself.*" And Miles had done so, in every sense of the word; perhaps the most vital result of his association with Benjy was the increased self-confidence with which he had come to regard himself. He remembered those wet February days, cycling through the rain and whistling because he felt necessary to someone else's existence; he remembered the compliment of Benjy's desire for his company, and for that matter, the compliment of Benjy's desire.

It was as though, Miles realised, he were at last overcoming an arrested development, as though he were growing wings and becoming airborne after years bivouacked as a chrysalis. Had he been able to see it, this confidence was obvious in his gestures; he no longer glanced aside so quickly, avoiding eye contact; his diminished nervousness made him seem lithe, rather than thin; and although he would never be handsome, he achieved a tanned distinction.

Which was why, when he lay reflecting on his satisfactory psychic development, Miles was so puzzled that Benjy did not come. He assumed that Olivia's presence must be the cause; but Olivia, if she was not already familiar with her brother's tastes, need never know. It seemed perverse to resent Benjy's absence after avoiding his presence all week, but Miles felt perverse. He needed something to relieve the tensions of the day, and he needed Benjy. He fell asleep resentfully, with feelings of neglect, and dreamt, in a world of fogs and icons, that he was chasing a fleeting female figure down some darkening London street.

After the rain, the weather around Bly became increasingly hot and dry, grass and cow parsley bleached in the ditches, and apples, suspended among the dry leaves of the orchard, flushed red. Doors and windows stood open, so that colonies of insects occupied the vicarage; mosquitoes and winged beetles clattered inside lampshades, caterpillars marched across the kitchen table; one evening, a death's head hawk-moth settled on Olivia's hair like a bow.

Miles typed interminably; he completed his index and corrected his final draft, tinkering with footnotes and intricacies of punctuation, constantly amazed at his own determination to finish the book at last. He would look up from his father's desk to see Olivia and Benjy stretched out among the grass, talking, or playing french cricket with a mangy tennis-ball.

Sometimes they were like twelve-year-olds, giggling over

some private joke in their family idiolect; sometimes they sat listlessly, like undergraduates, swopping gnomic pronouncements about recent books, a film both had seen. Miles would see projections of himself and Francesca, in shared summer vacations: grass-stained, idle, lost hot days.

Miles soon adapted to his role of indulgent supervisor, leaving them together as he devoted his attention once more to Burton. He would wave them off on one of their bicycle trips, enquire as to their day in Lowestoft or their visit to Norwich Cathedral, listen to Olivia's accounts of places and people. Miles learnt to treat Olivia a little distantly; she seemed impulsive, liable to fling her demonstrative arms round his neck as Benjy looked on. It was a not unpleasant sensation. Miles discouraged this, appealing to Benjy with a semaphore of eyebrow, as Benjy scowled. Miles was also surprised to find that Olivia did not repel him, although there was something a little eerie about her, the cunning eyes, the shiny, faintly green plaits.

A few days after her arrival, Olivia wandered over to the piano and asked Miles where the music was kept. He showed her, and retreated to the study, prepared for a sequence of standards in which the *Sonata Facile* and Chopin's *Nocturne in B* would figure prominently. Then it seemed for a moment as if Olivia had abandoned performance in favour of the radio. Three Brahms *Intermezzi* and an excerpt from the *Appassionata* followed in rapid succession. Miles went into the drawing room to find Olivia sitting back from the piano, rubbing her arms.

"Good God, that was you."

"Yes. Rather out of practice, I'm afraid."

"You were superb."

"Not really. I had some good tuition in France, but –"

"At the convent?"

"I went to the town for lessons."

"You must meet Francesca. I'm sure that you'd –"

Olivia shook her head, returned to the miscellaneous stack of music, and started on a Scarlatti sonata. Music moved through the house, poured through the open windows so that

Benjy emerged from the shadows of the garden, Crabbe under one arm, and leant in over the sill.

"Good, isn't she?"

"I don't know what you're going to Cambridge for," said Miles.

"Don't let her answer that."

"I wouldn't make it as a professional." Olivia raised her voice above the music.

Miles shook his head, as Olivia had done, and followed Benjy into the garden.

"I'd no idea –"

"Yes, she's got quite a talent there," Benjy said, throwing himself down among the grass, tattered panama over his eyes. "Oh Miles, I sometimes wish she hadn't come."

"Why?"

Miles sat down beside him, arms around his knees. A ladybird crawled laboriously along his wrist, took wing as Scarlatti glittered precariously among the leaves. Olivia broke off in mid-phrase, and after a brief silence played the opening staccato bars of the *Pavane Pour Une Infante Défunte*.

Benjy was murmuring under his breath. "'And all that famous harmony of leaves –'"

Miles leant over, gently raised the hat from his face. Despite the sun, Benjy seemed pallid, spectral. He looked up, eyes cupping the sky. "Benjy – why did you say that they kept you apart?"

Benjy shrugged, heavy-lidded and lazy in the chiaroscuro of apple leaves.

"They just did. No reason."

"But there must be some explanation."

"Perhaps they feared for the fate of the Underwood millions, or twenty-five thousand a year apiece, as it now stands. If something happened to us, it might go to some dreadful wicked uncle."

"That's not good enough, Benjy."

"It'll have to be." Replacing the hat over his eyes, as if to conclude the exchange. "You like her, don't you?"

"Like her? I'm not sure that *like* is the appropriate term. She's a little fey, isn't she?"

"Bloody spooky. *And* she knows it."

"You're getting on better than I expected."

"Yes, I think things are working out. After all, we've spent so much time apart. When *is* Francesca coming back?"

"I wish I knew."

The *Pavane* came to an end, leaving them to the clatter of leaves and the whirr of a cricket.

"Miles – Tears For Fears are coming to the Hammersmith Odeon."

"Who are they, and what has it got to do with me?"

"They're a band, Miles, you've listened to them. Robert's got tickets – comps – and he thinks he can get some backstage passes. His brother's in the music business."

"And you want to go?"

"Yes."

"Well, why ask me? I'm your supervisor, not your gaoler."

Benjy looked for a second as though the distinction were marginal.

"You don't – mind?" he asked at last.

"Mind? I'm in no position to mind."

"It's just that – I find it all a bit tense here, that's all. I feel as if I'm under a lot of pressure."

"That's curious. I find the atmosphere remarkably relaxed."

"You would."

"Good Lord, is this our first row?"

"You're impossible to row with." Benjy sat up and dissuaded the insects which had accumulated on his shirt. "I think I can leave you two together safely."

"Olivia won't come to any harm with me."

"It isn't Olivia I'm worried about."

Nevertheless, Miles felt curiously vulnerable as they waved Benjy off at the station a few days later. He hung out of the window, hand moving languidly, as the train disappeared and silence flooded back to the platform. The night before his departure, he had been morose and solemn; Olivia said that he was getting in the right mood for the concert, but Miles knew that he was sulking.

Then at the last minute he had been animated, talking about Robert's family and the friends they planned to visit. Olivia witnessed this with amusement. Now she stood beside Miles, making cabbalistic signs in the dust with the toe of her sandal, and Miles wondered what on earth he could do to entertain her. Just as she had alleviated the strain of being alone with Benjy, she now produced a one-to-one tension of her own.

"Do you want to go back?" she enquired.

"I think that would be a good idea, don't you?"

Olivia shrugged her brown shoulders. At first, Miles had wished that she wore more clothes, and not the sequence of singlets and shorts; then he had realised how successfully these garments complemented her figure, and that he was actually attracted by the smooth expanses of gold flesh which she emphasised with every gesture. Although she dressed as a boy, she was decidedly female, and therefore disturbing.

"On the other hand, why don't I take you over to meet Hilary Middlemass?"

"What, now? That'd be marvellous."

"It's after five. We could go over for a drink, and he might even give us a meal."

Olivia gave one of her smiles. "Don't you think I ought to change?" More than ever, she demanded Miles' attention: he found himself looking at her with pleasure.

"Don't ever change," he found himself saying, as they got into the car. "I'm sure Hilary will appreciate you just the way you are."

When they arrived, Charnwood was looking ruined and picturesque in the evening light. No-one answered the front door, but this was not unusual. Miles wandered to the side of the house: Hilary Middlemass might well be at the other end of the park, down by the deep, rather smelly lake. Olivia, who had slid her hand through his arm, kept looking round, although she was not, he noticed, as surprised and awed by it all as Benjy had been. She had a great deal more poise than her brother.

A few hundred yards away, in the shade of an immense cedar, Hilary and Louise were playing croquet on a bumpy lawn. There was something faintly absurd about the concentration both brought to the game, Louise measuring the lie of the land with the expression of a Caledonian engineer; Hilary, the mallet tiny as a baton in his hands, listening intently for the crack of ball on wood.

Louise played a precise stroke, watched the ball roll through its hoop, and leaning back on her mallet with satisfaction, saw Miles and Olivia. Hilary immediately looked up, as though she had made some comment, but Louise had not said a word.

"Miles! What a pleasant surprise!" He saw Olivia. "And this is even more of a surprise. What's your name, my dear?"

When Hilary sounded as paternal as this, the time had come to suspect him. But Miles smiled to himself and said nothing but: "This is Olivia. She's Benjy's sister."

They shook hands, Olivia's manner assured as Hilary's. Louise advanced, swinging her mallet in a controlled fashion which suggested that she was about to let fly in Olivia's direction. And yet there was no suspicion that she felt threatened by Olivia's presence: they made their exchanges politely, like contenders before a fight, or a pair of cats sizing one another up. There was an instinctive tensing of the muscles, charged eye contact. Miles gently detached Olivia's arm.

"We like to relax occasionally," Hilary was saying, looking at the mallet objectively as he turned it in his hands, as though he did not know quite what it was.

"You didn't look very relaxed!"

"No, well, Louise takes these things very seriously, you know. She's a competitive girl."

Miles could hear her talking to Olivia, the strophe and antistrophe of Olivia's lazy comments and Louise's polite interpolations.

"To tell you the truth, I've been working very hard recently. I'm doing a few Blake settings for a telly programme – some sort of documentary. Bloody awful film, but it pays well. You still haven't heard from Francesca?"

Miles shook his head in denial and they moved away, towards the lake, where sodden wrack floated on the dark surface of the water; occasionally Miles spotted a bubble that might have been a fish, or mere gas from rotting algae. The midges were out in force, and Miles resorted to his pipe.

"Miles, you never cease to amaze me."

"That's quite a compliment, coming from you."

"First of all you turn up with a page, and then you walk in with *that* on your arm –"

"What's wrong with that? I mean, Olivia?"

"'O when mine eyes did see Olivia first, methought she purg'd the air of pestilence –'"

Miles waved away several midges.

"She seems to be singularly ineffective round here," he observed. "And don't get literary, Hilary."

"You're a fine one to talk. Now you've done *Maurice*, we've got *Lolita*. Where on earth did you pick her up?"

"I resent the way you regard her as some sort of parcel, Hilary. If anything, she picked me up. She came to stay with Benjy."

"Oh yes, of course. And where is Benjy?"

"On his way to Hammersmith Odeon, for a rock concert. And stop looking at me like that."

"You've certainly made progress since our last session. Come back in a fortnight and let me know how you're getting on."

"If you're not quiet, I'll –"

Hilary moved a little away from the edge of the lake. "Well, I'm certainly delighted to make her acquaintance."

Miles sighed with exasperation. "If you only realise how incongruous you are," he said. "You stand there, looking distinguished and venerable, casting aspersions –"

"Oh, come and have a drink," said Hilary, managing to suggest that Miles had been making a fuss over nothing.

'Drinks' soon became extended to an invitation to dinner. Miles sat a little apart on the terrace, watching Olivia and Louise talk. Louise sat on the cracked balustrade, legs crossed precisely, hand propping her chin. Olivia lay along the balustrade itself, totally unconcerned by the twelve-foot drop on the other side, one knee raised.

Hilary moved about with a bottle of wine, and the faint suggestion that he was officiating in some rite; this almost sacerdotal air was enhanced by his habit of pausing in mid-step and gazing out over the park. Miles half-expected him to come out with some profound observation.

"Midges are rising again," he remarked, and went back to refilling glasses. Miles shook his head. It was a familiar gesture these days, since despite all the recent developments in his life, Miles still spent a great deal of time feeling puzzled. He wondered, for instance, what on earth Olivia and Louise found to talk about, for, although as thin, plaited, musical adolescents they fitted into the same category, in every other respect they were totally different.

Louise had a reserved, fastidious air, reminding him of one of Benjy's phrases, *too cool to fool*. She would become one of those musicians Francesca occasionally introduced him to, technical perfectionists full of passionate constraint, intimidatingly well dressed. Whereas Olivia's temperament seemed all too obvious: she lay there on the balustrade, in a lemma of her life, making some sly observation with a sheer drop to one side.

"I appreciate that you're distracted, but you should make some effort to get in touch with her."

Hilary stood beside him. Miles had not heard his approach.

"Francesca. I know. I keep meaning to, but –"

"I've written to her agent. And I'm trying to get hold of the tour manager. As far as I know, she's got something on at Lincoln Center next week."

"Oh, that's good. Yes, I knew there was a new recording contract –"

"*Cave.*"

"What? Oh, I see." Olivia and Louise came towards them. Even then, Miles wondered if the warning were directed against Olivia. Hilary was at his most charming, but Miles realised that he distrusted her.

★   ★   ★

128

Dinner was eclectic: there were several Indian dishes, including a dahl and chapattis, and semolina sweetmeats; but there was also an excellent claret (which Hilary had no qualms about drinking with exotic food), game pie, and a chocolate mousse in the form of a rabbit which, sitting among candles and glasses, achieved a totemic appearance. Miles and Hilary occupied themselves with further gossip, and Louise led a rather surprised Olivia off as soon as they reached the liqueur stage.

"They seem to be getting on."

"Louise is very politic."

"Actually, Hilary, I find Olivia rather a strain. Perhaps she'd like to come over to you for a few days."

"Novelty wearing off a bit, is it?"

"Well – she's got such a strong personality, and she's not the sort of person who can sit quietly with a book, the way Benjy does. She needs to have things happening, and when they aren't – she makes things happen. She's not a restful person, Hilary."

"She might come and upset things here."

"But I thought – with all the instruments –"

"Can she sing?"

"I don't know, I've never asked."

"Let's find out. Perhaps –"

After finishing their coffee, it took a little time to find Louise and Olivia. The unlit corridors and passages stretched before them like tunnels, the beam of Hilary's torch playing over dusty mouldings and reticulated cobweb. Miles had forgotten that Charnwood had the peculiar quality of seeming smaller from the outside. Inside, it consisted of countless rooms opening into each other, avenues of doors, stygian cellarage.

"Really shall have to do something about the wiring." Hilary Middlemass made this prosaic statement as he stood like the fatal bellman in a square of moonlight. There was a sudden suppressed giggle, and he opened a door. Louise, abandoned with uncharacteristic laughter, lay on a sofa; opposite her, Olivia sprawled in an armchair. The only light came from a black candle on the mantelshelf, and the little room, in common with the others, contained scarcely any furniture.

"I do hope I'm not disturbing you," said Hilary, "but I wondered – can you sing, by any chance, Olivia?"

"I'm an alto. Why?"

"You should feel honoured," Louise told Miles sententiously, as they followed Hilary to the music room. "This'll be the first performance of the Blake songs."

"Which ones?"

"*Innocence and Experience*, of course. What else?"

Miles could not tell, in the dark passage, whether Louise was smiling or not. He rather thought that she was.

The room Middlemass led them to had a sparse, electric light and piles of music on the floor, dog-eared sheets and bound scores, stray leaves, manuscript copies and photostated solos. A couple of stands marched across the boards, massive insects, and two concert grands, Steinway and Bösendorfer, stood nose to tail before a speckled, gilt-framed looking-glass which occupied an entire wall.

Miles remembered seeing Francesca in this room, hearing her play one of Hilary's sonatas. He remembered Hilary bringing her back in his car, and her refusal to ride her bicycle any more in case she damaged her hands; he remembered her in a pool of sunlight, knees grasping the cello, hair hiding her face. And he realised, watching Hilary distribute manuscript parts, that Middlemass was interested above all in performers, not people. He needed his singers and players, whatever their personal idiosyncrasies, and would tolerate curious behaviour if the musical balance was right.

Louise's function was primarily that of an apprentice, an amanuensis, as Hilary called her. Her other talents were unimportant. Perhaps Francesca had adopted this attitude, which would explain her patience with such diverse accompanists as Emily Deutsch and Charlotte Perkins. Even now, Olivia Underwood was being pressed into service as an extra voice.

But as soon as they started to sing, Miles realised the value of such expediency. Hilary Middlemass had set one particular poem as a part song, the metrically regular lines and repetitions circulating continuously, so that the result was like a madrigal for two people. The girls' voices rose and fell as they sang in continual pursuit:

> Never seek to tell thy love
> Love that never told can be;
> For the gentle wind doth move
> Silently, invisibly.
>
> I told my love, I told my love,
> I told her all my heart,
> Trembling, cold, in ghastly fears.
> Ah, she doth depart!
>
> Soon as she was gone from me,
> A traveller came by,
> Silently, invisibly:
> He took her with a sigh.

"Thank you for taking me," said Olivia, in consciously well-brought-up tones, as they drove back to Bly.

"Not at all. I'm glad you enjoyed it."

"Though I think that they should have been playing croquet with flamingoes and hedgehogs."

"Precisely."

"You know —" stretching her arm along the seat-back "— there's something a little frightening about Hilary Middlemass."

"I couldn't agree more."

"I don't think he likes me."

"I didn't get that impression."

"Oh no, I don't mean that he doesn't find me very attractive." Spoken with assurance. "I just don't think he likes me."

"He liked Benjy."

"Don't we all."

Miles attempted to move from the radius of Olivia's right arm.

"I didn't think you did. From what he's been saying, you argue quite frequently."

131

"That doesn't mean anything. Benjy can be very funny at times. Surely you've noticed? He takes things to heart. He's absolutely devoted to you, you know. His letters were –"

"Letters?"

"Oh yes. We always write."

"But I got the impression that –"

"He made a big scene about us not getting on, didn't he? When he went round to your house at Campden Hill Square?"

"Well, he was rather upset –"

"He does get distressed. Thank God he did well in Tripos. I'm always afraid –" letting her voice plunge dramatically "– that he might do something *silly*."

"He's done a lot of silly things," Miles replied, discouraging this theatrical approach. "But I don't think he'd ever do anything quite as silly as what you're thinking about."

"There was a time, though, wasn't there?"

"What time?" A gold hand, touched by moonlight, brushed Miles' shoulder, whether out of concern for Benjy or with some other emphasis, Miles could not tell. He felt irritated, tried to shrug it away.

"The time you found him, in that hotel. Or were you there together?"

"Scarcely. I don't make a practice of going to cheap hotels with my undergraduates."

"And what do you make a practice of, Miles?" The hand returned, the arm slipping round his shoulders. Perhaps because he'd drunk a quantity of Hilary Middlemass's arrack, Miles became very angry very suddenly. He stopped the car in the middle of the deserted road. Flat land stretched into infinity beneath the moon, its last slender quarter hanging in a clear sky.

"Oh, Dr Tattershall, why have you stopped?" Olivia's voice sounded ridiculously suggestive; she seemed to satirise her self-elected role of vamp.

"So that you can get out and walk," replied Miles, leaning across and opening the door.

"Oh." Dismayed, Olivia put her head on one side. Miles stared at her, hoping that he looked as grim as he felt, and Olivia started laughing. It began with a giggle that ran through her body; she cackled, then threw back her head convulsively, and laughed until the tears ran down her face. Miles watched, appalled by this sensual abandonment, yet oddly fascinated. Olivia clutched her arms together, bent double, gasped several times, and leant back exhausted, rubbing her face with her knuckles.

"Oh Miles, oh God, if you could see yourself –"

"Well, it's highly complimentary that you should go off into spontaneous fits of mirth, but really –"

"Oh, don't, you'll set me off again –" ˙

"I quite fail to see –"

"Of course you do. That's the whole point."

"I'm beginning to think that life is some huge private joke directed against me by the rest of the universe –" Miles was plaintive.

"And you're the fall guy. How true."

"And I'm the – yes."

"Oh, Miles, I'm so terribly, terribly, sorry." She laid her hand on his shoulder, another parodic gesture, one arm about his neck, and was quiet, apart from the occasional snort, for a while. Miles stared bewildered at the moon.

"I keep feeling as though I've missed a chapter," he said at last. "Or turned over two pages at once."

Olivia muttered something, her head sliding down. Miles patted her arm; she smelt, rather attractively, of Ambre Solaire. And as she slept, slumped against him, she felt warm and curiously vulnerable. Where Benjy had been taut and lean, her slim limbs were soft; almost experimentally he tried stroking the shoulder which was presented to him.

Sighing in her sleep, Olivia moved closer. Miles coughed loudly, and the moment was gone. She looked startled for a second, and then smiled.


By the time they reached Bly, it was almost dawn. The sky had lightened, and birds signalled to each other in the apple trees.

"It hardly seems worth going to bed," yawned Miles.

"It's always worth going to bed," said Olivia.

"Olivia, I do wish you wouldn't talk like that."

"Like what?"

"You know very well –"

"All I said was –"

"It's not so much what you say –"

"It's the way I say it. I know. But I can't help it."

"I don't see why not. You have excellent dramatic technique and I'm sure that with a few tricks of inflection –"

"What do you mean, *dramatic technique?*"

"Despite the unavailability of a stage, you're a fine actress."

"How do you manage to make your compliments so insulting?"

"It's all in the delivery, but you know about that. And now, if you'll excuse me –"

"Oh, I *hate* you!"

"That's rather a strong reaction when we've only been acquainted for a few days, isn't it?"

Olivia looked round for something to throw. What came to hand was a small Chinese vase which Miles had never liked much. He told her so and she froze in mid-gesture, vase raised above her head, like a discobolus.

"I could wrestle you to the ground and seize it from your grasp, if necessary," he suggested. Olivia's teeth fastened on her underlip, in her brother's mannerism, and she lowered the vase slowly, aware that she was absurd, sighing.

"I must admit, life's eventful when you're around," he continued, watching her replace the vase. "Still, you should get plenty of acting opportunities at Cambridge – oh, Olivia, oh God, don't, please, don't!" She had begun to cry, and not well: her face crumpled and she sniffed. This at least was a weapon men could not use on Miles, and he had never been wept at before. "'Consider how far you've come –'" drawing on memories of Lewis Carroll, "'– consider anything, only don't cry!'"

"Oh Miles, I can't bear it! I've had such a terrible life! I'm an orphan!"

"Well, so am I."

"What?"

"Technically speaking. My father's dead and my mother

ran off and left us when I was two years old. How do you think *I* feel?"

"But you haven't been hounded from country to country, alone, unwanted –"

"Neither have you. I'm sure you've always travelled in comfort and at great expense."

"Miles, dammit, I want you to feel sorry for me!"

"I can see that. And I do, Olivia, I do feel sorry for you." Allowing her to come closer, trying not to mind that she was making his jacket wet. "But, much as I hate travelling, I can't really sympathise with you because you've spent half your life on Air France."

"God, you're so reasonable!"

"Not as reasonable as I'd like to be."

"Are you always like this, or is it just women you dislike?"

"What an extraordinary question."

"If you were anybody else, you'd have kissed me by now."

It seemed futile to point out that he was not anybody else, had never been like anybody else, and would never remotely resemble anybody else, ever. Miles was beginning to be proud of the distinction. Perhaps being different was an advantage, after all. "Why don't you kiss me, Miles?"

"What for?"

This stopped her in her tracks.

"Isn't that a rather old-fashioned habit? I mean, don't people just leap into bed these days?"

"What a remark! Aren't you ever ruled by your feelings? Don't you ever let your responses have a chance?"

"Occasionally. And I haven't enjoyed it very much."

"Go on. Just try it. Just see what it's like. In a spirit of enquiry."

"I never do what I'm told. Only what I'm asked."

"Please."

"You know what'll happen, don't you? Look, Olivia, I'm convinced that this isn't a frightfully good idea –"

"This hasn't got anything to do with ideas."

"No – I know – but – look –" Miles realised that he ought to disengage himself, but already felt reluctant. He found Olivia's warm, soft body, the cat-like sensation of taut muscle

135

under smooth skin, the smell of her hair, more tantalising than he could ever have imagined. The house was utterly silent, and Olivia clung as though in sleep, which led him to wonder what sleeping wrapped in her arms would be like.

A spirit of enquiry: yes, Miles wondered what it would be like to make Olivia turn and stir, to dominate her at last and wipe the smile off her face; he wondered what it would be like to press down and possess her, silence her taunts, take her on his own terms. He had already been seduced once, and was determined that it would not happen again. He was also intrigued by the prospect of fucking a woman, and was mildly surprised by the ease with which that participle sprang into his mind.

Olivia looked up at him, features almost Benjy's, but eyes sly, with the glitter of a challenge. It occurred to Miles that he might be a complete failure.

The room was light, resonant now with birdsong.

"It hardly seems worth going to bed," she said.

Better to get it over with, Miles thought. After all, it might be quite a pleasurable experience, and – with a novel, competitive urge far stronger than his sexual one – he'd show her. Yes, he'd show her.

"It's always worth going to bed," he replied.

Olivia lay sleeping conscientiously in the half-light, intent on her dreams. Watching, Miles realised that she slept like her brother, lips slightly parted as though about to speak, and with grave facial repose. Propping himself on one elbow, Miles shook off the streamers of hair which bound them: Olivia had unfastened her plaits a few hours earlier, bending her head with a submissive gesture, shaking free a fall of viscous hair. She had become passive as they reached Miles' room, allowing him to undress her, removing the boy's singlet and shorts to discover the girl beneath, almost apprehensive as Miles had thrown back the patchwork quilt with the air of a man opening a door. It was as though, having decided that the act was inevitable, and having propelled Miles into desire by a variety of feints and ambuscades which would have seemed dated and obvious to anyone more experienced,

Olivia wanted to change her mind. Miles faltered at this prospect, seeing her lie before him as though for examination, cloaked in hair.

She had abandoned her self-consciously vampish air, and now seemed thin and innocent. At first terrified by her assurance, and determined to get the better of her, Miles now felt a potential violator. After all, he hardly knew anything about her. Perhaps the assumption of experience was a pose, and he scarcely saw himself as a successful sexual initiator. But at the same time, Miles was amazed by his own response: he wanted Olivia as much as he had ever wanted Benjy, and it was painfully obvious.

Miles pulled the covers up over Olivia's body, hands trembling a little.

"Look – try and get some sleep. I think I'll go for a walk."

"Miles –" She took his hands as he tucked the sheet round her, curling her fingers into his as he turned away.

"We've both had a lot to drink, Olivia. I think this is the best way."

"I can think of something better," she said, in her old voice. Miles could not shake free, sat down on the bed instead. Olivia lay back among the pillows, like a sick child; drawn by that analogy, Miles stroked her high, Tenniel brow, the line of the cheek which was a stencil of Benjy's, the little ridge above the upper lip. In symmetry to his gesture, Olivia reached upwards, took off his glasses. Immediately, she appeared to be reaching out of a mist, an androgynous wraith.

"I can't see –"

"You don't need to see." She guided his hand above the sheet, so that he felt her outlined by linen, warm flesh beneath the cool folds; she drew him forward, until he lay beside her, still fully clad, lulled by touch but determined to get away before anything happened.

"Lie here beside me – just for a little while. It'll stop the nightmares."

"Do you have them often?"

Her hands did not cease, leading him into exploration, tempting him onwards. "'Undiscovered country'," she muttered.

"Yes," Miles agreed. "'Undiscovered country'."

Olivia's fingers made his hands graze her hips, shelve down beneath her thigh. Leaving the expedition there, Olivia was making her own forays, ignoring Miles' protests, which were not particularly strong by this stage.

"Don't –"

"I'm sure you'll be much more comfortable if you take that off."

"I shall also be very cold."

"Not for long."

He felt the delicate scrape of buttons, Olivia's fingers along his chest and back.

"Just come and lie under the quilt for a while, until I get off to sleep."

He realised that this was an elaborate fiction, and began to enjoy it, kicking off his shoes and drawing the patchwork quilt across them.

"Hold me," Olivia said, imperatively, and rolled against him, cocooned in her sheet. Miles shuddered as she wrapped her hands around his neck.

"What's the matter?"

"Involuntary reflex action."

"Well, aren't you going to give me a good night kiss?" she demanded.

The chorus of birdsong was by now quite strong, and the bedroom had that granulated darkness of dawn.

"Yes," replied Miles politely, with a final bid at social convention before abandoning it altogether. Because as soon as their lips, tongues, skins, met, Miles' other preoccupations ceased to exist, and he was caught up in an ecstatic, fumbling determination to show her: he faltered and lunged, like an inexperienced rider, alternately exhilarated and terrified.

Realising immediately that Olivia was a great deal more experienced than himself was a relief, and a further strain: despite her obvious enjoyment of the proceedings, he worried about the speed and duration of his performance, and about its rank in Olivia's scale of comparison. Nevertheless, he delighted in possession, in the sensation of power that his ability to arouse and satisfy brought. The pleasure of seeing her lie drained and speechless beneath him was almost as great as the frisson of release.

Now, he leant above her, propped on one elbow, and reached for his glasses. He regarded her with the satisfaction of a completed paragraph read the day after its composition. And, while he realised that disillusion, tedium and loss must follow, he found it very hard to believe. Uppermost in his mind was a sense of achievement. He could take a woman.

Miles was fortunate in that Olivia never had the opportunity to tell him how mundane the performance had been.

Olivia opened her eyes, as though conscious of his scrutiny. She looked sad for a moment, her face retaining some of its sleeping gravity.

"Miles! You're looking at me as if I'm a first edition."

Miles apologised, taking off his glasses again and settling into the meshes of her hair.

"But you see, in a way, you are," he observed, losing himself again in sleep.

Throughout the day, enjoyable as it was, Miles had the conviction that some form of penalty was about to be exacted for the pleasures of the previous night. At first, he expected reproaches from Olivia, and felt that he had taken advantage of her; later, it seemed that she had taken advantage of him. But he was full of the satisfaction of having achieved something he had thought he would never accomplish.

Olivia's body was not so very different from Benjy's: apart from the obvious differences, she had the same thin frame, long limbs, broad shoulders, narrow hips; to a man accustomed to admiring other men, she did not present a great threat. And again, he sensed that his greatest pleasure was in tantalising her, watching her watching him, allowing her to excite him to a certain pitch before taking it out on her. Miles would have admitted that his instincts, not exactly sadistic, involved a strong desire for domination.

At intervals, lying beneath Olivia and amazed by her precocity (as far as he could tell), Miles considered that the

139

relationship would be obvious to Benjy the moment he returned. At other times, Benjy seemed so distant, already so limited, that Miles saw no reason for explanation, and, surprised by his own selfishness, considered that he had progressed beyond the boy in every way.

"You're quite good, for a beginner," she said later. "I was impressed. There's a lot of – ferocity there though. You shouldn't have kept yourself bottled up for so long."

"You sound like a supervisor."

"I suppose I am really," she admitted. "You'll probably go mad, now, for a bit. I know I did when I started."

"Go mad?"

"Prove you can do it. Go around scoring everything in sight." She lit a cigarette, one of Benjy's, holding it in her mouth just as he did, smoking like a man. When she lay stretched like that, hands behind her head, ribs taut, her breasts were no more than slight mounds. Miles was fascinated by her tomboy body. "You'll probably start seducing your students."

"You should see them."

"What did you do before? How did you cope without it for all that time?"

"I managed. The usual way. I tried to forget about it most of the time. In fact I'd given it up as a bad job."

"I'm glad you're making up for it now."

Miles tried to explain, rather as if he had to account for not having learnt to drive until he was thirty-three, or seen a performance of *Rigoletto*. "It's just something I didn't get round to. Lack of opportunity, I suppose."

"I can't cope without decent sex. Food, booze, drugs – no problem. But if I don't get enough sex I go up the wall."

"That's quite a statement for a convent girl."

"If you'd met more of us, you'd know why."

Miles knew that there was no love lost between them. For Olivia, he was a facility, a novelty, an alternative to masturbation, he thought bitterly at one point. He was an available man. It was an interesting attitude, one which he had only encountered in men talking about women; revealing to see

140

it reversed like this, he considered. Their relations had a comradely, no-nonsense air, and beyond the act itself, there was no sensation that they were performing an activity with any more emotional impact than a game of tennis. Miles found this reassuring, and wondered why he and Olivia had developed such a man-to-man attitude so quickly, when his relationship with Benjy involved such intense and profound complexities.

"I suppose you're very frightened of getting too entangled with people," Olivia said later.

"I never found anyone I wanted to get entangled *with*. I always wanted to stay as far out of reach as possible."

"Because they might let you down?"

"Something like that. Have some more wine."

They were sitting up in Miles' bed, afternoon sun pouring in over the patchwork quilt and a flood of newspapers.

"You know, this is rather like being ill in bed, but having company."

"I should think you were very lonely as a boy."

"I was, but I didn't realise that until I found out about everyone else."

"Everyone else? What do you mean?"

"Well, perhaps not everyone. But the ones who live in families and have best friends –"

"School must have been awful."

"Well, it was rather unpleasant."

"I hated it. The convent was all right, but then, when Arlette died –"

"Arlette?"

"Oh, she was supposed to be addressed by her novitiate's title, but she was always Arlette to me. She killed herself."

"Oh yes, you mentioned –"

"Did you have any close friends, Miles? Older boys?"

"Not really."

"Nobody you desperately admired, adored, wanted to be close to?"

"Nobody. Which explains just about everything that's happened over the last few weeks."

"The only person I have ever had is Benjy. And then our relations tried to keep us apart."

"Yes, I'm intrigued by that –"

Miles never finished this remark; his words were cut short by a resounding knock at the front door.

"Who's that?"

"Oh God, it's Benjy!" declared Olivia. "I *know* it is."

"Well, you stay there and I'll go and see."

"What shall I say?"

"Whatever comes into your head. That's what you normally do." Miles dragged on his cords and pulled on a shirt which was already buttoned. "Say that you're ill."

"In your bed?"

"I'm sure it won't be as farcical as you envisage."

"What a rational approach you have to everything, Miles." He saw her pouring a second glass as he disappeared downstairs, pulled on plimsolls as he ran towards the repeated drumming on the door. He noticed how perfect the intervals were and had already guessed who it would be.

Hilary Middlemass, dressed with characteristic eccentricity in blue jeans and a sweatshirt reading *ROLL OVER BEETHOVEN*, leant in the doorway. Miles noticed the black Porsche in the drive.

"Miles –"

"It's Francesca, isn't it?"

"You'd better come – or rather go – at once."

"Where is she?"

"In Manhattan. She collapsed last night in mid-performance."

"Is she in hospital?"

"At her apartment. But I believe that she's been asking for you. I've been in touch with the tour organisers, and I only got through an hour ago. Why the fuck can't you have a telephone here?"

"It never really seemed necessary. Until now."

"I've rung the airport, and made arrangements. Took quite a lot of doing on a Sunday, too. You're on the 8 p.m. from Heathrow, and they'll make arrangements at the other end."

"Do you know what's wrong with her?"

"Some form of nervous collapse."

"Christ, Hilary, I should have realised months ago. I knew last winter that –"

"There isn't time for reproaches now. You'd better stop whatever it is you've been doing, and get dressed. When's the next train to London?"

"Not for hours, and it's a Sunday service. Takes ages."

"I'll drive you down myself. Passport in order?"

"Yes – I've got a visa too – should have gone to the States before, but it was cancelled –"

"Right. I'll wait for you down here. What's Olivia going to do?"

Olivia appeared in the gallery, Miles' green bathrobe hanging about her in folds. Miles looked up at her wistfully, and both men sighed a little.

"Come over to Charnwood," Hilary suggested. "Louise would be delighted to see you."

Miles packed, aware of Olivia washing and dressing in the background. He glanced round to see her parting the waves of hair and spinning it into plaits, each strand brilliant in the late afternoon light.

She remained silent, impressing Miles by her restraint. His own curiosity raged as he changed, hunted socks, a tie which had slithered to the foot of the wardrobe, turned out the chest of drawers in search of his passport. He tried to imagine Francesca's condition, wondered what or who had precipitated such a reaction. Finally, when he clicked the locks of his case and straightened his tweed sports jacket, he went over to Olivia. She sat on the windowsill, lost in the view, turning one plait around and around her little finger.

Miles put his arms around her, a gesture now familiar as it had been inconceivable, but she turned aside resolutely, face a little grave.

"What *is* that depressing music you've put on the tape deck?" he asked, trying to lead her into conversation.

"It's called *Low*. I find it appropriate."

"It's a dreadful thing to have happened. I do hope you won't be bored. I hate to leave you like this."

She turned, full-face, eyes calculating once more.

"You're so polite, aren't you, Miles? The perfect gentleman. You hate to leave me."

Her tone chilled him, so that he turned hurriedly and ran downstairs, leaving her to the eerie music, twisting her plait around her fingers, staring after him.

Hilary stood without speaking, and followed him to the car.

"We should make it if I step on it," Hilary pronounced, pulling on an Aran sweater. The weather seemed to have grown several degrees colder since his appearance. Miles glanced up from the passenger seat at the occluded vicarage windows. From one, which had a series of yellowing paperbacks along the sill, a face gazed out: grave, immobile, haunting.

# Seven

Cramped into his narrow seat Miles yawned, glancing out of the window as he did so. Beneath, above, around him stretched an infinity of darkness. He found it hard to believe that somewhere below him the earth turned on its axis and people lay sleeping: Benjy, in some London suburb; Olivia, smiling at dreams in the Old Vicarage, Bly, or perhaps at Charnwood; Hilary, in the efficient arms of Louise, or slumped over a score; and Francesca, lulled by Nembutal or fast awake and standing at a window overlooking the Hudson.

The tickly airline blanket had slipped down, so Miles realised that he too had slept. He looked around the dim cabin, with its cargo of sleepers, and imagined their continued journey into the void. How long had he slept; indeed, how long had he been in this state of suspended animation?

Perhaps they would travel for ever, return to Earth light years later, mysteriously preserved by sleep like the seven men of Ephesus. 'Snorted we in the seven sleepers' den?' He smiled to himself: a quotation for every occasion, except perhaps this. He could think of no analogy for being precipitated several thousand miles across the globe in such conditions; only clichés seemed appropriate: it's all so sudden; if only I'd known; will I be too late? Will she be all right? Oh, my God.

However, this state of suspended animation left him curiously calmer than he would have expected. At first, hurtling down the motorway at Hilary's constant 110 m.p.h., Miles had no time for confusion.

His energies were concentrated purely on willing Middlemass not to crash. Alarm cancelled all other emotion, leaving no time to regret the loss of Norfolk, the tentacles of ribbon development reaching into the landscape, the highway litter of service stations and hoardings. But Heathrow had been a shock: he realised that rural seclusion had left him unprepared for the mass of people who surrounded him.

Miles wandered through check-in, passport control, and duty-free shops as at some vast costume ball: potentates in figured robes, Arabs in head-dresses, saried women pushing trolleys, milled about him. He stood, holding his little case and a book chosen at random from Bly, bewildered. Middlemass deserted him almost at once, anxious to leave London, which he hated, and return to Charnwood. Miles knew that he had wanted to come to New York too – and was unable to do so, as some minor political allegiance in his history did not allow him entry to the States.

It was not until Miles woke in mid-flight that he had the time or desire to think. Although his experience of flying had been limited, he enjoyed the actual take-off, the climax as the plane swung into the air; and the stewardesses were kind to him, amused by his shy and donnish manner. He realised that his charm worked as usual, and now he was perfectly aware of it. Miles occupied himself by looking at his fellow passengers, eating the meal on its tiny tray with doll's house cutlery, and drank three martinis, only realising after the third that in his naïvety he had not appreciated that they were mixed American style, with gin.

The businessman in the next seat, after scanning computer print-out and finishing an espionage romance, made desultory conversation. Miles enjoyed the interchange: they discussed wholly general topics, apart from Miles' mission, which prompted sympathy. "My girlfriend's interested in classical music. Got quite a few of your sister's records," he had commented. Miles found it a relief, after a month of Underwoods, to talk in such an impersonal, disinterested way to a complete stranger.

And then he began to realise how strong an emotion relief was to him: relief that Benjy had gone to Hammersmith Odeon; relief that he had proved himself capable of heterosexual intercourse (he only now acknowledged the anxiety); relief that he had been able to get away from Olivia; relief that he sat here now, albeit a little cramped, talking agreeably to a stranger while the stewardess brought another martini and addressed him, despite correction, as Professor Tattershall. And relief, almost, that Francesca's condition had declared itself, although in melodramatic circumstances. At least she would now admit to psychological disturbance and accept treatment.

Now he sat thinking. 'The one man left awake.' Quotes always drifted into his mind at this time of night, whatever time of night it was: his body insisted that it must be 2 a.m. but the stewardess, if called purely for the pleasure of being addressed by the title that he was unlikely to attain (unless he doubled his output and made a few useful friends), would tell him that it was 8 p.m. He thought again of Olivia, with concern, and wondered where she lay sleeping; his feelings were those of physical gratitude and completely un-romantic.

Whereas Benjy, whose white face still rose to meet him in dreams, seemed once more lost and unattainable. He still felt a thrust of desire, undiluted by his irritation and anger at Benjy's recent behaviour. He missed him, wished he were there at his side now, commenting on the passengers, making little jokes, offering observations from the English poets. He missed that pied beauty, the black and white looks, Benjy's constant chiaroscuro, negative and positive, dark and light. He missed him.

And really Olivia was no substitute. It had been interesting, he thought, that just as he was about to accept himself as a homosexual, he should be initiated into heterosexuality; it resembled his experience of learning primary Latin and Greek at the same time. Of course, a combination of both would be ideal but disruptive, especially during Full Term. He remem-bered Olivia's prediction that he would go wild for a bit, and could think of nothing more unlikely, particularly when he thought of the women he knew. It occurred to Miles that individuals attracted him, not species. Single faces disturbed more than galleries of physical beauty: Benjy's eyes, promising escape; Olivia's eyes, and her tongue as she moistened her lips like a cat; Melissa's boyish good-naturedness.

*I am bisexual.* It seemed an odd pronouncement, the kind of remark first-year undergraduates made, coming in sporting cropped haircuts or handkerchiefs, according to original sex. It was also the kind of pronouncement his father would have condemned.

Perhaps that was why he had never admitted it before.

Miles sighed. What *would* his father have said? What would his colleagues say? *How did you spend Long Vacation, Tattershall?* Oh, *usual things,* he would reply, *finished my book, drank a lot, got laid every night.* Conceivably, the majority of the English faculty spent their Vac like that anyway. He noticed that even his *lexis* had changed. *Got laid.* He would not have used that phrase six months ago. He foresaw a change in lecturing style, perhaps a shift to the didactic vernacular. And perhaps Benjy's comments about clothes had been right, too. He could go for brighter sweaters, a few strong colours. There was no need to dress like a lay preacher or a member of the local Conservative Association, as Benjy had described his current style. Yes, he could learn a lot still. Perhaps a scarlet pullover, loosely knotted about his neck. It would contrast well with an academic gown.

With these animadversions he fell asleep, and the plane droned on through wastes of night.

He woke to a woman's hand on his shoulder, and half-expected it to be Francesca. She had come to him, since he was ill and bronchitic under this unfamiliar blanket. He opened his eyes and realised that he had been dreaming. The kindly but vacuous stewardess stared down, picked up his spectacles from the floor. She had a full lower lip, like a dimpled pillow.

"Please fasten your seatbelt, Professor Tattershall. Coming in to land."

Miles did so, glancing out of the window not into blackness, but into a world of light. The East Coast spread beneath him, a lit fairground, a game on a board, a neon Mondrian. Luminous sequences flashed on and off, binary, tertiary, and the entire glittering plain sloped steeply as they banked.

Light continued to dazzle as the cab sped down the freeway from JFK. Vast signs beckoned in the distance: a moving, invisible figure wrote legends which vanished with the last letter and were interminably rewritten; lights flickered as though he were about to enter a Brobdingnagian pinball machine; tall buildings closed round him, reminiscent of *Metropolis*, which he and Benjy had sat through at the Arts Cinema, so long ago.

"You from England?"

"Oh, yes, actually," in accents that could leave no doubt.

"Bet you can't wait to get back there," remarked the cab-driver.

Ever given to literary allusion, Miles felt that he had entered some Coleridgean excess. Caverns measureless to man closed around them, canyons of glass and steel, the pleasure domes of Broadway, the sunless Hudson. Miles observed the number of people.

"Place to come for nightlife," replied the driver, and some of the life looked as if it only came out at night: curious animated bundles which, on closer examination, resolved themselves into shuffling figures, clothed in rags; a half-naked man screaming down Fifth Avenue; the malignant greenery of Central Park, stirring as though populated.

Francesca was staying in a gothic apartment block in the East Seventies. Miles paid off his cab, with the inevitable confusion about similar-seeming notes, and approached apprehensively. A commissionaire appeared and, after close scrutiny, Miles was conducted to the apartment.

A tall, sinuously attractive woman opened the door, her professional smile replaced by equally professional concern as she realised who he was.

"I guessed it was you from Hilary's description. Francesca is waiting to see you."

"Yes – of course – then she isn't in hospital?"

"God, no. She's up." Her soft accent was soothing, a little academic, and contrasted with the suede trousers and tough leather jacket she wore. "Francesca is right through there."

He wandered through a dim, labyrinthine apartment, noticing white, half-open doors and subdued table lamps; somewhere a radio played the orchestral version of Ravel's *Pavane*. To the suede-clad woman's taste, he supposed. There was a faint smell of roses, heavy, cellophane-wrapped roses which are delivered in congratulation or commiseration. Miles entered the last room, but there was nobody there apart from a thin, drawn woman in a paisley shawl.

He recognised the shawl before he recognised Francesca.

They sat opposite one another, Francesca on the square sofa, neat hands twisted in a parody of serenity, head down, and Miles in a deep armchair. He listened to the hum of air conditioning, waited for her to speak. He had not expected their reunion to be like this, had anticipated a run into each other's arms, the hugs and embraces of soap-opera reassurance, her tears on the shoulder of his tweed jacket. Instead, she simply sat before him, eyes half-closed, hands folded, daring him to come closer.

"I came as soon as I heard. Hilary came over and drove me to the airport. I wish I'd known sooner."

She did not reply.

"I couldn't imagine what had happened to you at all. I had horrible visions – isn't there an asylum called Bellevue? If only I'd known."

Her silence began to irritate.

"I knew something was wrong, that something like this would happen. If only you had accepted treatment earlier –"

She shook her head slowly from side to side, looking both older and younger: thin now, not slimly elegant; old as Inez Tattershyl, with the same marmoreal features, hair tucked back behind her ears. He had never seen her retreat into herself like this; evasion had always been his escape, a refusal to talk, self-immolation among the bookstacks. Francesca had raged, wept, stamped through adolescence, and then, returned from France, had become consciously serene.

Hearing a cautious footstep Miles turned to see the suede-clad woman in the doorway.

"Everything okay?"

It seemed such a prosaic enquiry, as though she expected Miles to ask for coffee or more ice in his drink. She trod

towards him, eyeing Francesca as if afraid of waking her, and
sat on the arm of Miles' chair. Miles was disconcerted by this
informality.

"I'm Gina Farrah," she announced. Miles shook hands
awkwardly. "How long has she been like this?" he asked.

"Couple of days. I knew something was up. She got kind
of excited. There was one evening when she got a marvellous
encore. Bernstein was going to come Back. She got very
animated and next day – well, she just started being this way."

"But Hilary said –"

"Yeah, well, she didn't collapse in so many words. More
couldn't go on – wouldn't. She was doing the Schumann and
refused to play."

"Oh God." Miles yawned inadvertently.

"*You* must be exhausted."

"I'm rather tired." He had scarcely slept since the night of
Benjy's departure.

"Let's get you to bed." This sounded remarkably commu-
nal, but Miles got up and followed her, aching for solitude,
pillows, and oblivion. He did not approach Francesca, who
remained still and half-staring as he left the room.

Miles lay under the duvet, wondering what the time really
was, and hearing Gina Farrah move about the apartment. He
wondered if she was getting Francesca to bed in the same
manner. She had pulled back the sheets, drawn the curtains,
insisted on hanging up his jacket and when he commented on
this, said:

"I take care of people. I enjoy it."

"Professionally? I mean –"

"I'm a friend of Hilary's. Also I work for Francesca's
recording company. They suggested I – keep an eye on her."

"Oh, I see." Miles passed his hand over his forehead. "I
wish you'd keep an eye on me."

"From what I've seen, you can take care of yourself."

"I'm learning." He sighed, deeply.

He woke next morning in confusion and a strange bed to
see an unfamiliar woman drawing curtains back from an

unfamiliar skyline. He had to be told, slowly, where he was and reminded of Gina's name.

"Has she said anything at all since she's been here?" Miles enquired, over a breakfast of croissants and coffee. Francesca was not present.

"Few things. Monosyllables, mostly."

"Has anything," he bit into a croissant, showering himself with crumbs, "been broken?"

"Funny you should say that. I woke up once – early hours – there was a sort of crashing coming from the kitchen. Lots of pots on the floor, all smashed. Francesca came in when I did, and it really upset her."

"I should think it did. This was – when?"

"A few weeks ago. Francesca was stopping over here on her way to Boston. Yes, it really upset her. When are you taking her home?"

"Home?" It seemed a strange word. He had never really considered Bly or Campden Hill Square as home.

"Back to England."

"I'm not altogether certain that it would be a good idea."

"But isn't that the best place for her?"

"Gina – has Francesca seen anything?"

"What sort of thing?"

Miles looked down at his plate. "I don't really know anything about mental illness. I've read a few books, but I couldn't claim to have any knowledge of the subject. When you hear that people have had nervous breakdowns, you expect – I suppose you expect screaming and hysterics, people shrieking and hallucinating and rolling around. Seeing Francesca like this – it's so much worse."

"She has been sedated, Miles. Remember, that means she's considerably quieter than she would be otherwise. Not that she was manic, or anything like that. She just became really withdrawn. I went to get her from the dressing room and she was just sitting there, tears streaming down her face. There was no way she could go out there and perform."

"Oh Christ. Look, the reason I asked about seeing things was this: Francesca has a history of these sort of problems. When we were both children – adolescents, I should say –

Francesca had trouble with – well, she claimed to have seen things. There were rumours in the village about her, but nothing that anybody could pin down. I suppose they found us all a bit suspicious – my father was an eccentric, and my mother disappeared, so we weren't exactly considered normal. She was found sleepwalking on several occasions. Things got broken –" He found it difficult, painful, to explain.

"But that's common enough, Miles. There's plenty of literature about it. Especially adolescent girls – they reckon poltergeists have something to do with sexual frustration."

"In that case, why haven't I been going around sleepwalking and seeing things for the last thirty years?"

"It's very unusual in men. And you're more practical, down to earth. I know you pretend not to be."

"You're very direct, aren't you?" He was not unimpressed with her manner.

"I saw it as soon as I met you. You like to play the helpless male, appeal to people's sympathy. But you're resilient enough. Nobody just walks into a fellowship at Cambridge without any effort. And a weaker guy wouldn't have taken that plane straightaway, just like that. They'd have found an excuse to come later, or stay at home."

"I should be very offended, Gina. But I'm not."

"Listen to me. I'm quite an expert on unusual personalities, I see a lot in my business. And out of you and Francesca, do you know who's the real winner? Do you know who's actually going to amount to something, eventually? You are. Once you pull your finger out, that is."

"Did you start your career as a baseball coach, by any chance?"

Gina smiled: she had an attractive, lean smile, broad below thin, expressive cheekbones. "No, I was an English major. Then I got into public relations and promotions, and went to work for the recording company. I minored in psychology, which helps."

"I can see why you and Hilary Middlemass get on."

"There is a certain resemblance," Gina agreed. "But listen, about Francesca. Something's got to be done about her. I mean, did you know that she's been on tranquillisers for *years*?

I just couldn't believe it, until I saw her hand luggage. She must have been taking dozens of the things every day. The body gets accustomed to them, you know."

"I didn't realise there were junkies on the classical music circuit, too."

"Anyone in this business can get addicted. Doesn't matter if you play Rossini or heavy rock. It's the pressure. Plus Francesca has this complex about appearing to be calm and serene to everybody, which is a big mistake. Your father must have slapped her down all the time."

"Yes, he was very oppressive."

"And you know she has weird relationships."

From anyone else, from the ghastly Charlotte, Miles would not have tolerated these remarks. But he liked and trusted Gina, and knew that her observations were based on shrewd insights, backed up by experience of human nature. "She has these *very* intense relationships with other women – younger ones, usually, who are just getting started. And she never does anything about it. Wouldn't offend anyone if she had a girlfriend – that's not shocking these days. But she can't. There's this invisible barrier she puts round herself, like an electric fence. It's just impossible to get near her."

"My father," Miles commented, "had a lot to answer for."

"Yes, certainly did. I can see a bit of it in you – but you're breaking out of it now. I can tell."

"Thank you. I suppose I've realised a lot of the things that you've mentioned. I've known for some time that things were going wrong – but I haven't done anything about it. Whenever I tried to, she would become very angry and distant, as though she resented my attempts to help."

"Don't blame yourself. There's nothing you could have done. And then there was that business of that poor girl who died – Emily Deutsch –"

"I don't think she ever really got over that. I suppose this is all some form of reaction –"

Miles poured himself another cup of coffee, feeling the caffeine rush through his bloodstream; in this new world, he felt charged with life and energy, more awake than he had done for years. It was definitely a place to come back to, in more enjoyable circumstances.

"I'm not certain that if she's – as she is now – Bly is the right place for her."

"Well, what are you going to do? She can't complete the tour in this condition, and she needs you around – or Hilary. She'd be lost in a – home."

"You think it's as bad as that?"

"I reckon that if she went into a sanatorium for observation, Francesca would really crack up. She wouldn't be able to cope. The last thing she needs is to be surrounded by other disturbed people."

"Then Bly wouldn't be a good place for her at all."

"Miles. You know what I mean. She needs familiar surroundings, and plenty of rest, and you. She needs you, because you're not a threat or a challenge, and you'll accept her."

"I can try," Miles agreed.

Brushing off the crumbs, and still blinking in the unaccustomed brilliance of the airy apartment, Miles went into Francesca's room. He found her huddled by the window, and she glanced up as he entered, turning away again, daring him to come closer.

"Francesca –"

Half afraid of that accusing shoulder, he put out his hands. As with Olivia, hours earlier, he stood behind her, sliding his arms round. Immediately, he realised it was the wrong gesture, a lover's gesture. She was taut with resistance, then gave an aggressive shrug, shaking off his affection. But Miles realised instantly that she had never known him physically demonstrative.

"Go away." Giving both words the same emphasis, she repeated flatly: "Go away."

"Francesca." He disengaged himself. "We shall be flying back together either tonight or tomorrow morning."

No reply.

"From what I can gather, you need a rest. I'm going to take you to Bly and then if you – if you can't settle there

155

we'll try somewhere else. I'll get a villa somewhere in the Mediterranean."

No reply. His style, accordingly, became telegraphic: sending messages out into the void.

"I have friends staying in Bly. Benjy's there. His sister, Olivia. She's an excellent pianist. There'll be distractions. Hilary Middlemass –"

"Hilary Middlemass thinks he's God."

"I wouldn't say that." Glad that she had spoken at all.

"Always ordering people about. Sick of it. He and Emily –"

Miles took her by the shoulders, half-turned her towards him. He shook her slightly, in a return of that new forcefulness that had been released with his sexuality. It was a melodramatic gesture, but Francesca did not seem to object.

"Did he meet Emily Deutsch?"

"Of course. After some concert somewhere. What about it?"

Miles dropped his hands. "I don't know. Francesca, do you really want to go back to England?"

"Why not?" She shrugged gracelessly. "I've had this place." She had acquired a few North American modulations, after only four months over here. The street-sharp speech no longer seemed incongruous; her glossy elegance had gone, replaced by misery and emaciation. She was thin and gauche now, like a middle-aged schoolgirl, and her hair had lost its sheen.

"You look the way you used to. I find it rather disturbing."

"That so?"

"Except for the phraseology, of course. Will you come?"

Francesca turned her head aside: submissive, amused. How Miles longed for her to turn and weep, to cry and stamp, as she had once done, as the Underwoods did all the time. And how he longed to put his arms around her, hold her, comfort her. But that force-field of isolation, that air of *noli me tangere* hung round her like an enchanted cloak.

"Haven't got much choice, have I?" she replied.

Somehow Miles must break her down. Taking her hands, sensing her flinch, he held them; they were stronger than his own, but he clung nevertheless. Echoes of another fairy tale assailed him: wasn't there some story where one had to hold a bewitched heroine through all her changes, if one were to get her back at all.

Miles held onto her hands, crouched down beside her so that they were at eye-level, charming consciously.

"Do come. I'm sure you'll like Olivia –"

"Who?"

"Benjy's sister. She –"

Francesca smiled for the first time, or at least attempted to turn her lips upward. "Quite a summer you've been having, Miles." And, for an instant, the magic worked. The other Francesca was there, accomplished and smooth, pushing back a lock of hair from her face, and the process had been reversed. Now he came to her, comforting, ministering, bringing all his new insight and power to reassure, describing her profile tenderly with his fingers. Francesca held his palm against her cheek for a moment, and suddenly turned aside. Giving a strange little chuckle, she got up and left the room.

"Are you certain we should have left her?"

"She'll be okay. Francesca would be much more upset if we hung about all the time." Gina Farrah stirred jam into her glass of tea.

Miles and Gina sat in the Russian Tea Room, after an exhaustive dash round Manhattan. Gina had argued that now he was here, Miles might as well see the place, and he was quite happy to let her take him. Alone, the size and speed would have appalled him, and he would probably have wandered block after block in increasing torpor. But Gina was an excellent guide, knew all the island's shortcuts and shortcomings, and now Miles was content to sit, having celebrities pointed out to him, exhilarated rather than tired.

Miles had come ill-prepared for the New York climate in August, and been dragged by Gina into several outfitters. Without his having mentioned it, she seemed to know that he had been considering a few new garments, and he now sat, self-conscious but assured, in a pale linen suit, darker shirt, and new, stylish shoes. He would never have dressed like this in Cambridge without a sensation of the ridiculous; but now the clothes seemed right to him, and he experienced an unfamiliar pride in his appearance. Over here, looking thin and bespectacled was appropriate; there were many others, dressed like Miles, visible at the tables around him.

"I couldn't wait to get you out of those clothes," Gina remarked, oblivious to the double entendre. "I guess you never bought anything new since leaving school."

"Well, they were new – but just the same as the old ones. Looking different is considered – well –"

"Your father wouldn't like it?" Gina grinned. "Then it just has to be fun."

"I'm enormously grateful to you, Gina. I'd never have had the nerve to do this alone."

"It's nothing. I just suspected the product had changed, and that you needed new packaging. It's my business to do this sort of thing. We're image-makers."

The conversation reminded him of something.

"What's up?"

"You just reminded me of a friend of mine – back in England. She's in the same line of business – a graphic designer. I haven't thought of her for ages."

"I think you should remember her more often."

"Why's that?"

"I reckon it would do you good. You looked quite pleased to be talking about her."

"*Really?*"

"Really. Tell me about her."

"Nothing to tell. She's a cousin of Benjy's." Gina had heard all about Benjy. "Come to think of it, you're rather similar. Another of what you'd call the movers and shakers."

"And you aren't?"

"Well, for the time being I'm fully occupied learning to walk."

"Would you like living here, Miles? You seem to have taken to it."

"I used to think I couldn't survive in somewhere much larger than Cambridge. Now, I'm not so sure. Yes – as long as I knew a few people. It could be rather exciting."

"Never thought of getting a teaching job out here? I know a lot of Brits do."

"It's an idea. I'd certainly get away from my father's ghost, wouldn't I?"

Gina nodded.

"You could enjoy it out here. You really could be quite something. Especially if you keep up that wonderful accent."

"What accent?"

"Look – there's Walter Cronkite."

"Who?"

"You're right, you've still got a lot to learn."

After dinner, they walked to the 59th Street Bridge which Miles admitted was romantic, but alarming. He expected imminent attack and sat back in the yellow cab with relief.

"It's okay. Once you're used to it."

"I could get used to it."

"Francesca loved it over here – at first. I hope she'll be able to come back some time."

"She'll get better. I'll see to it."

They arrived back at the apartment to find Francesca asleep, and for an instant the quality of that sleep disturbed him: the concentrated frown and deep breathing. But Gina touched his hand.

"She's all right. Do you think I'd go out and leave her alone with so much as a bottle of Aspro?"

Gina suggested calling a few like-minded friends, who would take Miles to a gay nightclub, but he declined. He felt as if he had had quite enough excitement for the time being. Coming out, he knew, was something to do with that old phrase about coming out of the closet. He felt more as if he had come out of prison: relieved, giddy, excited, and sometimes missing the comfortable regime which offered familiarity and no responsibility.

As he agreed to stay in, Gina produced a bottle of Bourbon, and they sat in one of the dim, soft rooms, talking and drinking.

"I get the impression you're not all that keen to go back to Norfolk, Miles."

Gina was right. Paradoxically, New York was far more restful than Bly. He longed to arrive there, Francesca on his

159

arm, and find the Old Vicarage peacefully deserted, with perhaps a brief note from the Underwoods announcing their unscheduled departure, but he knew it to be unlikely.

"Problems?" Gina pursued.

"I hope that if I don't think about them, they'll go away. What am I going to do about Benjy, Gina?"

"I can't solve everything for you, Miles. I can give you advice, get you into some new clothes, and boost your ego, but don't expect miracles. Things will resolve themselves, you'll see. What you've got to do now is concentrate on getting Francesca back into shape. She needs you."

Miles smiled, looking at her over the tops of his glasses. Earlier that day, she had advised tortoise-shell frames, and he was already considering it. He admired this strong, brave, suede-clad woman, enjoyed her resemblance to Melissa, and found that he had been thinking about the latter increasingly. The trip to New York had taught him a lot, and not just about Francesca.

They were at the departure gate, Francesca sitting sedately beside her cello, Miles brandishing a bottle of duty-free Bourbon.

"I hope you'll come back soon," Gina was saying. "New York's good for you."

"I've enjoyed it. I only wish we'd met for – happier reasons."

Gina smiled, competent and smooth, efficiently coaxing Francesca to her feet. His sister seemed totally uninterested in the exchange, and Miles wondered how much she noticed of what went on around her.

"You're freightfully nice, Miles," Gina remarked, mocking his accent but kissing him with warmth. "You'd better get going, or you'll miss it." She gave Francesca a gentle shove.

Miles looked back over his shoulder, to see Gina waving, and waved back, happily. He hoped he *would* see her again.

Francesca remained silent throughout the entire journey: or silent towards Miles. She gave the necessary affirmatives when offered trays of food, shook her head at drinks. Miles, pulling a blanket over himself as the cabin grew chilly, wondered if he was in disgrace.

They had taken a night flight, since he had been late waking that morning, Gina letting him sleep off his jet lag. Her presence had been immensely comforting, and he wished he had taken up the unspoken offer she had made last night. They had sat gazing at each other for a time, then Miles had shaken his head slowly, and gone to bed alone. He knew that such temporary shelter offered no solution. It did not effectively solve the problem of returning to Bly, and having to explain the Underwoods to Francesca, and Francesca to the Underwoods. In any case, he was far too tired to have acquitted himself well with Gina.

Miles had come to realise, nevertheless, that he liked women after all: their rationality, wit, essentially practical and unromantic approach to life. He wondered if his original fears had sprung from ignorance. Sex, like anything else, was really a question of study, and application.

The trouble was that he still wanted Benjy.

Miles wondered if Francesca had guessed at Gina's friendly gesture, and disapproved. He half-expected some comment from her, or some remark about his rapport with Gina. Instead, waking at what felt like four in the morning, he touched her shoulder. "Look, the Aurora Borealis," he said, but Francesca seemed unimpressed by the phenomenon, the great luminous stage-curtain draped over the heavens. "Look," he repeated, and turned to her in the dim-lit cabin.

Tears coursed silently down her face, and as he watched, a fragment of memory drifted back to him. He had comforted her like this years ago, back in another dawn. Back in that orchard.

Miles wiped her face gently, and lulled her asleep, blanket-swathed, in his arms. She remained silent for the rest of the flight, and after landing he had to steer her through customs and passport control, and carry her cello case diligently. Francesca's agent had been efficient in avoiding publicity, her mental state had been kept strictly confidential. No waiting cameras menaced them.

161

Hilary Middlemass appeared out of nowhere, in an old trenchcoat and trainers. Miles waited for some signal of reunion: surely Middlemass would provoke a response.

Instead, Francesca nodded to him, and allowed herself to be led away, like someone who has just been sentenced. Hilary had brought down a BMW to cope with Francesca's luggage. Hilary's driving did not alarm her either, but then, in the old days of music lessons at Charnwood, she had become accustomed to it. Awaiting imminent destruction with every passing mile, Miles realised that nothing could really shock Francesca any more.

# Eight

Miles returned to Bly on a sunlit but chilly evening, and the realisation that summer was over: trees had developed gilt; across Queen Anne brickwork the creeper darkened; shallows of light where he stood beside Francesca were cool. A copy of *Four Quartets* flapped its wings idly on the grass, emphasising the Old Vicarage's air of desertion.

Perhaps, Miles speculated, they had gone: perhaps a note waited for him on the kitchen table after all, propped up against a conciliatory bottle; perhaps, and it was an attractive thought, he would never see the Underwoods again.

Already dry, the leaves clattered above their heads. Francesca stepped forward, as towards applause.

"It's cold here."

"Just what I was thinking."

"You've had your summer."

Miles agreed. "I can't think where it's gone." Late July with Benjy, and what in retrospect seemed an infinity of long walks and hot afternoons in bed; August with Benjy and Olivia, her devious wit and Benjy's retreat into Trollope – 'August for the family'; now September, and the bright air sharp as wine.

"I feel as though I've been away for years," said Miles.

"I have."

Miles took her arm, and felt her shiver slightly.

Hilary approached, trenchcoat open to reveal another trendy sweatshirt, this time featuring Brahms and Liszt. He took Francesca's other arm, and they stood outside the Old Vicarage like three strangers.

The place seemed diminished: after only a few days Miles' time in New York had expanded, as though he had been away

163

for centuries. He remembered children's stories where the hero returns from some legendary world to discover that he has been absent for less than an instant.

"You've brought her back, Miles," said Hilary, following his train of thought. His words changed Miles' action from a mere flight to New York into a heroic quest. Miles looked down, embarrassed, and realised that he must leave them alone. Hilary and Francesca had scarcely exchanged a word throughout the drive from Heathrow.

Miles wandered up the drive and noticed a new cobweb slung like a hammock across the front door. Avoiding it, and its plush occupant, he allowed cool darkness to receive him. Walking forward over flags he heard what seemed to be a whisper; turning in expectation, the memory of Benjy, as so often more arresting than the actuality, he realised that the source of the sound was the open book flapping on the grass. Reaching through the low drawing-room window he fished the book up: the paperback cover sweated dew, suggesting that it had been left out all night.

> Moving without pressure, over the dead leaves,
> In the autumn heat, through the vibrant air . . .

Wondering with what cavalier gesture Benjy, or perhaps Olivia, had abandoned it, Miles took up the book tenderly to dry in his study. But it almost fell from his hands as he walked in and discovered the havoc there.

The horsehair sofa had been inverted, like a hide, and the feathers of his typescript were scattered throughout the room. In one corner, he heard the ominous drip of ink, and darting forward discovered with relief that only a mouldering clerical directory had been saturated with permanent Quink. His manuscript was intact.

Gathering the sheets systematically, he wondered if a freak wind had been responsible. He had probably left the window open. But the Burton papers had been left in a file, in his drawer. Perhaps Benjy had been impelled to a covert examination, or even Olivia. But why? In the middle of gathering the leaves, Miles turned at the echo of a footstep.

There was nobody there.

Miles seemed to be getting as nervous as Francesca. 'Footfalls echo in the memory.' Distraction often revealed itself in the random allusion: the sooner he got Burton off to the impatient publishers, and started something else, the better: it would not do for him to be nervous as well. Spooked, as Gina had put it. He smiled at the memory of Gina, and the thought cheered him.

Francesca appeared in the doorway, seeing Miles kneeling there among his papers, smiling vaguely.

"What's – what's all this?" Her interest was brief, flickering, faded almost as soon as she had finished speaking.

"You may well ask. I haven't a clue. Something must have got in. No, don't –"

Francesca got down to help, touching her forehead in a gesture he recognised as his own. "What is all this?"

"My book on Burton. Look, are you sure you shouldn't go upstairs and rest?"

"People are always telling me to rest. Sick of it." She touched her head again, with a blink of pain. "It's all right. Just one of my headaches."

"But you don't get headaches." He put his hand out to her brow and she held it there, with her hot fingers, Francesca curled among the typescript, Miles on one knee. "That's better," she said, closing her eyes with a little sigh, as Miles realised that they were being observed. Olivia stood in the doorway, regarding them through impudent eyes. His first impulse was to break from Francesca, leap to his feet with embarrassment; but that would be to put Olivia's interpretation on what he considered an innocent gesture.

"Olivia. How are you?" he enquired, still poised before his sister in a slightly balletic pose.

Olivia ran her tongue across her bottom lip, caught the lip briefly between her teeth in Benjy's gesture, and Miles sensed that enigmatic animosity which she had displayed when he left. He always felt as though she were daring him to do something impossible.

"I've been with Sir Hilary and Louise." Shading in the innuendo delicately. "This must be your sister."

Miles got up, slowly, effected introductions. Francesca was slightly ashamed, continuously pushing a lock of hair back behind one ear: her poise seemed lost before elegant Olivia, long brown legs emphasised by white shorts, hips thrown into relief by her pose. It was an intriguing display, and, Miles realised, turning, that it was not for his benefit. Francesca looked at Olivia in a bewildered, yearning way which wrung Miles with commiseration and made him want to carry her away for ever.

"How do you do, Francesca."

"I'm sorry – you – just reminded me of someone I once knew. I'm sorry." Francesca seemed unnecessarily apologetic, gauche and sad. Olivia smiled back, with an expression so cute that Miles was prompted to a violent response. He understood what was happening, that he was in a sense responsible, by allowing Olivia to come here. But he could do nothing to prevent it, and could not have foreseen it.

"I expect you'd like to lie down," he said to Francesca.

"Mrs Sedge has your room prepared," agreed Olivia, extending her long, golden hand as if to guide Francesca. Miles stepped between them, and the hand fell to Olivia's side.

"I'll take Francesca up. You could make a cup of tea, if you would." He caught her eye, the terrible amusement which prompted such anger, and felt like whispering: *I'll deal with you later.* Instead, he enquired after Benjy.

"Oh, Benjy's out," with a camp inflection. "He's gone to see the bookshops in Norwich."

"Who's that?" asked Francesca wearily, as they reached her bedroom. It still smelt damp with disuse, and the lead looking-glass had a mist of specks and blotches across it.

"Benjy's sister. He asked if she could –"

"She reminds me of someone. Someone I knew a long time ago. It isn't important."

"When was this?"

"Years ago. I don't remember much about her, to be honest. It's just a look – the hair."

Miles wondered again whether it had been wise to bring her back to Bly. "She's a bright girl," he said, keeping his feelings to himself. "Going up to King's next term. She –"

Francesca had stretched herself out on her old bed, looking round at faded chintz curtains, the bust of Bach, a yellowed certificate proclaiming her proficiency in swimming. She patted the bed beside her, and Miles sat down.

"What's been happening to you, Miles? I've been so self-obsessed – I'm sorry."

"There's absolutely nothing to be sorry about." Miles, relieved that she had started to talk again, and to respond, touched her shoulder. "And as for me – I can't even begin to explain all the things that have been happening –"

"Perhaps I shouldn't ask." Slightly offended and rolling aside. "You always were a late developer."

Ignoring the remark, Miles took her hand and examined the neat nails, the gleaming half-moons.

"I've always been fascinated by your hands. Look at mine. I could never play like you."

"I don't suppose I could write books, for that matter, or teach. By the way, what *was* all that down there?"

"Someone or something had thrown my manuscript about. It'll be all right. Perhaps a little crumpled, but it has to go to the typist in Cambridge anyway."

"Not just that. I mean Olivia." Francesca smiled, and reaching up with her free hand, removed his glasses and put them on. Suddenly, he saw their likeness, a similarity he had never been able to discover before: apart from a slight difference in colouring, his own features, newly famished, gazed back at him.

"You haven't looked like that since your fifteenth birthday," he remarked.

"I know. I've become so thin. Too thin, really."

"We'll feed you up, here. You'll soon feel better."

"And make an effort? Pull myself together?" Francesca spoke rather bitterly, and handed back his glasses. "Yes, I'll be all right when they've weaned me off all the pills and tablets. I've got some others now, to take instead."

"Hilary was pleased to see you." Miles made it sound as if her return had been a social call, and she actually laughed, uneasily.

"Hilary Middlemass. Hilary Middlemass made me what I am today."

"He helped you become very famous, Francesca."

"He also helped me become a nervous wreck."

Footsteps alerted Miles, and he went to the bedroom door to find Olivia outside with a tea tray. She looked down chastely, announcing: "I found some Earl Grey downstairs. And Mrs Sedge left a madeira cake. Benjy's home."

Miles' composite memory of those last days at Bly was like a cinematic still, an album photograph from their parody of family life. He had felt himself choke with rage when Olivia said *home*, because it implied that she had been received into the mysteries of his domain, when he regarded her as a mere interloper. But his hostility diminished as he watched Olivia with Francesca; his sister did appear to be recovering, and if that recovery was assisted by Olivia's attentions, he could scarcely complain.

And so the scene developed. Francesca, in a wicker chair on the terrace, invalid's plaid rug across her knees, a score on her lap, her poor hair which had become streaked with grey, fastened in a bun. Olivia, limbs stretched over the stone as she sunned herself like a chameleon. Benjy, hat over his eyes and book in his hands, lounging on the grass. And Miles, Miles who in a rush had finished his book and lay about in post-natal depression, unable to do more than re-read old detective stories in their comforting cream and green Penguin bindings.

It was a frequent scene. After nacreous mornings, the September afternoons were warm. They would drift out onto the terrace after lunch, and as it grew cool, Francesca would retreat again to the studio, and, occasionally at first, then as a matter of course, practise. Soon Olivia went to join her, and music would float out into the sultry autumn air as Miles and Benjy sat with their books.

Just as Bly had seemed different on his return, so was Benjy. Miles had anticipated change. Just as he had known that when Olivia arrived, nothing would be quite the same, he realised that after New York, their relationship would have altered yet again. Benjy arrived back from Norwich – or arrived home, as Olivia put it – in a distant mood. He clapped Miles on the shoulder, his parodic stalwart gesture, and cut a slab of cake.

"How was New York?"

"Did Olivia tell you what happened?"

"Yes. We went over to stay with Hilary for a while. He told me about Francesca."

"How was Hammersmith Odeon?"

"Okay, I suppose. They're better on record."

"And Robert?"

"He's – just the same. You know. Saw Mel, briefly. She and Tony have split up."

"I'm sorry to hear that."

He smiled at Miles cakily. "Thought you'd be pleased."

"I wouldn't put it quite like that. I thought they seemed quite – happy."

"Well, these things happen. You know what relationships are. Told her how much you fancied her –"

"Benjy –"

"'Course I didn't." With a swift tilt of the eyebrows. "But I'm sure you do."

"Of course." Miles added pedantically, "Ariosto has an enchantress called Melissa. Benjy – look – I'm – a lot has happened."

"I should hope so. You didn't come back from Sin City in the same state as I last saw you. Or the same suit. I really like that, Miles."

Miles had changed into one of the Manhattan outfits, and for the first time in his life was feeling mildly narcissistic.

"Blue's a good colour. I'll turn you into an exquisite yet."

"Benjy –"

"I want to hear *all* about it. How about a walk, after dinner?"

"Perhaps."

Dinner was not without its tensions. Miles could sense the ambivalent impulses running between Francesca and Olivia, a fascination on both sides made most evident by Olivia's attentions. She had appeared in a black dress with thin straps which Miles had never seen before, and addressed herself to entertaining Francesca with assiduity. Knowing what he now knew, Miles feared for his sister. He did not want her to be the victim of another of Olivia's sexual practical jokes, as he sensed he had been.

Simultaneously, she still charmed Miles with snaky movements of her tongue across her lips, while Benjy, apparently delighted to see Miles again, chattered about the first edition of Crabbe he had bought in Norwich, and described the audience who went to see Tears For Fears.

Occasionally, and this was new, he smiled at Olivia, and, instead of capping her anecdotes, offered observations of his own. At one point, a stockinged foot insinuated itself between Miles' knees, under cover of the dinner table. Since Olivia and Benjy were both seated opposite, averting their eyes, it was impossible to tell whose stimulation he was receiving. The gesture conjured various fantasies in his mind.

Leaving Francesca and Olivia to their coffee, Miles suggested a walk to the staithe. Aroused in spite of himself, he felt that he should explain. Quite what he meant to explain was another matter. He could sense Benjy's intentions as they strolled down the hill past the Chestnut Tree, and along the deserted road, and anticipated them with pleasure.

A new moon lit their progress as they walked along the dike, the air full of the susurration of waves and reeds. 'And two are walking apart forever.' What had set that running in his mind?

Miles stepped down into the sand, as far as the water's edge.

"I've been so randy," Benjy announced.

170

"Oh? That wasn't taken care of in London, then?"

"Scarcely. Robert isn't that way at all."

"I see."

"You don't exactly sound passionate." Miles had never heard him speak like this before, and was faintly repelled by his arch tone.

"I wish you wouldn't talk like this."

"Why not? Nobody here but me."

"Benjy – look – I don't know how to put this, but –"

"There's another man!" With mock histrionics.

"No, not at all –"

"Then what is it?"

Miles didn't know what it was: his body still wanted Benjy, but his desire had become hedged about with worries, diluted with anxiety. Benjy had reverted to his distant, slightly disturbing persona, gazing back with detachment like a polite but bemused visitor from another planet. It was impossible to reach him.

"Miles, what have you been up to? What happened in New York?"

"Nothing happened in New York, apart from a visit to Lord & Taylor. I suppose you thought I went round the dives, did you? All black leather and sado-masochism and – what's the word I want?"

"Cruising?" offered Benjy, lethally.

"Yes."

"I wouldn't have thought you had the guts for that."

"No, probably not, nor the inclination. It wasn't in New York, and it was something else."

"Christ, Miles, you haven't picked up an infection?"

"I've been to bed with a woman."

"Is that all?" Benjy shrugged.

"I thought you might be – a little shocked."

"Should I? After all, it's perfectly *natural*. We all have to try these things. No point in being narrow-minded. Your tastes are your own. But I think now you'll see my point. Women for duty, boys for pleasure and watermelons for ecstasy. It's an Arab proverb."

"What have watermelons got to do with it? Why can't I

talk to either of you without its degenerating into a double act —?"

Perhaps it was 'double act', the reverberations within Benjy's subconscious that did it, but Benjy picked up Miles' thoughts immediately.

"She got you, did she?"

"Who?" shivered Miles, who was beginning to feel chilly.

"Olivia. I knew she would. I could see it coming."

"Look, Benjy —"

"I should never have left you two together. She takes everything that's mine, sooner or later. *Everything*. Do you understand?"

Miles didn't, but he could understand that Benjy was almost hysterical. "She's not to blame, really, Benjy. It was my fault. I was drunk. I took advantage of her."

"Come off it, you never do anything when you're pissed. And nobody ever took advantage of Olivia. She knows every trick in the book."

"Oh, God."

"Did you get all the stuff about her unhappy childhood, and did she cry and tell you she was an orphan? Did she make you want to protect her? Did she hang back a bit to make you feel lovely and guilty?"

"This is disconcertingly accurate, Benjy."

"Oh, I've seen her go through it all before. I suppose you amused her."

"Amused her?"

"She's been through most of my friends by now, but anyone would want you on their list of conquests. Dear."

"Why have you dropped into that way of speaking?"

"It's Scene. This is the way we talk. Flower. Oh, bloody hell, Miles," reverting to his normal tone. "It's all done for. It's all finished." His distress seemed far out of proportion. "Why did she have to come and spoil it all?"

"She hasn't spoilt it all," lied Miles, anxious to preserve something he knew to be disintegrating about him: the contagion hung about in dark air. "It's just different, that's all."

Benjy turned aside, already immersed in shadows, and Miles was reminded again of old stories, distant myths. The hot August afternoons were gone, and in their place an enchantment; or had that been the magic, and was this now the reality?

Miles had felt nothing but confusion and distress since coming here. It had never occurred to him that a journey abroad would turn one's own country into a foreign land. He wanted to hold Benjy now, assure and reassure him, smooth the dark locks with his own nervous hand.

"Don't you realise?" he was saying. "She takes everything, and ruins it. She took my toys when I was younger, and broke them. Now she does the same thing with my friends."

The speech was absurdly melodramatic, allowing Miles to laugh. He put his arm round Benjy's shoulders, and Benjy retaliated with a gross gesture. Miles turned aside.

"Oh, I *see*. A victory for the ladies. Now you've proved you actually can get it up for a woman, you're not interested any more."

"I wouldn't have put it quite like that."

"Let's face it, you couldn't put it *anywhere* before you met me."

"Benjy, please don't go on like that."

'The scene begins to cloud.' Damn English literature as a means of making a living. He seemed to think in nothing but quotations tonight. Perhaps it was some escape from the unpredictability of his personal life. A comment from the poets for every occasion. Their dialogue had now become some unhappy comedy.

"How am I supposed to go on? My sister's taken my boyfriend. Suddenly you've found something more interesting, something more *socially acceptable*, you've found out you can lay a lady with the rest of them. You make me sick."

A few weeks ago this would have been enough to drive him into Benjy's arms, gross gestures and all, but Miles had grown wary of tears and pleas in any sex.

"You're just trying to make yourself normal!"

Seizing on words in his habitual manner, Miles asked: "Normal? Surely you don't consider yourself to be anything but normal? Wouldn't it be heresy to call yourself abnormal?"

"You know what I mean. Straight." His eyes were pale

173

with insecurity and an unknown fear. At the time Miles assumed it to be the legacy of guilt, guilt for what Benjy still regarded as aberrant behaviour. It was only later that he learnt the true cause. He went to Benjy, who stood at the water's edge.

"Do you remember we came here, a few weeks ago? Remember?" Benjy's voice was insistent. "That time?"

Miles nodded, at the recollection of Benjy mouthing him among the twisted grass and crumbling dunes. Memory brought half-hearted desire, but he dissuaded Benjy's hands.

"You don't realise, Benjy. I think I do –"

"Would you rather have a platonic relationship? Mind you, when you think what Plato probably got up to, it sounds ironic." He giggled miserably.

"We'd better get back. They'll be wondering what's become of us."

"They know. Don't they? Don't they?"

"Well – I – I don't suppose they talk about it."

"Miles – let's walk a bit further down –"

"No. No, Benjy. This whole – this evening – has just turned me right off."

"Probably guessed what we're up to, anyway."

"I'm sure Francesca would be very shocked –"

"Francesca? You've got to be kidding. She's – well – she's a –"

Benjy staggered as Miles struck him.

"Good God, Miles. You've still got a sense of decency. And a good right hook." Recovering his balance. "Nearly fell off the dike. *Sorree.* How flippant I've become. You've made my nose bleed," he added in astonishment, smiling at Miles in the moon-flooded road, wiping blood with the handkerchief which was curtly offered. "Love you when you're angry."

And, Miles realised, looking at the trio on the terrace one afternoon, he did love Benjy. Changeling Benjy, full of contradictions and inconsistencies, unpredictable from one moment to the next.

174

He remembered the loop of seasons through which they had pursued one another, Benjy's shy materialisations and disappearances among the alleys and bridges of Cambridge, the frustrated months when Miles had wrestled alone with unfamiliar desire. Now his appetite had vanished: Benjy's new mannerisms repelled him. It was only when Benjy lay asleep under a tree, the panama hat cast aside and Crabbe fluttering in the breeze, that he felt any of the old passion; and even then, Benjy would wake and wink at him, so that Miles turned aside in embarrassment.

He had brought Benjy back to the Old Vicarage that night with a bloodied shirt. Francesca and Olivia looked up from their Benedictine in horror as they came in through the french windows, Benjy's head bowed over crimson and white. Olivia, who seemed to have summed up their dialogue at a glance, muttered softly:

"No rough stuff, I hope, Miles?"

Again, Miles realised what it was to be moved to violence. It was never what Olivia said, so much as the way she said it, the subtle emphasis on certain words, the supple enquiry of your *sister* when she met Francesca, the intonation of *rough stuff* on this occasion.

During the first days of Francesca's return, Miles had attempted to slough off his anger. Olivia seemed to have such a therapeutic effect on Francesca, drawing her into the studio to play, accompanying her, proffering old sheet music from the cupboard, anything from a Bach partita to a faded *Indian Love Lyrics*. Francesca appeared to thrive on these attentions, but by the weekend Miles realised that she was bewildered. He had never watched anyone fall in love before, and decided that perhaps the term was not an adequate description of what was going on. The expressions which succeeded each other across Francesca's face filled him with commiseration. One evening under the trees, while their sisters were playing, Miles said as much to Benjy. The Franck *Sonata* transposed for cello, drifted out into the night.

"It's different for women," said Benjy. "Perhaps Francesca just likes to encourage her."

"She's in love, Benjy, and that's the same for everyone. I don't like it at all."

"Well, there you go. Can't all be tolerant, can we? Or are you saying my sister isn't good enough for yours?"

"No – not at all –" Again, Miles was brought up sharp by the contrast between Benjy's physical beauty, notably his long black lashes, and his unaesthetic, clumsy way of talking.

"It's just that there's an element of – manipulation. I can't quite think of the word I mean –"

"At a loss for words, Miles? That'll never do."

Miles discovered the word he wanted a few days later. He had been disturbed by some tension whenever Olivia and Francesca were present. Francesca had reached the stage of dazed stupor which he remembered so well from his own experience, and Olivia, posing on the balustrade or executing dance-steps, seemed to delight in promoting this state while seemingly oblivious of the distress which she was causing.

One afternoon, Miles returned from the post office and, instead of going through the front door as usual, walked round to the french windows. Francesca sat in a flood of sunlight on the terrace, paisley shawl around her shoulders, and Olivia at her feet. Francesca was combing the girl's hair, which crackled and spun in autumn light, sank and lifted on the breeze. Olivia reached back idly and stopped Francesca's hand in mid-stroke. The comb, which had been swooping like a cello bow, fell to the ground with a clatter. Lifting aside the curtain of hair, Francesca bent to kiss Olivia's nape.

Olivia leapt to her feet and turned on Francesca with fury. "My God! You're filthy! You're disgusting! You're *sick!*"

Francesca turned aside, hand on her forehead in the gesture Miles remembered as his own. "You're perverted!" Olivia screamed, and was ugly, hair spinning in snakes about her head. She advanced on Francesca, who seemed to diminish with every word. "I should have *known* what you were after! You were just playing on my sympathy! My God, I wouldn't have bothered to come here if I'd known what a bunch of perverts you all were! You're corrupt! All of you!"

176

"Go away," said Francesca, quietly. "Just go away. Please."
Olivia was looking round for something to throw. Instead, Miles stepped forward between them, seized her by the wrist, and was about to slap her when he recognised that she was not hysterical. Confessing to the performance, she winked slyly, running her tongue over her lips. Miles stepped back, astonished.

"Apologise," he managed to say. "Apologise to Francesca immediately, or get out."

She smiled at him, and, kneeling before Francesca in a gesture of supplication, took her hands.

"Francesca – there – I'm *so* sorry. Suppose I got a bit out of control there. But you must understand –"

Miles hurried away to his study, almost shaking with what he thought was rage and then realised was sexual excitement. He sat at his desk, head in hands, while his feelings subsided, and longed for Cambridge, the Rare Books Room of the University Library, peace. The weariness which came with finishing his book, combined with jet lag and the dialectics of sexuality, would succeed in driving his little world apart. He felt like a domestic cat during some family crisis, walking from room to room with its ears twitching in bewilderment, unable to understand the harsh words and slamming doors surrounding it.

As he sat there, drawing out his analogy, a polite knock came at the door.

"Come in."

Olivia entered, hair still hanging to her waist, thumbs hooked into the belt of her shorts.

"What was the meaning of that little display?" he enquired, wearily.

"Your sister," sitting on the edge of his desk, "asks a lot."

"She deserves a lot."

"But there are some things I just can't do."

"You disappoint me, Olivia."

He was studying her golden knees, and wondering how they came to be so bruised.

"Miles, you're getting awfully nasty these days."

"If you'll excuse me, I've got rather a lot of work to do."
"Miles –" noticing the cognac bottle by the window, "aren't you going to offer me a drink?"
"No, I'm not. You can wait until six, like the rest of us. Now, if you'll please –"
"Leave you in peace? That's all you want, isn't it? To be left alone. And I did so much for you." She moved closer, insinuatingly, putting not-overclean sandalled feet onto the bars of his chair.

Miles got up and walked over to the window. Turning his back, he said: "Go away, Olivia. I don't want to play any more."
"Oh but Miles, why so hostile? I thought you were my friend."
"Don't rely on it." He turned round, began to light his pipe, detached, academic. "I know what game you're playing. You'd like me to get angry so that I'll screw you. Isn't that it?"
"You've become so gross, Miles. I used to like it when you were shy."
"Very well. *On certain occasions anger may be considered to be a strong sexual stimulant. Discuss.* Do you prefer that?"
"That's more like your old self, Miles."
"Well, this is my new self, and I'm asking you, as politely as possible, to get out."

Olivia turned on her heel and left, amazed. Miles fetched the cognac and poured a large glass, sitting on the window ledge to drink, looking out across the gilded fields and dreaming of escape. He could ring Woodville now, and his rooms would be ready by nightfall: he could drive into comfortable darkness and leave the Underwoods to sort themselves out in isolation. Ordering them from the house was an impossibility. But then, who would protect poor, bewildered Francesca?

He watched Olivia ride out into the road on one pedal, throw her golden thigh across the bicycle and glide away down the hill, hair skimming the wind; he thought of her, tongue darting between her lips in the sunlight, and realised how he would later describe her presence and influence: she was sinister.

The following evening Miles walked, alone, through the
fields. The stubble had been burnt, and now the ground
was striated with black scorchmarks; a rivulet of flames still
glimmered in the darkness, and smoke hung heavy as incense
in the autumn air. He walked, hands in pockets, relishing the
solitude, and it was some time before he sensed somebody
walking behind him.

"Hilary!" He had spun round, to see Middlemass dressed
in black and almost invisible against the field of darkness.
"Why, you're getting positively gregarious. When did you
arrive?"

"They don't know that I'm here."

"So I can't offer you a drink?"

"I thought we might go down to the Chestnut Tree."
Hilary had dropped into a sombre, sober, tone.

"Fine. You sound far from animated, tonight."

Miles could not see his expression in the darkness: he simply
followed, until both were ensconced in a gloomy recess of
the lounge bar, Hilary nursing a Guinness which complemented his dark clothes.

"Look, Miles, there have been – rumours – in the village."

"Rumours? What sort of rumours?" He wondered if any
of their activities had been witnessed. "What do you mean?"

Abandoning periphrasis, which was his usual tactic, Hilary
explained. "Louise mentioned it. Someone at the post office
told her. There have been lights in St Peter's, late at night,
and flitting figures."

"Couldn't it just be local youths? Couples?"

"I doubt it. Local myth is still strong enough to invest the
church with superstitious awe after dark."

Miles nodded. "They think that it might be – what,
ghosts?"

"Not quite. Mrs Sedge, whose sister-in-law cleans for
us, told Louise that there was an atmosphere at the Old
Vicarage."

"Well, she was right there. Not quite the sort of atmosphere
which interests the psychic research society, perhaps, but
certainly an atmosphere!"

"Don't be flippant, Miles. Mrs Sedge is a Sensitive."

"Mrs Sedge is always finding cold spots, and haunted corners, and chilly sensations," replied Miles. "Simply because my father fell downstairs and broke his neck fifteen years ago, people seem to think that the place is an epicentre of supernatural activity. It's rather absurd."

"Mrs Sedge spoke of goings on."

"Yes, but there isn't anything spooky about them –"

"Isn't there?"

"Gives an entirely new interpretation to *The Turn of the Screw*, doesn't it?"

Middlemass placed his palms flat on the tabletop, spanning the octaves of oak-grain.

"All this may be nonsense, Miles, mere superstition, but if it's affecting Francesca in any way, I want it stopped. If anything's disturbing her, I want it stopped."

Miles drank, listening for a while to the shuffles and clatter around them.

"Olivia torments her, doesn't she?"

"Yes. How did you know?"

"I've gathered from Louise that she had a – vicious streak."

Miles nodded.

"I don't want to tell you this, Hilary, I feel as if I'm admitting something – it might be a sort of jealousy on my part, but –" He described the incident the previous afternoon.

"And how does Francesca react?"

"She's so bewildered, Hilary. I don't think she's ever met anyone like Olivia before."

"Fortunately, few of us have."

"Or want to. It's rather a relief discussing this, Hilary. I did so appreciate knowing Benjy – having him with me – you can't understand how much that meant to me. But now – it's horrific."

"Perhaps I should come back with you."

"I'd be glad if you did. Come back for dinner, Hilary, and see for yourself."


If Olivia was at all surprised to see Hilary, she hid it well. Tripping forward to meet him, as Miles put it, she gave a virtuoso display of girlish ingenuousness, whilst Benjy, who appeared out of the shadows, smiled to himself and shook Middlemass by the hand.

"Where's Francesca?"

"She went to have a rest when we'd finished practising," gushed Olivia. "She still gets awfully tired, you know."

"Is she upstairs?"

"I suppose so. Shall I take you?"

"I can find my own way," he said ungraciously, and went.

Miles followed Olivia into the kitchen.

"Benjy and I were just going to have something on our own," Olivia said. "Mrs Sedge left plenty, and you simply disappeared. But there should be enough to go round."

"Quite the little hostess, aren't you?"

Olivia slipped her arm round his waist.

"Be nice to me, Miles. Go on, do yourself a favour. We had a good time together." She looked up at him, a hungry adoring cat.

Miles found it hard to resist her fawning expression, patted her head, just as he would have that of some simpering domestic feline.

"Miles – why doesn't Hilary like me?"

"He'd probably like you better if you didn't keep vamping him."

"Didn't *what*?"

"It seems an appropriate word."

Olivia disengaged herself and dumped a pile of blue Italian plates in his hands. "Take these through," she ordered. "I must go and change."

"Into what?"

When Miles returned to the drawing room, it was to find Hilary and Francesca on the sofa. Francesca had been talking quickly, in her low, vibrant voice, but was silent as soon as he entered. Miles began to feel excluded. Benjy came in, smiling to himself, the inevitable Crabbe under one arm.

"I don't know why you always gravitate to the most boring and mediocre specimens of literary history," commented Miles, feeling bitchy and needing to hit out.

"Your shining example, petal," replied Benjy, with venom.

The tone succeeded in communicating their relationship to everyone present. It didn't matter that they all, from Olivia in the doorway to Hilary on the sofa, knew anyway. It was the exposure in Benjy's camp retort which made Miles shut his eyes with embarrassment, and sink into a chair with his hand over his forehead.

"All present and correct?" enquired Olivia. "Dinner's ready."

Miles looked through his fingers to see that Olivia had indeed changed, and into the black, Grecian-style dress which made her look like a figure from a tragedy. She had bound her hair about her head in a style which emphasised the resemblance. With a flash of intuition, Miles understood: Olivia looked like a figure in a sacrificial ceremony.

"You're not forthcoming tonight, are you, Miles? You aren't with us," Francesca murmured, halfway through the meal. Miles didn't even notice what he was eating. He was conscious that Olivia made no headway at all with Hilary, and as a result was putting herself out more than ever.

She had a brilliance about her that evening, reminding Miles of their trip to Charnwood and the argument which had followed. Francesca watched, hypnotised, as Olivia talked and glittered, undismayed by Hilary's laconic observations and his obvious preference for Mrs Sedge's lemon meringue pie, rather than Olivia's flashing gestures. But it was Benjy's reaction which Miles found most informative. He turned to look at the boy twice, first seeing him watch Olivia with his usual contempt, and on the second occasion meeting an expression not far from despair.

Benjy caught Miles' eye, glanced heavenwards, and winked. Miles turned aside.

Escaping to the orchard at the first opportunity, Miles wandered among the trees in the darkness. Apples cracked like skulls beneath his feet. He sat down in the grass, under muttering branches, and wondered if he would ever be left alone again. After some time, he sat up with a shock, realising that he had been asleep. He sighed, as he did not seem to be getting enough sleep any more, and was about to climb to his feet when he heard voices.

"What's wrong with you?" demanded Olivia. There was no reply. "Anyone else would be glad to." Silence. "Past it, are you?"

Miles wondered whether to intervene. As he rose, damp and cramped, he heard the other voice. It spoke briefly, and the following silence was intense. He walked forwards, blundering into trees as his glasses were moist with dew, towards a gasping sound. Something hurled itself out of the darkness and he realised that it was Olivia.

"Miles! Miles, oh thank God! It's Hilary – he said something awful to me!"

"What did *you* say to him?"

"He – he –"

"I'm not going to believe he propositioned you. I simply won't."

"He didn't. But it's so insulting – Oh Miles, Miles, take care of me –"

"Where is he now?"

"I don't know. He's gone. Vanished."

Miles heard a car start in the distance.

"You'd better come and have a drink or something. Were you blabbing about Francesca?" Surprised at his own severity, as he was occasionally these days.

Olivia's surprise, however, was quite genuine.

"Francesca? What's she got to do with it?"

Miles wanted to tell her: he had received two insights that evening, and, like theories, they demanded exposition: but there was nobody to whom they could be propounded.

He felt her attraction most when she hung on him like this, demanding comfort and attention, but now Miles realised it to be as much a gambit as any other gesture. He brought her into the drawing room, where Benjy and Francesca, deep in conversation, received her with exclamations.

"Did he insult her?" Benjy demanded, looking positively Italian.

"Yes, but there's no need to look as if you're about to

challenge Hilary to a duel. Poor old Hilary." Poor old Hilary indeed: Miles wondered what he was up to. Leaving Olivia to lie on the sofa and enjoy the situation, he walked out of the Old Vicarage, and down to the staithe, resuming the solitary walk which he had started earlier.

He knew. He had always known, but his conscious mind had rejected it: now, lying under the patchwork quilt, arms behind his head in the familiar position, he was almost at peace: he knew and had seen; there was a curious relief in having his suspicions confirmed.

It was after four in the morning, and light quickened beyond the window, although dawns were coming later now; summer was almost over. First light filtered in, just as it had done those months ago in Benjy's room, when they sat waiting for morning after the incident at the hotel. He remembered Benjy among the pillows, a sickly prince; he had realised then, watching light strike across the spines of King's, and yet the possibility had frightened him. And he remembered other aubades, waking and waiting at Benjy's side in summer darkness.

Miles lay, relaxed and ready for sleep to take him, if knowledge did not prevent it; the exhaustions of an entire summer had caught up with him, and he longed to sleep for weeks. Suspicion had drained him like a long illness: confirmation brought crisis and recovery.

Miles had returned from his long walk just before midnight, and found the Old Vicarage in darkness. Someone had cleared the dishes, straightened the books in the drawing room; he stepped through the french windows into a world of sleep, and, tired but wary, crept upstairs. The boards of the gallery creaked a little, and the cracks rebounded through the night as he reached Francesca's door.

He closed it after him and walked over to the bed. She lay muffled in blankets, shored up against the cold September air, and for an instant he thought her breathing too heavy. Miles touched her pulse, found it steady under the warm skin, and was about to creep away again when she flung out her hand and caught his wrist. He wondered what she dreamt about, muttered to, before she released him without waking.

Miles went into his room and stretched out on the bed, but with no intention of sleep. From time to time he let his eyelids droop, and once jerked awake after a brief nightmare: it had lasted a fraction of a second, but he had seen Olivia raise her dripping head, hair in coils, a smile on her lips. *Be nice to me, Miles.* The words hung in the air, as if she had been at his bedside, speaking them. And the innocuous phrase was full of horror.

Going to the window, and standing well aside, like an agent, he waited: he wondered from time to time if he had slept longer, and missed his opportunity, or perhaps chosen the wrong night. But, a little after two fifteen, as he began to doze at his post, the first light, dim as marsh gas, glided through the darkness beneath him. Miles monitored its progress, over the lawn, competing with faint moonlight along the path to the churchyard, through the lychgate. For an instant, a flame flared and dipped, as though a match had been lit, and the first light resumed its progress.

For some minutes, darkness ebbed back, and Miles wondered again whether he had dreamt on his feet. But from his room the stalwart bulk of the church was visible, its square tower silhouetted by the moon's first quarter, and, as he doubted his own eyes, the windows glowed and darkened with a passing beam, steadying as it reached the chancel. The light might have been strong enough within: outside, since the windows were deep set and the glass old, it had a decidedly ethereal quality.

Miles stole downstairs, unwilling to wake anyone who was still there, and out into the darkness. He had camouflaged his white shirt with a black sweater, and he picked up an ancient felt hat from the hall-stand to shade his face. Turning to catch his image in the glass, he gave a faint cry; disturbed by this quasi-supernatural activity, he felt as though he was seeing his own fetch. He also seemed to see not himself, but his father's ghost: the dark crew-neck, glimpse of collar, shadowy hat, gave a clerical appearance. Perhaps, he thought, that was not inappropriate, and he stepped into the night, conscious not of an unknown fear, but of the greater horror that he expected. Dry leaves muttered about the lychgate as he walked through the churchyard: gravestones, each of which might shade some crouching figure, leant domino-like above mounded ground. The moon sailed serene as he gained the porch, with its faded Women's Institute notices and flower rotas. Miles stepped onto the coconut matting, turning the cast-iron ring with his fingers; he had learnt long ago to open the heavy door without a sound, catching it as it swung back on its hinges.

He slipped into darkness redolent with beeswax, dead-flower water and decay, knowing that the occupants would not see or hear him as he shrank into a recess near the font, an invisible man.

Candles had been lit on the altar, and were the only light source; beyond the transept Inez Tattershyl watched from her tomb, and the bronze plaque of *Thom. Will. Tatterſhalluff, D.D.*, gazed down in Augustan tolerance at the pair of figures, one silver and one gold, who knelt in a naked embrace.

Miles woke in the safe light of an autumn morning and rubbed nightmares out of his eyes, convinced that last night's lights and rituals had been an illusion. He had never witnessed any secret or forbidden mysteries: he had dreamt. Shivering in spite of sunlight, he dressed and was about to go downstairs, to the air filled with the harmonics of normality. Mrs Sedge banged through the kitchen, Francesca repeated a phrase continuously, the coffee-grinder whirred. Suddenly, he noticed something hanging from the end of the bed: an ancient felt hat.

Picking it up, he twisted its worn brim between his fingers, realising that he had not seen an ignis-fatuus. For the first time, he sensed danger, realising that knowledge made him vulnerable, aware of that pervasive sensation of fear which is as powerful in full daylight as at midnight. Miles walked downstairs like one of his childhood heroes dissembling in an enchanted palace.

Miles was prepared to spend the day in quiet shock, perhaps walking down to the staithe or taking the Morris into Norwich on some pretext. It was essential that he avoid contact with either of them unless strictly necessary. However, he was defeated in this plan soon after entering the kitchen. He had settled with coffee and the paper, unable to eat, when Olivia came down. He knew she was there without looking up, and when he lowered *The Times* for verification, she stood, posing, in the doorway, waiting to be discovered.

"Morning, Miles. Sleep well?"

He made a non-committal grunt.

"Not very talkative this morning, are we?" She helped herself to some coffee, forcing his attention.

"You seem to have recovered from last night's events."

Olivia looked up quickly.

"What do you mean?"

"After dinner. Your – post-prandial contretemps, as Middlemass might put it."

"Oh yes. Hilary. He was trying it on, wasn't he?"

"I don't know. You're the expert."

"And what exactly is that supposed to mean?"

"People presumably try it on with you all the time."

"Oh, Miles. He's really rather old and pathetic, you know."

"Then why did you go to Charnwood?"

"I wasn't after the old man. I don't like him, and he doesn't like me."

"So why did you go there?"

Head bent, Miles wondered why he asked these questions; he had not realised how painful it would be to make Olivia talk, to wait as she picked her way through his verbal ambushes.

But almost as if sensing his traps, she declared: "I was interested in Louise."

They both knew that she was lying. Selecting the last barb.

"Pity you haven't got television here, Miles. There's a Joseph Losey film tonight that I'd like to see."

"*Accident?*"

"*Secret Ceremony.*"

And she tripped out into the orchard, the back door banging after her in a wind which sprang from nowhere.

★　　★　　★

Unable to stay at Bly a moment longer, Miles drove to Norwich. The normality of the town, shoppers with trolleys and small children, buses, newspaper shops and continual evidence of prosaic, boring, everyday life, reassured him. For a few hours he kept his fears in abeyance by visiting book-shops, discussing first editions, bindings and engraved title pages with leathery old booksellers he had known for years. In a spirit of adolescent bravado he visited a brightly lit man's outfitters, one of a high-street chain, and bought another three vivid new jumpers. Wearing one, he wandered round the Cathedral and lunched with a retired Woodville Fellow who lived near the Close.

Most of the afternoon was spent discussing the life-cycle of local butterflies and moths.

Finally, rested and confident, full of lunch and tea and early evening drinks, he forced himself to drive back to Bly. The air was already darkening, and he seemed to have the B road to himself. Glimpses of fire from the scorched and burning fields still lit his way, as though he were in the rearguard of a marauding army. The sky was infinitely blue and vacant, as Benjy's eyes had been, but offering greater promise of escape. There was nothing, he realised, to prevent his driving on through Bly, to the coast, and settling in a hotel until the Underwoods had gone.

His passport was still in his wallet – he had been reluctant to take it out – and he was perfectly free to take off to the Continent. The possibilities were limitless. He had money, no responsibilities, a need for freedom. For the second time that week, he thought very seriously about leaving.

Months ago, in a momentary phase of disillusion with Benjy, Miles had applied for a one-year stint at an East Coast univer-sity, lecturing on the seventeenth century: he knew that he was on the short list, but had seriously considered turning down the appointment if it were offered, because he did not want to lose Benjy. Now, he wondered if there had been any news. Another visit to the States would be very welcome.

Perhaps euphoric at the prospect of being rid of the Under-woods for ever, Miles drove more quickly than usual, only noticing the black Mercedes as it was almost upon him.

Distracted, he motioned for it to overtake, moving further to the left to make room. The Mercedes stayed on his tail, but building up to a speed which the little Morris could not match.

Miles signalled for it to overtake again, waving it past with his arm, but was answered by the blare of the other's horn, and further acceleration. Miles ran before it, trying not to panic and watching for an opportunity to slip into a turning and let it pass. But the road twisted ahead, uncertain and empty.

About to pull in to the side and risk a dent, Miles heard the distant clatter of the level crossing. He and the Mercedes sped downhill towards the tracks, the bell sounded and the barriers responded: the train gained on the distance. Speeding to the railway lines as if to challenge the crossing, Miles swung aside at the last moment; the Mercedes sped on, missed the barriers by an instant, and was on, out of sight, before the express rushed between them with a clatter of lighted carriages.

Miles reversed quickly, the little Morris choking and complaining, and drove back to Bly by another route. On the outskirts of the village he stopped and bent over the wheel, exhausted. Defensive driving was scarcely his line, and, bewildered by the incident, he had not taken the Mercedes' number. In his disturbed state, it had also seemed as though the car had no driver.

Miles walked to the Chestnut Tree and had a solitary double, wondering what sort of lunatic had been let loose in Norfolk, and why he played games with innocent motorists like himself. He was beginning to feel more than a little paranoid: his house was not his own, his sister was a drug addict, his lover was – Miles could not even think about what his lover was. And now he was not even safe on the roads. Life in the States could not possibly be any worse.

Miles had another, which he hadn't planned to, but leaving the little Morris where he had parked it, he walked cautiously home, yellow pullover glowing in the dusk. The soft warm wool, and its friendly, egg yolk brightness, gave some consolation. At least he was beginning to cut a better figure, he thought.

Returning, he found the Old Vicarage in darkness, its windows open and a table laid as though its occupants had taken fright and fled some mysterious intruder. Miles, too tired and depressed to respond to imaginative explanations, stretched out on the sofa with a third Scotch and hoped that everyone had gone for an impromptu walk. He did not even turn on the table lamps: his head ached, his shoulders were strained from driving, and any light would have dazzled.

However, as soon as he lay down, images coursed through his mind: he saw candles fatten and stretch in a draught, growing erect in the darkness; the roodscreen throwing its cruciform shadow across the vaulting, and a fall of hair across a boy's silver back, a thin-ribbed back so familiar to him. He had moved soundlessly, as though awed, and the figures had been quiet as apparitions; the stillness had been unnatural, total. Unlike the night beyond the windows which he could hear now, with its susurration of reeds counterpointed by signalling birds; unlike the faint, but, to Miles' sharp ear, perceptible footsteps on the terrace.

He sat up and knew she was there. He called out as she appeared, silhouetted in the french windows, her black dress stirring in the breeze which sprang from nowhere.

"Come in." Miles attempted normality. "Have a drink, sit down."

He spoke as though to a troubled student, one of the sad girl undergraduates who had been infatuated with him and been treated with compassion.

"I've got one." Wineglass raised like a chalice, she moved forward, and then hung back. At last, she settled on the arm of a chair, close enough to touch but infinitely distant. Miles felt very sorry for her.

"You know about us, don't you?"

"I can't help knowing," he replied. Then: "I'm sorry."

"For whom?"

"I – I guessed that it must be like this. Before last night."

"You should not have been there. You should not have gone to the church." Her tone was formal, deadly: it discarded his attempts at kindness.

"I wanted to be certain."

190

"I knew that you would discover us, sooner or later. You're too clever not to realise what was happening."

Olivia's very stillness and self-control disturbed Miles: cool formality had always been his defence, but it demanded an opposition of tears and insults to be seen at its best. Olivia met him on his own ground, and behaved now like a proud murderess confessing her guilt before disposing of the detective.

"I was afraid of what was happening between you and Benjy," she admitted. "And so I had to part you. You do understand?"

"Why are you telling me all this?"

"You were there. In the church. You saw us. Didn't you? Didn't you?" It was Benjy's old trick of reiteration.

"I could see what you were doing, before that," Miles replied. "The night before I went to New York. I realised you were playing some sort of game with me. But I thought that it was motivated by pure spite."

"Miles, that is very unkind." Again, that tense, over-controlled language, as though she were speaking in a foreign tongue. This conversation would have sounded better in French, reflected Miles: revenge, destruction, a poised rhetorical tirade.

"We have to be together, Miles. You do understand that, don't you? Nothing must come between me and Benjy. They've tried for so long to keep us apart. But not any more. Not now."

"What will you do?"

She raised the glass, and her lips glistened in the darkness. "I shall find a way for us to be together. I have to go away. I'm leaving. Benjy will join me very soon."

She stood, stylised as a vase-painting in that dark light, and as full of fatal dignity. Despite himself, and all he knew about Olivia, Miles was horribly impressed.

"Did you see Hilary Middlemass today?" he asked.

"How omniscient you are, Miles."

"What did he say to upset you in the garden last night? Has he guessed what's happening between you and Benjy?"

"But of course. You're very *clever*, Miles." Her old tone:

insolent, seductive; he expected to see her glance at him slyly, running her tongue across her lower lip; instead she stood immobile, deadly.

"I know what I have to do."

Miles was still filled with sympathy: he had a very good idea of what Olivia intended, and though he had no reason for it, he pitied her.

"Think it over," he suggested. "Don't rush into anything. There's no point in doing anything silly –"

She lookèd at him with contempt.

"What do you know about it?"

"Your brother asked me that, once."

"How would you ever know? You've never felt deeply about anything in your life. Not deeply enough to prove it."

"And you're going to prove you care? Now?" And by a stupid, histrionic and self-gratifying gesture, he added to himself: But why should I attempt to stop her?

"I'm going to prove it," she agreed, so that Miles almost went to her, after all. It would take very little effort to seize her now, hold her in his arms, give her a strong drink and talk sense. But he knew that these methods were ineffectual: that to prevent her making this gesture now would not prevent her from carrying it out as soon as she had the opportunity. And he had wanted to be rid of her, after all.

"How would you ever understand?" she repeated, drinking off the wine. Turning, flinging the glass into the fireplace where the crystal shattered on the cold hearth, she walked out into the night.

She had gone. Miles did not know how long he sat there, bewitched, watching fragments of crystal glitter among the ashes, but when voices sounded in the passage he jumped up, fell over something, and saw Francesca. Flicking on the lights, she stood windswept and brilliant, hair flying and shawl slipping about her shoulders, like a well-intentioned witch.

"Ah, Miles! I didn't realise anyone was here. What's been happening?" She bent down to the fireplace, the shattered glass on the hearth. "Miles?"

192

"I – don't ask me. What time is it?"

"About nine – I say, Miles!"

Drawn by her warmth and beauty, flushed pink face and glowing, intelligent eyes, Miles had walked over to his sister and hugged her. He felt that a spell had been broken.

"It's so good to have you back," he said. "You really do look like your old self now."

"Yes," smiled Francesca, patting the yellow pullover with approval. "There have been quite a few changes round here, haven't there?"

"You've been for a walk?" he enquired, beginning to realise that there was something wrong in the drawing room. He had been too preoccupied to notice before.

"Benjy and I went down to the staithe for some fresh air." She was vivid with the intensity of an autumn night, colour whipped up into her face. "Miles, you look as if you've seen a ghost."

"There's an element of truth in that."

"I don't know where Olivia is. She must have gone off somewhere. Quite frankly –" dropping into a tone of *pas devant les enfants* "– I shall be glad when she's left." Looking about her again, taking an alert and lively interest in everything. "But what's been *happening*?" She saw what darkness had hidden from Miles: the vase had fallen off the piano and littered the rug with rowan berries; books, which had flown from their cases, lay spreadeagled on the floor, amongst a depopulated chess-board; chessmen had broken ranks and lay in all directions, defeated; a watercolour hung askew, its glass fragmented.

"I don't know. I had the lights out. I didn't really notice."

"Miles! I couldn't miss a thing like this if I tried."

"That depends what there was to distract you."

"Are you sure you're feeling all right?"

"I didn't, but I do now. I nearly had an accident with the car. Some maniac in a Mercedes tried to overtake," he rationalised skilfully, anxious not to alarm. "I couldn't think straight for a while."

"Poor Miles. I think Hilary mentioned something like that

the other day – someone's been reported for dangerous driving around here. Never mind. We'll clear this up and have something to eat. I expect Olivia's popped over to Charnwood."

"Why's that?"

"Isn't she keen on Louise, or something?"

"Something like that. Francesca, you're warm: you haven't caught a chill?"

"I haven't felt so well for ages. I'm going to practise again after dinner. I feel so full of energy suddenly – it must be giving up those tranquillisers. I'm not taking anything now. But where have you been? Clothes shopping?"

"I went to Norwich to visit old Dr Hughes. Just to escape for a few hours. By the way, where's Benjy?"

As though invoked, Benjy replied: "I'm here." He stood thin and dark in the doorway, in one of his remoter moods. Perhaps Miles imagined the faint expression of reproach in his eyes. "Why didn't you tell me you were going?"

"I didn't know I was going until I went – if you see what I mean."

There was silence.

"Angel passing overhead?" commented Francesca.

"Something like that," agreed Miles. Again, he was reminded of the set from a play: the third act of the mystery; the actors stand grouped, waiting for the sound of screeching tyres and colliding metal offstage, which will thunder through the stalls and astonish the audience.

But there wasn't the faintest noise.

Although improvised and bizarre, the meal was one of the most relaxed Miles had ever eaten in the Old Vicarage. Francesca, looking suddenly younger, glowed and joked, hair glossy against a silk blouse the colour of rowan berries. Benjy, impressed and out to impress, responded. He had changed into an old rugby shirt – Miles could not imagine where he had got it from, as the boy was completely unathletic – and appeared to be happy, uncomplicated, studentish, making a good dinner. Miles, too exhausted to join in, watched and smiled weakly, head on hand. Both attributed this to his near-accident with the black Mercedes.

Miles had tried to obliviate serious thought in domestic details, clearing the disordered drawing room, washing lettuce, opening bottles of wine; he admired the manner in which Francesca had trained Benjy to cook, even if his efforts only amounted to peeling hard-boiled eggs and getting out the cheese. Tenderly, Miles returned a spider to the garden and dissuaded a phalanx of creatures which emerged from the blackberries Francesca had picked that afternoon: and he listened, continually, for footsteps outside, for the announcement, knowing that the night's events were by no means concluded.

While Francesca was taking coffee into the drawing room, Benjy came into the kitchen and hugged Miles as the latter scooped nervously through the washing up.

"What was that for?"

"Just felt like it. I'm sorry I said all those horrible things the other night. Can we be friends?"

Miles hugged back, with soapy hands, and shrugged. He knew that after tonight Benjy's attitude would be totally changed: but the boy was in one of his warm, approachable moods, and Miles could not resist affection.

"Course we can."

"You've changed a lot, you know, Miles. You even speak differently."

"I hadn't noticed."

"You're much less measured. You don't sound as if you're conducting a seminar any more."

"And that's a good thing?"

"It's a very good thing." Benjy went over to a plastic bag in the corner. "Look, I bought you this. I meant to leave it when I went but – well, I thought we'd have it now." Miles took the bottle of pure malt, and glancing at Benjy saw that doggy admiration there which he remembered from long ago, and which he had not seen for a long time. He wondered what expression would replace it, soon. Probably that remote, indifferent gaze, like someone from another planet, Miles thought. That total lack of concern.

"Thanks, Benjy. That's very thoughtful. Would you like to get some glasses out?" He was faintly embarrassed.

"I thought we ought to toast somebody," Benjy remarked, as the three of them sat in the drawing room.

"Such as?" sighed Miles.

"Hilary's Blake *Songs* are being played at the Proms this month," said Francesca. "Let's drink to that. After all, he's done a lot for me. For all of us."

Miles could not speak. Dissembling a cough, he nodded.

"That's a great idea," Benjy agreed. "I was just thinking –"

The theatrical nature of the occasion which Miles had noticed earlier, table lamps ablaze and chintz curtains wafting in the breeze, was more than he could bear. He knew that soon – perhaps at any minute – somebody would appear with news of Olivia. There was no telephone, and someone would come on foot. Or by car, perhaps with the blue blaze of sirens. He was almost shaking with anxiety, welcoming news of disaster rather than no news at all.

Even as he thought of this, an engine slowed and died outside, and a door slammed. Middlemass entered through the open french windows, pausing for an instant, like a well-known actor timing his round of applause: at the same moment, his eyes met Miles' in brief confirmation.

"I've found Olivia," he announced. "She must have been going down the hill on a bicycle, and collided with a car. I found her on my way over here, and it's lucky I did. A hit-and-run accident. No – don't get up. There's nothing anyone can do for her now."

Hilary sat opposite Miles in the study, Benjy's bottle of Glenlivet between them on the desk, half full. A moth glided through the open window and flung itself inside the lamp-shade, battering between cloth and bulb until Miles caged it in his hands and released it into the night.

"What arrangements have been made?"

"The body's been taken to Norwich, to the Hospital," said Hilary. "There's to be a post-mortem, and an inquest, but I should imagine that it will be very straightforward."

"And will they catch – whoever did it?"

"I was coming to that."

"What do you mean?"

"It looks as if Olivia was hit by a car. I found her lying, with her bicycle, at the foot of the hill. At first I thought she'd simply fallen off, and been concussed. She had no lights, you know, and bad brakes. You shouldn't have let her ride that old bicycle of yours."

"I couldn't stop her."

"I should think there'll be a verdict of accidental death."

"But what about this hit-and-run driver? I mean, only tonight, I was nearly mown down by some lunatic –"

"Miles, I said that it looked as if she'd been hit by a car."

"What are you suggesting?" Miles knew very well, but wanted it confirmed.

"I'm not the most practical of men, Miles, but it occurred to me to glance at her eyes. Olivia's pupils were tiny. Pinpoint. She was on a large dose of something when she went down that hill. I'm surprised she could even sit on a bike."

"Then – she wasn't hit by anything?"

"Even if she had been, it wouldn't have made any difference. I know very little of these matters, but I should think she was past help long before I found her."

Miles swallowed another gulp of whisky, sensing that Hilary Middlemass knew everything, wondering whether to admit it. He longed for Hilary's comfort and reassurance.

"Pretty hard on you – wasn't it? Finding her, I mean?"

"I didn't. I was driving over here to see Francesca – I just wanted a chat – and came on the scene quite late. Nobody seemed to know what to do, so I telephoned for an ambulance from the pub, and tried to remember the first aid they taught me in the Intelligence Corps forty years ago. But I knew it wouldn't be any good."

"They'll find out – at the post-mortem – if she took anything, and when she took it?"

"They're bound to. It surprised me, to be honest. I didn't think Olivia was the sort to get her kicks from drugs. Other things perhaps, but not drugs."

"She didn't."

"Miles, I don't want you to say anything which you might

regret." Hilary's tone was compassionate, but carried a warning. "If anything was ever to get into the papers –"

"I think it would just be regarded as an unfortunate accident."

"I see. Well, perhaps if you can throw any light on it, you should tell me."

"'Brief as the lightning in the collied night'."

"I'm not with you – ah, yes, perhaps so. 'So quick bright things come to confusion.'"

"Did you tell them that she was on her way to see you?" Miles asked.

"It seemed like a good idea."

"But we both know that she was going nowhere. Agreed?"

"Miles –"

"I've got to talk, Hilary. I didn't realise how terrible this was going to be. You see, I knew she was going to do it, and I let her."

"Miles, there was nothing you could have done. If you had prevented her this time, there would have been a next, and a time after that. You can't blame yourself."

"But I wanted her to. I let her. I knew bloody well she'd taken something, but I was so – overawed by her, and frightened, I let her go ahead. I just didn't realise how guilty it would make me feel."

"It was the best thing. For all of us."

"Hilary! We're talking about a girl of – a girl who was only nineteen. How can you say that? You make her sound like a criminal."

Miles went to the window, breathed night air still thick with smoke from the fields. Sitting on the sill, he pressed his aching head against cool glass.

"Miles, absolutely no blame attaches to you. If she chose to take an overdose of something – tranquillisers, I imagine – and ride a bike down a steep hill after drinking the best part of a bottle of wine, that's her business."

"But I could have stopped her!"

"How were you to know?"

"I let her get on with it. I didn't question *why* she wanted to make a gesture like this – for some reason the act had its own logic, seemed to me to contain a glorious defiance. She had a kind of look tonight which I couldn't help admiring."

"Olivia Underwood was an unpleasant little Schiz. Manipulative, neurotic, killing everything she touched – I'm not sorry to be rid of her, and I don't suppose many other people will be, either."

"Hilary, for God's sake." Tears sprang unbidden and unwanted into his eyes, hovering there, threatening to spill. How often one was betrayed by one's emotional responses, he thought.

"Oh, don't be sanctimonious. Of course, it'll upset Benjy, but he'll get over it. As for Francesca – she was tying the poor woman up in knots."

"She was an accomplished pianist."

"Even I don't believe that being an accomplished pianist excuses everything."

"You're right. No-one really will be very sorry. That's what's so sad. And she had everything – looks, talent, money –"

"And she was driving her brother almost insane. Charming combination of attributes."

"Don't you ever care about anyone, Hilary?"

"A few individuals. Yourself. Louise. And Francesca. Francesca particularly."

"When did *you* realise – what their relationship was?"

"As soon as I saw Olivia and Benjy together. You can always tell. I wasn't certain whether to believe my own instincts at first – but I soon realised."

"Are you sure Benjy will survive without her?"

"I don't think Olivia planned it that way, but I think he will."

Miles was suddenly, intensely, angry; Hilary's detachment and self-control had become unendurable. As always, his expression of the emotion was in hostile formality.

"It didn't occur to you that you could have stopped events reaching this pitch? I mean, what sort of state could she have been in, to have been driven to an act like this?"

Miles had completely forgotten his own, recent anger with the girl.

"It would have happened, sooner or later," Hilary repeated.

"As for her state of mind – I think she probably acted in a fit of pique. Olivia probably had quite a supply of drugs, of one sort or another. Just to give others pleasure, you understand. I should imagine she avoided them, herself. Or she might have taken a few bottles of Francesca's tranquillisers, to assist her journey into the next world. She didn't mean to go there alone, either. Remember what happened to Benjy, back in Cambridge?"

Miles felt sick, blaming it on too much whisky, knowing it to be fear.

"I'm taking Francesca over to Charnwood for the night. Louise will take care of her."

"That won't be necessary. Francesca is perfectly all right here. In any case, she's taking care of Benjy."

"You take care of Benjy."

"But –"

"There's no reason that he should ever know about what you said to Olivia. There's no reason for you to admit that you suspected she was out to – take her own life. That I am afraid will come out at the inquest – they'll find the traces of drugs in her system. But Benjy need not know that she virtually warned you what she was going to do."

"Please go. Take Francesca – you're right, she'll be happier with you, and can telephone the Underwood relations from Charnwood. I need to be on my own, now."

"Of course, it was tragic." Without conviction. "*Ne nisi bonum*, etcetera, but all the same –"

At this Miles turned his back.

"I shall probably be over to visit Francesca tomorrow. We'll talk then."

"Miles –"

"Please go."

He stood, facing into darkness until he heard Hilary's car start, and then wandered out of the study, too exhausted to sleep. The Old Vicarage had that preternatural calm which follows fatality, for what had surprised Miles more than Hilary's announcement had been its reception: Francesca and Benjy had greeted the news in total silence.

Benjy had gone white, and remained silent as though holding his emotions in tight check. Francesca had lowered her head, as though in prayer, before speaking and demanding the practical details. She had packed quietly and left without saying goodbye.

He walked aimlessly through to the drawing room, and found Benjy face-down on the sofa, arms huddled close. A lonely child, used to death and isolation, turned in on himself for comfort. Benjy reminded Miles of himself now, so quiet and self-possessed in grief.

Bringing the patchwork quilt from upstairs, he made a cup of tea and settled next to Benjy on the sofa. The boy stirred unhappily and moved closer, wrapping his arm round Miles' waist and resting his head against Miles' shoulder.

Huddling them both in the quilt, Miles sat silent, hand stroking Benjy's hair. It was a day which had lasted for months, and he realised that one grew older in instants, not years. Benjy's turned-away face had a new grimness now, had learnt another lesson. But he was here, and alive, and almost well, and had some sort of a chance, and that was all Miles cared about.

Tears again rose on the brink of his eyelids, and he took off his glasses to rub his lashes with the back of his hand. It seemed strange that he, sitting here now, the last man left awake, should shed tears for Olivia.

# *Nine*

Miles woke alone next morning, cramped and anxious, eyes gummy and mouth foul with the aftertaste of whisky and misery. He went into the kitchen, worried about Benjy, and saw him beyond the window, half-hidden among the trees of the orchard. There were empty cups on the table, remains of coffee, and no attempt at food.

He showered thoroughly, as though trying to wash away the miasma of death, and put on fresh clothes. The new jumpers lay forlorn on the bed, garish now, but he chose one anyway, dressing for courage, and went back downstairs clad in bright, brave, electric blue.

It was still early – barely eight fifteen, and the high Norfolk sky was full of late summer brilliance. Miles felt that this promising, optimistic, cheerful weather was almost tactless.

He stepped out into the orchard, where wasps circled about fallen fruit, and crawled through ruined palaces of apples which cracked underfoot. Ashamed of his own dreamless sleep, Miles went to Benjy, finding him paler than ever in his now appropriate black.

"Benjy –"

It was the first time they had actually spoken since Hilary's appearance. Last night, Benjy had simply turned blindly for comfort, burrowing into a protective embrace which would let him sleep for a few hours.

"I suppose you're going to say that you're sorry and is there anything you can do?"

Miles looked aside. "Yes, that's what they said to me at school, when my father died. All the same, I *am* sorry, and there is a lot I can do. Francesca seems to be organising most things from Charnwood – ringing up, and so on."

"She's a very kind woman." Tonelessly. He turned towards

Miles, almost spindly in the strong sunlight, a lock of hair falling into his eyes. It seemed for an instant that as Miles had grown stronger and more confident, Benjy had visibly wasted away. Perhaps just an illusion, caused by grief, fear, confusion. He was also astonished as his desire reasserted itself. His body really had no sense of occasion, Miles reflected: producing tears and anger one moment, then brightly dressed and erect the next.

He touched the boy's shoulder, in a gesture as much of propitiation as lust, but his hand was shrugged away.

"You know about it, I suppose."

"Know what?"

"About Olivia and me."

"Yes," agreed Miles. "Yes, I think I always knew."

Benjy's voice was quiet, flat, the voice of an undergraduate expounding an indifferent essay. "Olivia was afraid that you'd find out. We both were. That's why we had to be so careful: that's why we used the church."

"How long – I mean –"

"It's always been like this. We've always –" he corrected himself smoothly "– we had always loved each other. We didn't have anyone else, because our father was so busy. He had a series of girls after our mother died but – he hadn't much time for us."

Miles settled in the long grass beside him, ready to listen at last to his story.

"Olivia worshipped me," Benjy continued, "we were very close. We had to be, just to survive. I think my father guessed, even then, and our relations. *They* realised we didn't fight, and squabble, like ordinary brothers and sisters. We weren't normal siblings." Miles noticed the emphasis on *normal*.

"Olivia was very precocious, even as a child. She – she used to – manipulate people. She was so extraordinarily erotic – the original nymphet. I've seen her twist people twice, three times her age up in knots, people you'd think were completely straight and – *normal* – and who probably were until she arrived on the scene. Like Francesca – I mean – I don't want to offend you, Miles, I don't know what Francesca – but anyway, men, women, other children at school – she could

203

always get something on them, somehow. If it wasn't sexual, then it would be in some other way. I suppose she did it for power. She loved to have power over other people."

"And you? She had a great deal of power over you, didn't she?"

"Imagine it, Miles. It isn't difficult to understand how we started – to get involved. We were alone, and basically unhappy, and in a foreign country when we weren't away from each other at separate schools – that was the worst bit. Our relations always tried to keep us apart. You know – or perhaps you don't, because you aren't typical – but you start to change, and experiment, and sex is a great, fascinating mystery. She came back from some girls' school one summer when she was about twelve anxious to demonstrate her new-found knowledge and – well, I suppose really she seduced me. I – you know what it's like – she just has – had – the most amazing sexuality. I was completely obsessed by her. I still am."

"And I suppose your father's death –"

"Under mysterious circumstances, as the Consul put it. He fell off a roof, as you know. They passed it off as an accident, but –"

"You think that he committed suicide?"

"I don't think anything of the sort. It was when Olivia was about fourteen. I've never admitted this before to anyone, but I think – there were more plans to split us up, you see – I think Olivia assisted him in that fall."

Miles did not want to believe such a ludicrous story, but knowing Olivia as he had done, he did. He remembered Hilary's acerbic comment. *An unpleasant little Schiz.*

"What about last Christmas? When you came to Campden Hill Square you were terrified. Hagridden."

"We – you know what Olivia is – was – like."

"Did she threaten you in some way?"

"I'll come to that in a minute. I've never told anyone about all this before. I mean, I've wanted to protect her. I've known for some time something was wrong with her, but – I didn't admit to myself how wrong."

His tone had that dramatic flatness Miles remembered from

204

the night of the accident in Cambridge. His pedestrian language emphasised the intensity of feeling, rather than reduced it.

"I never wanted anyone else, you know. Not another girl, that is. School was different, of course, and trying things out – well, that started as a bit of a pose, as you guessed, and then I got to enjoy it. We – we need each other, you see. Needed, I mean." Pedantically anxious to make everything clear. "I just couldn't get enough of her. Fucking her, holding her down – she had that way of clenching you deep inside her – but you know that –"

Miles nodded. There was no animosity between them about this, rather a strong camaraderie which he found arousing.

"She used to be very jealous of Mel. God knows why, I don't fancy her. I like her, and she's wonderful, really kind, but Olivia is literally the only woman I've ever screwed. It never worked with anyone else. A girl tried a couple of times in Cambridge, and I couldn't do a thing. With guys, no problems. But I really belong to Olivia."

He stopped, staring into the middle distance, as if he saw something moving among the leaves. "We were so close, Miles. I could have died with it, sometimes. After that row in London, we were closer than ever. She came to see me last term – after she'd finished at the convent, and before she went to Paris – and we – we made a pact. Only I couldn't go through with it."

"That hotel in Cambridge – that girl?"

"You've guessed. She came shortly before Tripos – that's why I didn't see much of you – and she said she'd found a way for us to be together, always. No-one would be able to touch us, ever again. We'd be safe. She met me in the hotel with the pills and the bottle and – I couldn't go through with it. She kept taunting me and calling me a coward – you know how cruel she could be. Goading me. Miles, I felt so ashamed. She left me to get on with it, and I almost did.

"If only I'd had the guts to join her last night."

"What – what do you mean?" Miles was unwilling to admit how much he knew.

"Don't you realise? That was no accident. She must have

decided – I don't know – just felt she couldn't stand it any more. Just wanted to be rid of the lot of us. She always was keen on grand gestures. If only I'd gone with her." Eyes full of distant vistas. "I should have gone with her, but I let her go alone."

Benjy sat apart, isolated as he had ever been. Miles wanted to reach forward, but knew that Benjy was escaping. Soon all contact would be broken.

"I can't follow her now, Miles."

"Probably because you have a healthy sense of self-preservation," observed Miles tartly. The boy was growing self-indulgent now: time to stop.

Music drifted through the air. For a moment Miles found it eerie, before remembering that Benjy had left the radio on. That familiar pre-morning news choice, Ravel's *Pavane*, floated out into the orchard, like a signature tune.

Benjy startled.

"I thought for a minute –"

"So did I," agreed Miles, as strains from the piano recording reached them. "She had talent, you know."

Benjy nodded.

"When did you find out about us, Miles?"

Sunlight filtered through the branches, and gorged wasps, drunk on apples, crawled between their feet.

"Instinct. And you left a clue." Sounding like one of the protagonists in one of his green-spined detective stories, during the last stages, the final pages. "You left a book outside one night. Do you remember? No? Let me remind you.

'Sudden in a shaft of sunlight
Even while the dust moves
There rises the hidden laughter
Of children in the foliage . . .'"

Benjy nodded, and for an instant seemed about to reach towards him. But he dropped his head and Miles understood that all further communication would be discouraged; he remembered Benjy's aphorism, 'not drowning but waving', and wondered now if its original would not be more appropriate.

He was prepared for an emotional mayday.

"You see, I'm on my own now," Benjy said. "The terrible thing is that I've got what I want. I'm free. She can't do anything to me now. I'm free."

Last words, thought Miles, as full of allusion and illusion as if they had been sitting in his room at Woodville. Benjy was signing off: they had reached emotional incommunicado as Benjy's eyes paled with the vision of such precipitous liberty.

Some other half-remembered phrase drifted into his head: something about the lily-white boys. Ah, that was it. How appropriate. He could always rely on his subconscious for the apt quotation.

'One is one and all alone and ever more shall be so.'

As Hilary Middlemass had predicted, a verdict of accidental death was returned at the coroner's inquest. Olivia Underwood, anxious and worried about her forthcoming start at Cambridge, had ill-advisedly been taking tranquillisers, and, unconscious of the dangers of alcohol, had fallen from her bicycle at speed and sustained fatal injuries.

Hilary, weighty and sombre in black, gave his account of the scene of the accident. Benjy testified to his sister's apprehension about Cambridge, and her habitual disregard for brakes and lights when out cycling, as well as her cavalier style of sailing downhill with her arms outstretched. The bicycle itself, a poor crushed thing which had belonged to Miles, was described; the mysterious black Mercedes, which had by now troubled many local residents, was invoked.

The burial took place two days later, in Brompton Cemetery. Intrigued by the prospect of meeting Underwood relations, Miles had no particular feelings about the ceremony itself. He had attended several interments purely out of courtesy, and did not expect Olivia's to be any different. Francesca, standing beside him in the second pew, had her pre-performance expression on: a tightening of the eye-muscles and a set to the corners of her mouth. Benjy, standing with the family, was sombre. Within days he had assumed an air of shy formality which had impressed the spectators at the inquest and now made a favourable impact on the mourners. His hair, still floppy, had been modified by an expensive barber, and he wore a black double-breasted suit and silk tie. He stood elegant and mournful, occasionally pushing back the flap of hair over his forehead, epitomising the virtues of somebody *taking it well*. Only Miles could have said that Benjy's sentiments were not those of grief, but of profound relief, a sensation he was so familiar with himself.

"He leadeth me beside the still waters," intoned the vicar, in faintly querulous Anglican tones. Miles, evaluating his performance with professional acumen, decided that his heart was not in it; which saddened him, since it seemed that someone should mourn Olivia.

The mention of 'still waters' started some current in his consciousness: glimpsing Benjy he thought suddenly that these lovers, incestuous and doomed, should have drowned in one another's arms rather than be separated in this fashion. Instead, they had lost each other, and Benjy, his destiny evaded, was condemned to life.

He had forgotten his chagrin that Benjy had come to Bly only to meet Olivia; he tried to forget Olivia's sly cruelty and his conviction that she was evil; he was overwhelmed and disarmed by the familiarity of the burial service as earth drummed on the coffin lid. Miles attributed the moisture in his eyes to the sudden cutting wind which rustled the banks of flowers: he never cried.

But it surprised him, as a girl stepped forward and threw a torch of chrysanthemums into the grave, standing among those other Underwoods, the earlier Underwoods buried beneath their feet among the trailing ivy and ornate stone-work, that he should lament Olivia.

The girl stepped back, and Miles recognised Melissa. He had looked for her in the church, and in the cars arriving on Fulham Road, and only now saw her. She was wearing a man's black felt hat, like a gangster, and looked uncomfortable in a dark skirt and high heels. He expected a fall of hair as she swept off the hat, walking away from the graveside; but instead, there was a golden shining crop, short as a boy's, which threw her bone-structure into relief. She looked like – he had dreaded that with those Underwood features and that hair, she would resemble Olivia – but instead, the collar high against her neck, she looked like Benjy: a stronger, fitter Benjy, a warm creature from a real world, and not a phantom.

"Miles! How are you? Isn't it awful? I could do with a drink."

"When I said I'd hoped to see you again, I didn't think it would be in these conditions."

"You remember that? God, it was ages ago, wasn't it? I'm bloody hungry too. I was up half the night. Got a deadline."

"Well – I don't think the Underwoods are – I don't think there are any –"

"No, they aren't laying on anything. Couldn't really. I mean, everyone's upset but sort of *relieved*, you know. Poor old Olivia. It's like those thrillers where no-one ever really liked the victim."

He was amazed by her perception. She seemed to pick implications out of the air, and she did not play games of let's-pretend with her insights, either. Miles was very glad to see Melissa again.

"Would you like to – come and have lunch or something? I've driven down from Norfolk, so I can't really suggest we go back to the place in Campden Hill – it's all closed and dusty at present."

"Love to. You parked round here?"

"No. I left my car – some way out of London. The traffic's a little too much for me, I'm afraid."

"No kidding. Don't worry, there's plenty of places round here. I'm glad to see you again, Miles. This isn't the place to say it really, but you look so much better!"

"Better? In what way?"

"Sort of – well, the circumstances are *not* ideal, but you look much more together. In control of things. Benjy's been telling me all about your book."

"Yes – there's some chance it might be published. They

think it can be fitted in to one of a series on prose stylists that's being put together."

"That's terrific. Look, let's get out of here. Hanging around among all these dead people gives me the creeps."

"I hadn't realised how many Underwoods there were."

"Heaps of them. All buried here. Made a fortune in the garment trade and became respectable in the nineteen hundreds. They've even got a sort of mausoleum. Just the sort of thing to appeal to Benjy. Hang on a sec."

Melissa's father and mother, a cadaverous journalist and an author of cookery books respectively, were introduced, and seemed to Miles both likeable and reasonably sane. They had none of the haunted Underwood glamour shared by Benjy and Olivia. After being introduced, Miles felt someone pat his arm, and turned.

"Don't suppose I'll see much of you next term, Miles."

It was Benjy, in all his black and white beauty, suddenly very grown up, and very unobtainable. Someone had told Miles once that one grows accustomed to good looks, that attractiveness soon loses its appeal: he had never found this to be so. Every time he looked at Benjy he experienced a jolt of love and awe. It was none the less strong now.

"I'll be very busy," agreed Miles. "I'm lecturing on Vaughan and Crashaw."

"But I expect we'll run into each other, now and then."

That would be the worst part of it.

"This is it, Miles." They might have been standing on a railway platform, or a dock. Benjy gave a traveller's shrug, waiting for the whistle and slamming of doors, wondering what to say. "It's been fun."

"That's not really an accurate value judgement, Benjamin."

"Well – you know what it's like."

"I do indeed."

He stuck out his hand; it was a not impersonal handshake. "Goodbye, Miles."

He turned, and walked out of Miles' life.

"Miles?" Melissa's voice. "You look a bit grim."

"This *is* supposed to be a funeral."

Making excuses to Francesca, who was preoccupied with Hilary Middlemass, he waved to the Underwoods and walked, with Melissa at his side, out of the cemetery and into the dusty normality of Fulham Road. They found a wine bar, noisy and empty before the lunchtime rush, and settled at a table. The amplifiers belted out some rock ballad with the reprise 'everybody's gotta learn some time'.

"Well, I'm glad that's over. Can't see the point of pretending I'm sorry. Just hope poor old Benjy will be all right, that's all."

"I'm sure Benjy can look after himself," replied Miles, certain of that now. "I like your hair like that. It really suits you."

Melissa patted the crop self-consciously. "Are you sure? I only had it done a couple of days ago. It's been so hot, and long hair is a lot of bother. I don't spend much time on my appearance, I'm afraid. I'm always a bit of a mess."

"It's rather attractive." Miles surprised himself by reaching over and touching her hair with his fingertips. It had a soft, furry texture which he found very appealing.

"I'm sorry to hear about – was it Tony?"

"Oh, that was *ages* ago. I'm not too upset – he was a bit of a wimp. Quite sweet, but nothing special. Anyway, I've been too preoccupied with work recently – that's probably why we split up – he never saw anything of me. I'm working on this new account and –"

It did not occur to Melissa that she might be boring him, or showing insufficient grief at her cousin's death. It did not occur to her that getting through more chilled dry white wine than Miles, or paying for lunch, would cause offence. It did not. Miles was impressed, delighted, relieved, to spend time with somebody so obviously lacking in guile and deviousness. The resemblance to Benjy, far from being disturbing, reassured; she had Benjy's best characteristics, of enthusiasm and volubility, with none of his more unsettling traits.

Miles was enjoying himself for the first time in weeks. They chattered on – Miles discovering that he was doing just as much gossiping and speculation as Melissa after the wine had relaxed his guard – and had to be turned out of the wine bar at closing time.

"I thought it was about lunchtime!" exclaimed Melissa. "Shit! It's nearly half past three!"

"Do you have to be back at work?"

"Some time this afternoon. I can stay late – it's not like an office job, but there's a lot to do. Look, do you want to come back for another coffee?"

"But we've already had three."

"A liqueur then."

"You're on."

Had he really said that? Happily, tipsily, he tripped out into the street with her, to find her battered Citroen, and drive off into the wilds of Balham to drink brandy for the rest of the afternoon. Miles had a lot to thank Benjy for.

A year ago such a programme, mundane by many standards, would have been inconceivable.

Melissa – he was learning to call her Mel now – peeled off her jacket with some relief, and kicked off the high-heels, throwing them into the back seat of the car. She sat beside him, skinny and brown, driving with confidence, occasionally reckless, bare feet deft on the pedals. Miles stretched happily, revelling in her tomboy attractiveness, reflecting that this was a strange way to spend the afternoon of a funeral.

# Ten

Miles stood alone in the rich autumn afternoon, sniffing the afterscent of rain. For it really was autumn now, not the hot and dusty foretaste of the Fall (he loved that post-lapsarian Americanism), and those leaves which remained were crisp and gilt, curled on the trees as though twisted out of metal. Rowan berries still glowed, soaked with moisture, and the mountain ash boughs still had that unearthly sheen to their bark, like torn silk curtains left flapping in the breeze.

The Old Vicarage was empty now, and likely to remain so for a few months to come. There were no yellowed paperbacks on the windowsill of his bedroom, and a zealous neighbour had husbanded most of the apples in the orchard when the For Sale notice went up.

Miles was not sorry to see the house go out of the family. Other voices and other footsteps would fill the rooms, the boards would resound to unfamiliar feet, children would call to one another from the gallery, and the studio become a playroom. The domestic rituals of ordinary families would exorcise the Old Vicarage.

He had stopped here, not knowing quite why he had come, why he had paused on the journey back to Cambridge. Would it have been better to leave the place alone, his memories intact? Miles had driven through sweeping rain to get here, persistent, East Anglian rain, drumming on the roof of the old Morris, creeping in through the sills. It had been raining all day, and Miles had driven to Charnwood from Cambridge that morning, to news he had expected.

When Miles had visited Woodville before the beginning of Michaelmas Term, it was to find his old rooms dank with disuse and unutterably depressing. The deepset windows and

213

colony of spiders, the dark panelling and heavy mahogany bookcases filled him with dismay; he had even stronger reservations about his bedroom, with its faded Indian quilt and pentatonic mattress springs; the gyp-room had an ineradicable smell of gas.

Wondering why he had never noticed, or objected to, these features before, Miles immediately put in a request for a set which had become vacant on the other side of the college. These rooms, reputedly haunted by the decapitated shade of Anthony Rivers, Lord Scales, were less disturbing than those Miles had left. He had no reservations about sharing with the shade of the college's founder: his objection to his old rooms was that they were haunted by the phantom of Benjy.

As though seeing eidetic images, Miles could not free the dank staircase, sagging armchairs and tiled fireplace from the vision of Benjy eating, walking and disputing, or simply sitting by the gas-fire, eyes on Miles, cigarette unlit. In these conditions, he would never forget Benjy.

The college agreed to the transfer, and Miles spent an agreeable, dusty weekend moving his books and chattels to R2. Installed on Sunday night, he lay down in his new bedroom (a room that, unlike the previous one, he would not be ashamed to take people back to) and waited for psychic manifestations. Instead, he slept peacefully, and forgot his dreams.

Soon afterwards, Miles had travelled to the South of France. It had taken a bit of hectic last-minute booking, and Francesca had obscurely objected, reminding him that he hated travelling.

Miles had loved it. His new confidence asserted itself, and he travelled down through Italy, spending far more than he intended, eating, sleeping, drinking too much, and falling into bad company, which had been most enjoyable of all. There had been one or two intrigues, and he had realised that the proud, rather adolescent statement, reeking of bravado, *I am bisexual*, was quite applicable. He was different, and happy to be.

Miles had returned to Cambridge that autumn sunned, highly sexed and self-assured. Before long, a rumour spread among his colleagues and throughout the Faculty that Miles Tattershall was better; the nature of his former illness was never determined, but there was general consent that, whatever disabilities Dr Tattershall had suffered, he was now fully recovered. He became popular with his students, found his lectures well attended, and was flattered when one boy began to imitate his style of dress. (Miles had become a frequent customer of the Italian outfitters on Trinity Street.)

Within Woodville, these conclusions were somewhat substantiated by the suspicion, despite the discretion of both parties, that Miles Tattershall was on terms of intimacy with the Bursar's wife. Of course, nothing was ever proved.

Miles for his part still had memory to contend with. Sometimes he woke at night with the recollection of Benjy; occasionally he saw the boy in the street. These chance meetings were painful but not externally evident; he suffered a slight, tolerable pain, a seizure of spiritual angina, and realised that it was worse to see Benjy a few yards distant, walking parallel to him down King's Parade, with the knowledge that they inhabited separate worlds, than if Benjy had been dead and buried beside his sister. But he also realised, with a flash of insight that lit up one melancholy autumn night, that he had undergone a belated form of that malaise which afflicted his undergraduates: the Cambridge love affair.

As term progressed, Miles saw Benjy less about the streets, or, perhaps, with his new preoccupations, failed to notice him. He heard indirectly that Benjamin Underwood had been accepted for the Diplomatic Corps, and received the information as impassively as it had been imparted.

And so, one Saturday deep in November, as rain poured down over the fens, Miles drove down to Charnwood.

Hilary was out but Francesca waited at the open door as he drove through the saturated park towards the house. Rain beat down on the lake, and the croquet lawn where, aeons ago now, he had watched Middlemass and Louise stand with their mallets. Some bird rose from the reeds and flapped away with a dispirited cough, as Miles remembered standing at the water's edge with Hilary.

"Miles. I'm so glad you could come." She kissed him warmly, breath full of smoke. The cigarettes were a recent habit, a betrayal perhaps of tension, but preferable to bottles of pills.

Francesca had gained a subtle radiance: her hair shone; the attempted serenity had been replaced by an energetic glow; and she surprised Miles with her warmth and enthusiasm every time he met her.

Francesca had never come back to Bly after Olivia died. She had visited, of course, collected clothes and books, and carefully transported her cello. But to all intents and purposes she had been living with Hilary ever since the night of the accident.

Francesca's influence on Charnwood was already evident: there were soft furnishings now, curtains and cushions and tiny trophies and souvenirs on every surface. Carpets covered the chilly floors, and afternoon tea was strictly conventional. Charnwood's eclectic charm had given way to the sybaritic comforts of Campden Hill Square. Miles thought it rather a pity.

"When's the wedding?" he asked, balancing the porcelain teacup precariously on the arm of his chair, so that Francesca came and moved it to the table.

"December. It's to be in a Registrar's office, since Hilary's lapsed. He wants it all over before I start my Far East tour."

"Lady Middlemass. It doesn't sound like you at all."

"I'm sticking to my own name for professional purposes. Though his reputation is big enough for both of us. I suppose I could always hyphen it."

Miles stopped, looking across the deserted lawns to sopping brown trees. He felt depressed, rather than elated by the news, as though he had hoped for something better for Francesca, was sad that she would be incarcerated in Charnwood.

"How is Louise?"

"She's gone back to the Academy. Hilary is very proud of her. They think she'll win a scholarship to the Juilliard School."

"And – what is her reaction to all this?"

"She'll get used to it. After all, her mother's been married three times."

"What's that got to do with it?"

"Well, she can scarcely object if her father –"

"Louise is Hilary's *daughter*?"

"Yes, of course. Didn't you realise? That's why she was staying here. They hadn't met for years, and then Hilary realised how musical Louise was, and started to encourage her."

"Good God, I assumed she was –"

"His mistress? Not at all. Hilary loves to puzzle and mystify, but that's all there was to it. All very straightforward."

"Perhaps I read too much into things."

"I think it's understandable. Hilary told me about – those two. I suppose after all that, you're bound to misinterpret even the most normal relationships."

"Are there any *normal* relationships?"

Francesca shrugged. "Have you seen much of Benjy, these past weeks?"

"Scarcely anything. We don't – that is – I've been very busy."

They had prowled warily around the topic of Olivia's death, conscious of each other's suspicions but avoiding too much reference to the subject, unless related to practical considerations. Now that she was dead and buried, he wanted to say nothing more about her.

"Poor Miles. You've had a hard time, haven't you?"

"Not particularly. I saw Mel last week – we had lunch together while I was up in London to visit the British Library. Cheerful as ever."

"Do you think you'll get over it? Ever?"

"I don't think we should discuss this any further."

"I suppose it would all have been different – if we'd been different."

"What *are* you talking about?" He took a second slice of cake, irritated. "Different in what way?"

"I suppose that if we'd seen more people when we were younger, and hadn't been so wrapped up in each other, you wouldn't have been a – late developer. We were so close, Miles. Too close. Remember when I thought something, and you thought it, too? Or how you always knew –"

"Well, it didn't work when you were – ill – in New York, did it?" Miles was acerbic. "I didn't know a thing until Hilary found out. It's Hilary who really – who really looks after you, you know."

"That's because we've lost sympathy, Miles."

"Whatever do you mean, lost sympathy? Look, I think you're a bit overtired. Hadn't you better –"

"You see, I keep remembering how it used to be," she continued, dreamily. "When I was fifteen and those odd things happened. You came back from school –"

"Don't dwell on it." Miles had detected a definite early warning and was anxious to avoid a full verbal attack. "Lots of people experience poltergeists and phenomena. It's very common, especially among girls –"

"I promised Father not to talk about it."

"Then don't."

"Miles, why don't you want to discuss this?"

"There's nothing to discuss."

"I tried to get you to talk about it at Christmas, and you wouldn't. What are you so afraid of?"

Again his instinct warned him: it was as though he saw a dorsal fin draw closer in the water.

"After my dream," she persisted. "You woke me. You sat by me. And you wouldn't talk about it."

"Francesca –" waiting for the sound of a car, wishing that Hilary would come back and provide distraction. "Francesca, you've had a very trying time. I'm sure you're over-excited, and –"

"But I've been sitting here thinking, Miles, and I've realised why you guessed about Benjy and Olivia. You knew about them, because of us."

For a minute Miles could not speak, and then he bluffed.

"Don't be ridiculous. I hate to think what you imagine they got up to together, but there's nothing like that –"

"Don't you remember? I'd been sleepwalking and they sent people to search for me. Don't you remember coming to me in that orchard, and finding me –"

"Francesca, you're very disturbed. You don't know what you're –"

But even as he spoke he was drawn to her, coming closer in order to take her shoulders and stop her talking. Whatever she knew must never take verbal form or be given definition. "Nothing happened, Francesca," he declared, but the impulse between them denied it.

"Almost," she whispered. "Almost – and ever since –"

Footsteps echoed on the terrace, and Miles broke away. They stood looking at each other, appalled, as Hilary entered. "Miles! How are you! You've heard our news?"

Hilary had interpreted the scene in an instant, and Miles, looking at them together, Francesca turning her face up trustingly to be kissed by Middlemass, realised that he had lost her.

He would not come back to the Old Vicarage again. This time next year, Miles reflected, he would be on the East Coast, a visiting lecturer specialising in seventeenth-century English prose, with one book behind him and another on the way. If the climate was favourable, he would probably stay there.

There was nothing in England for him.

He did not know quite why he had called in at Bly on the way back to Cambridge, what had made him turn off the road and drive up the hill to the church, or go through the creaking lychgate, raindrops soaking his palm as he touched the greenish wood.

Miles had wandered into the garden, caught sight of his own image in a pane of glass. Electric blue jumper, hornrims, well-cut hair: there was no danger of his resembling his father, now.

Damp cat's tail grasses brushed against his pale corduroy trouser legs, soaked the Italian shoes. It really was just as well his publishers had accepted the book on Burton, he thought; life was expensive now that he had become a dandy.

But it had stopped raining, and the clouds had rolled away, as though at the order of some celestial art director. Miles smiled. He had learned a lot from Mel, not least a new terminology. The rain had given over to a bright, pixillated pre-Raphaelite evening glow, which illuminated rowan berries and roseships in almost hallucinogenic iridescence. The rain had left him feeling rinsed, cleansed, refreshed, and he stood now in the brilliant air with a new sensation of freedom. Alone, but not lonely. Still a little detached, but not afraid or yearning for a cloak of invisibility. He thought back to a comment of Hilary's, made just as he was leaving, earlier that day.

"You *have* made up for lost time. What an evolution. Miles Tattershall, *homo erectus*."

He smiled, the boy hero of some childhood story, having survived the journey through a world of mystery and enchantment. He had pushed aside the gnarled briars to discover a hidden country, and come back, changed, to tell the tale: older, stronger, braver: the Visible Man.

Cambridge was a little parochial now, life more of a challenge.

'Be not solitary, be not idle.'

Burton's parting words to the reader: Miles had profited from them, and now intended a life of demanding social and academic activity. He had gone to a party with Mel the other night, and found it less horrifying than expected. He had invited people in for dinner, and they had come, and they had actually enjoyed themselves. He had even bought the familiar runner a pint in the college bar, seeing him come in one evening streaming with rain and cold.

He folded back the roof of the little Morris Minor, relishing the cold rain against his palms. The prismatic sunset had resolved itself into a golden haze. Surprised at the time, for he had to be back in Cambridge for a promising dinner, Miles jumped into the car and drove away without looking back.

LAKE COUNTY PUBLIC LIBRARY
INDIANA

THIS BOOK IS RENEWABLE BY PHONE OR IN PERSON IF THERE IS NO RESERVE
WAITING OR FINE DUE.

LCP #0390